She couldn't look at him.

"After all we've planned, how could you believe those lies?"

"I said I was sorry."

Libby forgot that she'd meant to hide her tears, and looked him full in the face. "Sometimes being sorry isn't enough, Jess!" She turned away.

His hands came to rest on her shoulders. "What can I say? I was jealous. That may not be right, but it's human."

Perhaps because she wanted so desperately to believe that a marriage to this wonderful, contradictory man would succeed, Libby set aside her doubts and turned to face him. The depth of her love for this erstwhile enemy still staggered her.

* * *

"Her characters come alive and walk right off the pages and into your heart."

—*Rendezvous*

Dear Reader,

I'm so pleased to have the chance to reintroduce some of my early titles in this special series of reissues. *Wild About Harry, Just Kate, Part of the Bargain* and *Daring Moves* take place around the globe, from New York to Seattle—even Australia—and I hope you'll enjoy the journey as much as I did. And the gorgeous new cover art makes a terrific setting for these classic tales…as well as just a taste of my upcoming hardcover for HQN Books, *McKettrick's Choice!*

You've met my wonderful McKettrick men (and women) before, in *High Country Bride, Shotgun Bride* and *Secondhand Bride*, but many of you wrote and e-mailed to say you were *very* intrigued with Holt, the eldest brother. You wanted his story, and I very much wanted to tell it.

McKettrick's Choice is a big-scope story, with all the elements of a classic Western and many new ones, as well. It's longer than the earlier books, so you'll get to spend more time with Holt, his wonderful lady, Lorelei—has he *ever* met his match, and that's saying something, with a hardheaded McKettrick!—and a crop of secondary characters who really stole my heart. Living with these people was a delight, and I hope you will share my enthusiasm as you read. My goal was to take you along on the big cattle drive, as well as several other adventures, and to give you a place at the McKettrick table, where you will always be warmly welcomed.

In the not-too-distant future you will meet more McKettrick men—the modern variety. For further updates, check out my Web site at www.lindalaelmiller.com. You'll find some other interesting information there, too, including my scholarship program for women and a variety of fun contests. You might also enjoy following my blog, if you're interested in following the day-to-day saga of life at Springwater Station.

Last but not least, I would like to thank my longtime readers for their support and interest, and welcome the new ones. Let's sit down around the kitchen table and talk about cowboys.

All best,

Linda

Part of the Bargain

LINDA
LAEL
MILLER

HQN™

If you purchased this book without a cover you should be aware
that this book is stolen property. It was reported as "unsold and
destroyed" to the publisher, and neither the author nor the
publisher has received any payment for this "stripped book."

ISBN 0-373-77092-8

PART OF THE BARGAIN

Copyright © 1985 by Linda Lael Miller

All rights reserved. Except for use in any review, the reproduction or
utilization of this work in whole or in part in any form by any electronic,
mechanical or other means, now known or hereafter invented, including
xerography, photocopying and recording, or in any information storage
or retrieval system, is forbidden without the written permission of the
publisher, Harlequin Enterprises Limited, 225 Duncan Mill Road,
Don Mills, Ontario M3B 3K9, Canada.

All characters in this book have no existence outside the imagination of
the author and have no relation whatsoever to anyone bearing the same
name or names. They are not even distantly inspired by any individual
known or unknown to the author, and all incidents are pure invention.

This edition published by arrangement with Harlequin Books S.A.

® and TM are trademarks of the publisher. Trademarks indicated with
® are registered in the United States Patent and Trademark Office, the
Canadian Trade Marks Office and in other countries.

www.HQNBooks.com

Printed in U.S.A.

Classic tales from
Linda Lael Miller and HQN Books

WILD ABOUT HARRY
JUST KATE
PART OF THE BARGAIN
DARING MOVES

and look for her brand-new hardcover

McKETTRICK'S CHOICE

available in bookstores now!

For Laura Mast
Thank you for believing and being proud.

1

The landing gear made an unsettling *ka-thump* sound as it snapped back into place under the small private airplane. Libby Kincaid swallowed her misgivings and tried not to look at the stony, impassive face of the pilot. If he didn't say anything, she wouldn't have to say anything either, and they might get through the short flight to the Circle Bar B ranch without engaging in one of their world-class shouting matches.

It was a pity, Libby thought, that at the ages of thirty-one and thirty-three, respectively, she and Jess still could not communicate on an adult level.

Pondering this, Libby looked down at the ground below and was dizzied by its passing as they swept over the small airport at Kalispell, Montana, and banked eastward, toward the Flathead River. Trees so green that they had a blue cast carpeted the majestic mountains rimming the valley.

Womanhood being what it is, Libby couldn't resist watching Jess Barlow surreptitiously out of the corner of her eye. He was like a lean, powerful mountain lion waiting to pounce, even though he kept his attention strictly on the controls and the thin air traffic sharing the big Montana sky that spring morning. His eyes were hidden behind a pair of mirrored sunglasses, but Libby knew that they would be dark with the animosity that had marked their relationship for years.

She looked away again, trying to concentrate on the river, which coursed beneath them like a dusty-jade ribbon woven into the fabric of a giant tapestry. Behind those mirrored glasses, Libby knew Jess's eyes were the exact same shade of green as that untamed waterway below.

"So," he said suddenly, gruffly, "New York wasn't all the two-hour TV movies make it out to be."

Libby sighed, closed her eyes in a bid for patience and then opened them again. She wasn't going to miss one bit of that fabulous view—not when her heart had been hungering for it for several bittersweet years.

Besides, Jess had been to New York dozens of times on corporation business. Who did he think he was fooling?

"New York was all right," she said, in the most inflamatory tone she could manage. *Except that Jonathan died,* chided a tiny, ruthless voice in her mind. *Except for that nasty divorce from Aaron.* "Nothing to write home about," she added aloud, realizing her blunder too late.

"So your dad noticed," drawled Jess in an undertone that would have been savage if it hadn't been so carefully modulated. "Every day, when the mail came, he fell on it like it was manna from heaven. He never stopped hoping—I'll give him that."

"Dad knows I hate to write letters," she retorted defensively. But Jess had made his mark, all the same—Libby felt real pain, picturing her father flipping eagerly through the mail and trying to hide his disappointment when there was nothing from his only daughter.

"Funny—that's not what Stace tells me."

Libby bridled at this remark, but she kept her composure. Jess was trying to trap her into making some foolish statement about his older brother, no doubt, one that he could twist out of shape and hold over her head. She raised her chin and choked back the indignant diatribe aching in her throat.

The mirrored sunglasses glinted in the sun as Jess turned to look at her. His powerful shoulders were taut beneath the blue cotton fabric of his workshirt, and his jawline was formidably hard.

"Leave Cathy and Stace alone, Libby," he warned with blunt savagery. "They've had a lot of problems lately, and if you do anything to make the situation worse, I'll see that you regret it. Do I make myself clear?"

Libby would have done almost anything to escape his scrutiny just then, short of thrusting open the door of that small four-passenger Cessna and jumping out, but her choices were undeniably limited. Trembling just a little, she turned away and fixed her attention on the ground again.

Dear heaven, did Jess really think that she would interfere in Cathy's marriage—or any other, for that matter? Cathy was her *cousin*—they'd been raised like sisters!

With a sigh, Libby faced the fact that there was every chance that Jess and a lot of other people would believe she had been involved with Stacey Barlowe. There had, after all, been that exchange of letters, and Stace had even visited her a few times, in the thick of her traumatic divorce, though in actuality he had been in the city on business.

"Libby?" prodded Jess sharply, when the silence grew too long to suit him.

"I'm not planning to vamp your brother!" she snapped. "Could we just drop this, please?"

To her relief and surprise, Jess turned his concentration on piloting the plane. His suntanned jaw worked with suppressed annoyance, but he didn't speak again.

The timbered land below began to give way to occasional patches of prairie—cattle country. Soon they would be landing on the small airstrip serving the prosperous 150,000-acre Circle Bar B, owned by Jess's father and overseen, for the most part, by Libby's.

Libby had grown up on the Circle Bar B, just as Jess had, and her mother, like his, was buried there. Even though she couldn't call the ranch home in the legal sense of the word, it was *still* home to her, and she had every right to go there—especially now, when she needed its beauty and peace and practical routines so desperately.

The airplane began to descend, jolting Libby out of her reflective state. Beside her, Jess guided the craft skillfully toward the paved landing strip stretched out before them.

The landing gear came down with a sharp snap, and Libby drew in her breath in preparation. The wheels of the plane screeched and grabbed as they made contact with the asphalt, and then the Cessna was rolling smoothly along the ground.

When it came to a full stop, Libby wrenched at her seat belt, anxious to put as much distance as possible between herself and Jess Barlowe. But his hand closed over her left wrist in a steel-hard grasp. "Remember, Lib—these people aren't the sophisticated if-it-feels-good-do-it types you're used to. No games."

Games. *Games?* Hot color surged into Libby's face and pounded there in rhythm with the furious beat of her heart. "Let go of me, you bastard!" she breathed.

If anything, Jess's grip tightened. "I'll be watching you," he warned, and then he flung Libby's wrist from his hand and turned away to push open the door on his side and leap nimbly to the ground.

Libby was still tugging impotently at the handle on her

own door when her father strode over, climbed deftly onto the wing and opened it for her. She felt such a surge of love and relief at the sight of him that she cried out softly and flung herself into his arms, nearly sending both of them tumbling to the hard ground.

Ken Kincaid hadn't changed in the years since Libby had seen him last—he was still the same handsome, rangy cowboy that she remembered so well, though his hair, while as thick as ever, was iron-gray now, and the limp he'd acquired in a long-ago rodeo accident was more pronounced.

Once they were clear of the plane, he held his daughter at arm's length, laughed gruffly, and then pulled her close again. Over his shoulder she saw Jess drag her suitcases and portable drawing board out of the Cessna's luggage compartment and fling them unceremoniously into the back of a mud-speckled station wagon.

Nothing if not perceptive, Ken Kincaid turned slightly, assessed Senator Cleave Barlowe's second son, and grinned. There was mischief in his bright blue eyes when he faced Libby again. "Rough trip?"

Libby's throat tightened unaccountably, and she wished she could explain *how* rough. She was still stung by Jess's insulting opinion of her morality, but how could she tell her father that? "You know that it's always rough going where Jess and I are concerned," she said.

Her father's brows lifted speculatively as Jess got behind the wheel of the station wagon and sped away without so much as a curt nod or a halfhearted so-long. "You two'd better watch out," he mused. "If you ever stop butting heads, you might find out you like each other."

"Now, that," replied Libby with dispatch, "is a horrid thought if I've ever heard one. Tell me, Dad—how have you been?"

He draped one wiry arm over her shoulders and guided her in the direction of a late-model pickup truck. The door on the driver's side was emblazoned with the words "CIRCLE BAR B RANCH," and Yosemite Sam glared from both the mud flaps shielding the rear tires. "Never mind how I've been, dumplin'. How've *you* been?"

Libby felt some of the tension drain from her as her father opened the door on the passenger side of the truck and helped her inside. She longed to shed her expensive tailored linen suit for jeans and a T-shirt, and—oh, heaven—her sneakers would be a welcome change from the high heels she was wearing. "I'll be okay," she said in tones that were a bit too energetically cheerful.

Ken climbed behind the wheel and tossed one searching, worried look in his daughter's direction. "Cathy's waiting over at the house, to help you settle in and all that. I was hoping we could talk…"

Libby reached out and patted her father's work-worn hand, resting now on the gearshift knob. "We can talk tonight. Anyway, we've got lots of time."

Ken started the truck's powerful engine, but his wise blue eyes had not strayed from his daughter's face. "You'll stay here awhile, then?" he asked hopefully.

Libby nodded, but she suddenly found that she had to look away. "As long as you'll let me, Dad."

The truck was moving now, jolting and rattling over the rough ranch roads with a pleasantly familiar vigor. "I expected you before this," he said. "Lib…"

She turned an imploring look on him. "Later, Dad—okay? Could we please talk about the heavy stuff later?"

Ken swept off his old cowboy hat and ran a practiced arm across his forehead. "Later it is, dumplin'." Graciously he changed the subject. "Been reading your comic strip in the funny papers, and it seems like every kid in town's wearing one of those T-shirts you designed."

Libby smiled; her career as a syndicated cartoonist was certainly safe conversational ground. And it had all started right here, on this ranch, when she'd sent away the coupon printed on a matchbook and begun taking art lessons by mail. After that, she'd won a scholarship to a prestigious college, graduated, and made her mark, not in portraits or commercial design, as some of her friends had, but in cartooning. Her character, Liberated Lizzie, a cave-girl with modern ideas, had created something of a sensation and was now featured not only in the Sunday newspapers but also on T-shirts, greeting cards, coffee mugs and calendars. There was a deal pending with a poster company, and Libby's bank balance was fat with the advance payment for a projected book.

She would have to work hard to fulfill her obligations—there was the weekly cartoon strip to do, of course, and the panels for the book had to be sketched in. She hoped that between these tasks and the endless allure of the Circle Bar B, she might be able to turn her thoughts from Jonathan and the mess she'd made of her personal life.

"Career-wise, I'm doing fine," Libby said aloud, as much to herself as to her father. "I don't suppose I could use the sunporch for a studio?"

Ken laughed. "Cathy's been working for a month to get it ready, and I had some of the boys put in a skylight. All you've got to do is set up your gear."

Impulsively Libby leaned over and kissed her father's beard-stubbled cheek. "I love you!"

"Good," he retorted. "A husband you can dump—a daddy you're pretty well stuck with."

The word "husband" jarred Libby a little, bringing an un-
welcome image of Aaron into her mind as it did, and she
didn't speak again until the house came into sight.

Originally the main ranch house, the structure set aside for
the general foreman was an enormous, drafty place with
plenty of Victorian scrollwork, gabled windows and porches.
It overlooked a sizable spring-fed pond and boasted its own
sheltering copse of evergreens and cottonwood trees.

The truck lurched a little as Ken brought it to a stop in the
gravel driveway, and through the windshield Libby could
see glimmering patches of the silver-blue sparkle that was the
pond. She longed to hurry there now, kick off her shoes on
the grassy bank and ruin her stockings wading in the cold,
clear water.

But her father was getting out of the truck, and Cathy Barlowe, Libby's cousin and cherished friend, was dashing down
the driveway, her pretty face alight with greeting.

Libby laughed and stood waiting beside the pickup truck,
her arms out wide.

After an energetic hug had been exchanged, Cathy drew
back in Libby's arms and lifted a graceful hand to sign the
words: "I've missed you so much!"

"And I've missed you," Libby signed back, though she
spoke the words aloud, too.

Cathy's green eyes sparkled. "You haven't forgotten how
to sign!" she enthused, bringing both hands into play now.
She had been deaf since childhood, but she communicated
so skillfully that Libby often forgot that they weren't convers-
ing verbally. "Have you been practicing?"

She had. Signing had been a game for her and Jonathan
to play during the long, difficult hours she'd spent at his
hospital bedside. Libby nodded and tears of love and pride

gathered in her dark blue eyes as she surveyed her cousin—physically, she and Cathy bore no resemblance to each other at all.

Cathy was petite, her eyes wide, mischievous emeralds, her hair a glistening profusion of copper and chestnut and gold that reached almost to her waist. Libby was of medium height, and her silver-blond hair fell just short of her shoulders.

"I'll be back later," Ken said quietly, signing the words as he spoke so that Cathy could understand too. "You two have plenty to say to each other, it looks like."

Cathy nodded and smiled, but there was something sad trembling behind the joy in her green eyes, something that made Libby want to scurry back to the truck and beg to be driven back to the airstrip. From there she could fly to Kalispell and catch a connecting flight to Denver and then New York....

Good Lord—surely Jess hadn't been so heartless as to share his ridiculous suspicions with Cathy!

The interior of the house was cool and airy, and Libby followed along behind Cathy, her thoughts and feelings in an incomprehensible tangle. She was glad to be home, no doubt about it. She'd yearned for the quiet sanity of this place almost from the moment of leaving it.

On the other hand, she wasn't certain that she'd been wise to come back. Jess obviously intended to make her feel less than welcome, and although she had certainly never been intimately involved with Stacey Barlowe, Cathy's husband, sometimes her feelings toward him weren't all that clearly defined.

Unlike his younger brother, Stace was a warm, outgoing person, and through the shattering events of the past year and a half, he had been a tender and steadfast friend. Adrift in waters of confusion and grief, Libby had told Stacey things that she had never breathed to another living soul, and it was true that, as Jess had so bitterly pointed out, she had written to the man when she couldn't bring herself to contact her own father.

But she wasn't in love with Stace, Libby told herself firmly. She had always looked up to him, that was all—like an older brother. Maybe she'd become a little too dependent on him in the bargain, but that didn't mean she cared for him in a romantic way, did it?

She sighed, and Cathy turned to look at her pensively, almost as though she had heard the sound. That was impossible, of course, but Cathy was as perceptive as anyone Libby had ever known, and she often *felt* sounds.

"Glad to be home?" the deaf woman inquired, gesturing gently.

Libby didn't miss the tremor in her cousin's hands, but she forced a weary smile to her face and nodded in answer to the question.

Suddenly Cathy's eyes were sparkling again, and she caught Libby's hand in her own and tugged her through an archway and into the glassed-in sunporch that overlooked the pond.

Libby drew in a swift, delighted breath. There was indeed a skylight in the roof—a big one. A drawing table had been set up in the best light the room offered, along with a lamp for night work, and there were flowering plants hanging from the exposed beams in the ceiling. The old wicker furniture that had been stored in the attic for as long as Libby could remember had been painted a dazzling white and bedecked with gay floral-print cushions. Small rugs in complementary shades of pink and green had been scattered about randomly, and there was even a shelving unit built into the wall behind the art table.

"Wow!" cried Libby, overwhelmed, her arms spread out wide in a gesture of wonder. "Cathy, you missed your calling! You should have been an interior decorator."

Though Libby hadn't signed the words, her cousin had read them from her lips. Cathy's green eyes shifted quickly from Libby's face, and she lowered her head. "Instead of what?" she motioned sadly. "Instead of Stacey's wife?"

Libby felt as though she'd been slapped, but she recovered quickly enough to catch one hand under Cathy's chin and force her head up. "Exactly what do you mean by that?" she demanded, and she was never certain afterward whether she had signed the words, shouted them, or simply thought them.

Cathy shrugged in a miserable attempt at nonchalance, and one tear slid down her cheek. "He went to see you in New York," she challenged, her hands moving quickly now, almost angrily. "You wrote him letters!"

"Cathy, it wasn't what you think—"

"Wasn't it?"

Libby was furious and wounded, and she stomped one foot in frustration. "Of course it wasn't! Do you really think I would do a thing like that? Do you think Stacey would? He *loves* you!" *And so does Jess,* she lamented in silence, without knowing why that should matter.

Stubbornly Cathy averted her eyes again and shoved her hands into the pockets of her lightweight cotton jacket—a sure signal that as far as she was concerned, the conversation was over.

In desperation, Libby reached out and caught her cousin's

shoulders in her hands, only to be swiftly rebuffed by an eloquent shrug. She watched, stricken to silence, as Cathy turned and hurried out of the sunporch-turned-studio and into the kitchen beyond. Just a moment later the back door slammed with a finality that made Libby ache through and through.

She ducked her head and bit her lower lip to keep the tears back. That, too, was something she had learned during Jonathan's final confinement in a children's hospital.

Just then, Jess Barlowe filled the studio doorway. Libby was aware of him in all her strained senses.

He set down her suitcases and drawing board with an unsympathetic thump. "I see you're spreading joy and good cheer as usual," he drawled in acid tones. "What, pray tell, was *that* all about?"

Libby was infuriated, and she glared at him, her hands resting on her trim rounded hips. "As if you didn't know, you heartless bastard! How could you be so mean...so thoughtless..."

The fiery green eyes raked Libby's travel-rumpled form with scorn. Ignoring her aborted question, he offered one of his own. "Did you think your affair with my brother was a secret, princess?"

Libby was fairly choking on her rage and her pain. "What affair, dammit?" she shouted. "We didn't *have* an affair!"

"That isn't what Stacey says," replied Jess with impervious savagery.

Libby felt the high color that had been pounding in her face seep away. *"What?"*

"Stace is wildly in love with you, to hear him tell it. You need him and he needs you, and to hell with minor stumbling blocks like his wife!"

Libby's knees weakened and she groped blindly for the stool at her art table and then sank onto it. "My God..."

Jess's jawline was tight with brutal annoyance. "Spare me the theatrics, princess—I know why you came back here. Dammit, *don't you have a soul?*"

Libby's throat worked painfully, but her mind simply refused to form words for her to utter.

Jess crossed the room like a mountain panther, terrifying in his grace and prowess, and caught both her wrists in a furious, inescapable grasp. With his other hand he captured Libby's chin.

"Listen to me, you predatory little witch, and listen well," he hissed, his jade eyes hard, his flesh pale beneath his deep rancher's tan. "Cathy is good and decent and she loves my brother, though I can't for the life of me think why she condescends to do so. And I'll be *damned* if I'll stand by and watch you and Stacey turn her inside out! Do you understand me?"

Tears of helpless fury and outraged honor burned like fire in Libby's eyes, but she could neither speak nor move. She could only stare into the frightening face looming only inches from her own. It was a devil's face.

When Jess's tightening grasp on her chin made it clear that he would have an answer of some sort, no matter what, Libby managed a small, frantic nod.

Apparently satisfied, Jess released her with such suddenness that she nearly lost her balance and slipped off the stool.

Then he whirled away from her, his broad back taut, one powerful hand running through his obsidian hair in a typical gesture of frustration. "Damn you for ever coming back here," he said in a voice no less vicious for its softness.

"No problem," Libby said with great effort. "I'll leave."

Jess turned toward her again, this time with an ominous leisure, and his eyes scalded Libby's face, the hollow of her throat, the firm roundness of her high breasts. "It's too late," he said.

Still dazed, Libby sank back against the edge of the drawing table, sighed and covered her eyes with one hand. "Okay," she began with hard-won, shaky reason, "why is that?"

Jess had stalked to the windows; his back was a barrier between them again, and he was looking out at the pond. Libby longed to sprout claws and tear him to quivering shreds.

"Stacey has the bit in his teeth," he said at length, his voice low, speculative. "Wherever you went, he'd follow."

Since Libby didn't believe that Stacey had declared himself to be in love with her, she didn't believe that there was any danger of his following her away from the Circle Bar B, either. "You're crazy," she said.

Jess faced her quickly, some scathing retort brewing in his eyes, but whatever he had meant to say was lost as Ken strode into the room and demanded, "What the hell's going on in here? I just found Cathy running up the road in tears!"

"Ask your daughter!" Jess bit out. "Thanks to her, Cathy has just gotten *started* shedding tears!"

Libby could bear no more; she was like a wild creature goaded to madness, and she flung herself bodily at Jess Barlowe, just as she had in her childhood, fists flying. She would have attacked him gladly if her father hadn't caught hold of her around the waist and forcibly restrained her.

Jess raked her with one last contemptuous look and moved calmly in the direction of the door. "You ought to tame that little spitfire, Ken," he commented in passing. "One of these days she's going to hurt somebody."

Libby trembled in her father's hold, stung by his double meaning, and gave one senseless shriek of fury. This brought a mocking chuckle from a disappearing Jess and caused Ken to turn her firmly to face him.

"Good Lord, Libby, what's the *matter* with you?"

Libby drew a deep, steadying breath and tried to quiet the raging ten-year-old within her, the child that Jess had always been able to infuriate. "I hate Jess Barlow," she said flatly. "I hate him."

"Why?" Ken broke in, and he didn't look angry anymore. Just honestly puzzled.

"If you knew what he's been saying about me—"

"If it's the same as what Stacey's been mouthing off about, I reckon I do."

Libby stepped back, stunned. "What?"

Ken Kincaid sighed, and suddenly all his fifty-two years showed clearly in his face. "Stacey and Cathy have been having trouble the last year or so. Now he's telling everybody who'll listen that it's over between him and Cathy and he wants you."

"I don't believe it! I—"

"I wanted to warn you, Lib, but you'd been through so much, between losing the boy and then falling out with your husband after that. I thought you needed to be home, but I knew you wouldn't come near the place if you had any idea what was going on."

Libby's chin trembled, and she searched her father's honest, weathered face anxiously. "I...I haven't been fooling around with C-Cathy's husband, Dad."

He smiled gently. "I know that, Lib—knew it all along. Just never mind Jess and all the rest of them—if you don't run away, this thing'll blow over."

Libby swallowed, thinking of Cathy and the pain she had to be feeling. The betrayal. "I can't stay here if Cathy is going to be hurt."

Ken touched her cheek with a work-worn finger. "Cathy doesn't really believe the rumors, Libby—think about it. Why would she work so hard to fix a studio up for you if she did? Why would she be waiting here to see you again?"

"But she was crying just now, Dad! And she as much as accused me of carrying on with her husband!"

"She's been hurt by what's been said, and Stacey's been acting like a spoiled kid. Honey, Cathy's just testing the waters, trying to find out where you stand. You can't leave her now, because except for Stace, there's nobody she needs more."

Despite the fact that all her instincts warned her to put the Circle Bar B behind her as soon as humanly possible, Libby saw the sense in her father's words. As incredible as it seemed, Cathy would need her—if for nothing else than to lay those wretched rumors to rest once and for all.

"These things Stacey's been saying—surely he didn't unload them on Cathy?"

Ken sighed. "I don't think he'd be that low, Libby. But you know how it is with Cathy, how she always knows the score."

Libby shook her head distractedly. "Somebody told her, Dad—and I think I know who it was."

There was disbelief in Ken's discerning blue eyes, and in his voice, too. "*Jess?* Now, wait a minute…"

Jess.

Libby couldn't remember a time when she had gotten along well with him, but she'd been sure that he cared deeply for Cathy. Hadn't he been the one to insist that Stace and Libby learn signing, as he had, so that everyone could talk to the frightened, confused little girl who couldn't hear? Hadn't he gifted Cathy with cherished bullfrogs and clumsily made valentines and even taken her to the high-school prom?

How could Jess, of all people, be the one to hurt Cathy, when he knew as well as anyone how badly she'd been hurt by her handicap and the rejection of her own parents? How?

Libby had no answer for any of these questions. She knew only that she had separate scores to settle with both the Barlowe brothers.

And settle them she would.

2

Libby sat at the end of the rickety swimming dock, bare feet dangling, shoulders slumped, her gaze fixed on the shimmering waters of the pond. The lines of her long, slender legs were accentuated, rather than disguised, by the old blue jeans she wore. A white eyelet suntop sheltered shapely breasts and a trim stomach and left the rest of her upper body bare.

Jess Barlow studied her in silence, feeling things that were at wide variance with his personal opinion of the woman. He was certain that he hated Libby, but something inside him wanted, nonetheless, to touch her, to comfort her, to know the scent and texture of her skin.

A reluctant grin tilted one corner of his mouth. One tug at the top of that white eyelet and...

Jess caught his skittering thoughts, marshaled them back into stern order. As innocent and vulnerable as Libby Kincaid looked at the moment, she was a viper, willing to betray her own cousin to get what she wanted.

Jess imagined Libby naked, her glorious breasts free and welcoming. But the man in his mental scenario was not himself—it was Stacey. The thought lay sour in Jess's mind.

"Did you come to apologize, by any chance?"

The question so startled Jess that he flinched; he had not

noticed that Libby had turned around and seen him, so caught up had he been in the vision of her giving herself to his brother.

He scowled, as much to recover his wits as to oppose her. It was and always had been his nature to oppose Libby Kincaid, the way electricity opposes water, and it annoyed him that, for all his travels and his education, he didn't know why.

"Why would I want to do that?" he shot back, more ruffled by her presence than he ever would have admitted.

"Maybe because you were a complete ass," she replied in tones as sunny as the big sky stretched out above them.

Jess lifted his hands to his hips and stood fast against whatever it was that was pulling him toward her. *I want to make love to you,* he thought, and the truth of that ground in his spirit as well as in his loins.

There was pain in Libby's navy-blue eyes, as well as a cautious mischief. "Well?" she prodded.

Jess found that while he could keep himself from going to her, he could not turn away. Maybe her net reached farther than he'd thought. Maybe, like Stacey and that idiot in New York, he was already caught in it.

"I'm not here to apologize," he said coldly.

"Then why?" she asked with chiming sweetness.

He wondered if she knew what that shoulderless blouse of hers was doing to him. Damn. He hadn't been this tongue-tied since the night of his fifteenth birthday, when Ginny Hillerman had announced that she would show him hers if he would show her his.

Libby's eyes were laughing at him. "Jess?"

"Is your dad here?" he threw out in gruff desperation.

One shapely, gossamer eyebrow arched. "You know perfectly well that he isn't. If Dad were home, his pickup truck would be parked in the driveway."

Against his will, Jess grinned. His taut shoulders rose in a shrug. The shadows of cottonwood leaves moved on the old wooden dock, forming a mystical path—a path that led to Libby Kincaid.

She patted the sun-warmed wood beside her. "Come and sit down."

Before Jess could stop himself, he was striding along that small wharf, sinking down to sit beside Libby and dangle his booted feet over the sparkling water. He was never entirely certain what sorcery made him ask what he did.

"What happened to your marriage, Libby?"

The pain he had glimpsed before leapt in her eyes and then faded away again, subdued. "Are you trying to start another fight?"

Jerry shook his head. "No," he answered quietly, "I really want to know."

She looked away from him, gnawing at her lower lip with her front teeth. All around them were ranch sounds—birds conferring in the trees, leaves rustling in the wind, the clear pond water lapping at the mossy pilings of the dock. But no sound came from Libby.

On an impulse, Jess touched her mouth with the tip of one index finger. Water and electricity—the analogy came back to him with a numbing jolt.

"Stop that," he barked, to cover his reactions.

Libby ceased chewing at her lip and stared at him with wide eyes. Again he saw the shadow of that nameless, shifting ache inside her. "Stop what?" she wanted to know.

Stop making me want to hold you, he thought. *Stop making me want to tuck your hair back behind your ears and tell you that everything will be all right.* "Stop biting your lip!" he snapped aloud.

"I'm sorry!" Libby snapped back, her eyes shooting indigo sparks.

Jess sighed and again spoke involuntarily. "Why did you leave your husband, Libby?"

The question jarred them both: Libby paled a little and tried to scramble to her feet; Jess caught her elbow in one hand and pulled her down again.

"Was it because of Stacey?"

She was livid. "No!"

"Someone else?"

Tears sprang up in Libby's dark lashes and made then spiky. She wrenched free of his hand but made no move to rise again and run away. "Sure!" she gasped. "'If it feels good, do it'—that's my motto! By God, I *live* by those words!"

"Shut up," Jess said in a gentle voice.

Incredibly, she fell against him, wept into the shoulder of his blue cotton workshirt. And it was not a delicate, calculating sort of weeping—it was a noisy grief.

Jess drew her close and held her, broken on the shoals of what she was feeling even though he did not know its name. "I'm sorry," he said hoarsely.

Libby trembled beneath his arm and wailed like a wounded calf. The sound solidified into a word usually reserved for stubborn horses and income-tax audits.

Jess laughed and, for a reason he would never understand, kissed her forehead. "I love it when you flatter me," he teased.

Miraculously, Libby laughed too. But when she tilted her head back to look up at him, and he saw the tear streaks on her beautiful, defiant face, something within him, something that had always been disjointed, was wrenched painfully back into place.

He bent his head and touched his lips to hers, gently, in question. She stiffened, but then, at the cautious bidding of his tongue, her lips parted slightly and her body relaxed against his.

Jess pressed Libby backward until she lay prone on the shifting dock, the kiss unbroken. As she responded to that kiss, it seemed that the sparkling water-light of the pond danced around them both in huge, shimmering chips, that they were floating inside some cosmic prism.

His hand went to the full roundness of her left breast. Beneath his palm and the thin layer of white eyelet, he felt the nipple grow taut in that singular invitation to passion.

Through the back of his shirt, Jess was warmed by the heat of the spring sun and the tender weight of Libby's hands. He left her mouth to trail soft kisses over her chin, along the sweet, scented lines of her neck.

All the while, he expected her to stiffen again, to thrust him away with her hands and some indignant—and no doubt colorful—outburst. Instead, she was pliant and yielding beneath him.

Enthralled, he dared more and drew downward on the uppermost ruffle of her suntop. Still she did not protest.

Libby arched her back and a low, whimpering sound came from her throat as Jess bared her to the soft spring breeze and the fire of his gaze.

Her breasts were heavy golden-white globes, and their pale rose crests stiffened as Jess perused them. When he offered a whisper-soft kiss to one, Libby moaned and the other peak pouted prettily at his choice. He went to it, soothed it to fury with his tongue.

Libby gave a soft, lusty cry, shuddered and caught her hands in his hair, drawing him closer. He needed more of her and positioned his body accordingly, careful not to let his full weight come to bear. Then, for a few dizzying moments, he took suckle at the straining fount of her breast.

Recovering himself partially, Jess pulled her hands from his hair, gripped them at the wrists, pressed them down above her head in gentle restraint.

Her succulent breasts bore his assessment proudly, rising and falling with the meter of her breathing.

Jess forced himself to meet Libby's eyes. "This is me," he reminded her gruffly. "Jess."

"I know," she whispered, making no move to free her imprisoned hands.

Jess lowered his head, tormented one delectable nipple by drawing at it with his lips. "This is real, Libby," he said, circling the morsel with just the tip of his tongue now. "It's important that you realize that."

"I do…oh, God…Jess, *Jess.*"

Reluctantly he left the feast to search her face with disbelieving eyes. "Don't you want me to stop?"

A delicate shade of rose sifted over her high cheekbones. Her hands still stretched above her, her eyes closed, she shook her head.

Jess went back to the breasts that so bewitched him, nipped at their peaks with gentle teeth. "Do you…know how many…times I've wanted…to do this?"

The answer was a soft, strangled cry.

He limited himself to one nipple, worked its surrendering peak into a sweet fervor with his lips and his tongue. "So…many…times. My God, Libby…you're so beautiful…"

Her words were as halting as his had been. "What's happening to us? We h-hate each other."

Jess laughed and began kissing his way softly down over her rib cage, her smooth, firm stomach. The snap on her jeans gave way easily—and was echoed by the sound of car doors slamming in the area of the house.

Instantly the spell was broken. Color surged into Libby's face and she bolted upright, nearly thrusting Jess off the end of the dock in her efforts to wrench on the discarded suntop and close the fastening of her jeans.

"Broad daylight…" she muttered distractedly, talking more to herself than to Jess.

"Lib!" yelled a jovial masculine voice, approaching fast. "Libby?"

Stacey. The voice belonged to Stacey.

Sudden fierce anger surged, white-hot, through Jess's aching, bedazzled system. Standing up, not caring that his thwarted passion still strained against his jeans, visible to anyone who might take the trouble to look, he glared down at Libby and rasped, "I guess reinforcements have arrived."

She gave a primitive, protesting little cry and shot to her feet, her ink-blue eyes flashing with anger and hurt. Before Jess could brace himself, her hands came to his chest like small battering rams and pushed him easily off the end of the dock.

The jolting cold of that spring-fed pond was welcome balm to Jess's passion-heated flesh, if not his pride. When he surfaced and grasped the end of the dock in both hands, he knew there would be no physical evidence that he and Libby had been doing anything other than fighting.

Libby ached with embarrassment as Stacey and Senator Barlowe made their way down over the slight hillside that separated the backyard from the pond.

The older man cast one mischievously baleful look at his younger son, who was lifting himself indignantly onto the dock, and chuckled, "I see things are the same as always," he said.

Libby managed a shaky smile. *Not quite,* she thought, her body remembering the delicious dance Jess's hard frame had choreographed for it. "Hello, Senator," she said, rising on tiptoe to kiss his cheek.

"Welcome home," he replied with gruff affection. Then his wise eyes shifted past her to rest again on Jess. "It's a little cold yet for a swim, isn't it, son?"

Jess's hair hung in dripping ebony strands around his face, and his eyes were jade-green flares, avoiding his father to scald Libby's lips, her throat, her still-pulsing breasts. "We'll finish our…discussion later," he said.

Libby's blood boiled up over her stomach and her breasts to glow in her face. "I wouldn't count on that!"

"I would," Jess replied with a smile that was at once tender and evil. And then, without so much as a word to his father and brother, he walked away.

"What the hell did he mean by that?" barked Stacey, red in the face.

The look Libby gave the boyishly handsome, caramel-eyed man beside her was hardly friendly. "You've got some tall explaining to do, Stacey Barlowe," she said.

The senator, a tall, attractive man with hair as gray as Ken's, cleared his throat in the way of those who have practiced diplomacy long and well. "I believe I'll go up to the house and see if Ken's got any beer on hand," he said. A moment later he was off, following Jess's soggy path.

Libby straightened her shoulders and calmly slapped Stacey across the face. "How dare you?" she raged, her words strangled in her effort to modulate them.

Stacey reddened again, ran one hand through his fashion-ably cut wheat-colored hair. He turned, as if to follow his fa-ther. "I could use a beer myself," he said in distracted, evasive tones.

"Oh, no you don't!" Libby cried, grasping his arm and holding on. The rich leather of his jacket was smooth under her hand. "Don't you *dare* walk away from me, Stacey—not until you explain why you've been lying about me!"

"I haven't been lying!" he protested, his hands on his hips now, his expensively clad body blocking the base of the dock as he faced her.

"You have! You've been telling everyone that I...that we..."

"That we've been doing what you and my brother were doing a few minutes ago?"

If Stacey had shoved Libby into the water, she couldn't have been more shocked. A furious retort rose to the back of her throat but would go no further.

Stacey's tarnished-gold eyes flashed. "Jess was making love to you, wasn't he?"

"What if he was?" managed Libby after a painful strug-gle with her vocal cords. "It certainly wouldn't be any of your business, would it?"

"Yes, it would. I love you, Libby."

"You love *Cathy!*"

Stacey shook his head. "No. Not anymore."

"Don't say that," Libby pleaded, suddenly deflated. "Oh, Stacey, don't. Don't do this..."

His hands came to her shoulders, fierce and strong. The topaz fever in his eyes made Libby wonder if he was sane.

"I love you, Libby Kincaid," he vowed softly but ferociously, "and I mean to have you."

Libby retreated a step, stunned, shaking her head. The reality of this situation was so different from what she had imagined it would be. In her thoughts, Stacey had laughed when she confronted him, ruffled her hair in that familiar brotherly way of old, and said that it was all a mistake. That he loved Cathy, wanted Cathy, and couldn't anyone around here take a joke?

But here he was declaring himself in a way that was unsettlingly serious.

Libby took another step backward. "Stacey, I need to be here, where my dad is. Where things are familiar and comfortable. Please…don't force me to leave."

Stacey smiled. "There is no point in leaving, Lib. If you do, I'll be right behind you."

She shivered. "You've lost your mind!"

But Stacey looked entirely sane as he shook his handsome head and wedged his hands into the pockets of his jacket. "Just my heart," he said. "Corny, isn't it?"

"It's worse than corny. Stacey, you're unbalanced or something. You're fantasizing. There was never anything between us—"

"No?" The word was crooned.

"No! You need help."

His face had all the innocence of an altar boy's. "If I'm insane, darlin', it's something you could cure."

Libby resisted an urge to slap him again. She wanted to race into the house, but he was still barring her way, so that she could not leave the dock without brushing against him. "Stay away from me, Stacey," she said as he advanced toward her. "I mean it—stay away from me!"

"I can't, Libby."

The sincerity in his voice was chilling; for the first time in all the years she'd known Stacey Barlowe, Libby was afraid of him. Discretion kept her from screaming, but just barely.

Stacey paled, as though he'd read her thoughts. "Don't look at me like that, Libby—I wouldn't hurt you under any circumstances. And I'm not crazy."

She lifted her chin. "Let me by, Stacey. I want to go into the house."

He tilted his head back, sighed, met her eyes again. "I've frightened you, and I'm sorry. I didn't mean to do that."

Libby couldn't speak. Despite his rational, settling words, she was sick with the knowledge that he meant to pursue her.

"You must know," he said softly, "how good it could be for us. You needed me in New York, Libby, and now I need you."

The third voice, from the base of the hillside, was to Libby as a life preserver to a drowning person. "Let her pass, Stacey."

Libby looked up quickly to see Jess, unlikely rescuer that he was. His hair was towel-rumpled and his jeans clung to muscular thighs—thighs that only minutes ago had pressed against her own in a demand as old as time. His manner was calm as he buttoned a shirt, probably borrowed from Ken, over his broad chest.

Stacey shrugged affably and walked past his brother without a word of argument.

Watching him go, Libby went weak with relief. A lump rose in her throat as she forced herself to meet Jess's gaze. "You were right," she muttered miserably. "You were *right*."

Jess was watching her much the way a mountain cat would watch a cornered rabbit. For the briefest moment there was a look of tenderness in the green eyes, but then his expression turned hard and a muscle flexed in his jaw. "I trust the welcome-home party has been scheduled for later—after Cathy has been tucked into her bed, for instance?"

Libby gaped at him, appalled. Had he interceded only to torment her himself?

Jess's eyes were contemptuous as they swept over her. "What's the matter, Lib? Couldn't you bring yourself to tell your married lover that the welcoming had already been taken care of?"

Rage went through Libby's body like an electric current surging into a wire. "You don't seriously think that I would...that I was—"

"You even managed to be alone with him. Tell me, Lib—how did you get rid of my father?"

"G-get rid..." Libby stopped, tears of shock and mortification aching in her throat and burning behind her eyes. She drew a deep, audible breath, trying to assemble herself, to think clearly.

But the whole world seemed to be tilting and swirling like some out-of-control carnival ride. When Libby closed her eyes against the sensation, she swayed dangerously and would probably have fallen if Jess hadn't reached her in a few strides and caught her shoulders in his hands.

"Libby..." he said, and there was anger in the sound, but there was a hollow quality, too—one that Libby couldn't find a name for.

Her knees were trembling. Too much, it was all too much. Jonathan's death, the ugly divorce, the trouble that Stacey had caused with his misplaced affections—all of those things weighed on her, but none were so crushing as the blatant contempt of this man. It was apparent to Libby now that the lovemaking they had almost shared, so new and beautiful to her, had been some sort of cruel joke to Jess.

"How could you?" she choked out. "Oh, Jess, how could you?"

His face was grim, seeming to float in a shimmering mist. Instead of answering, Jess lifted Libby into his arms and carried her up the little hill toward the house.

She didn't remember reaching the back door.

"What the devil happened on that dock today, Jess?" Cleave Barlowe demanded, hands grasping the edge of his desk.

His younger son stood at the mahogany bar, his shoulders stiff, his attention carefully fixed on the glass of straight Scotch he meant to consume. "Why don't you ask Stacey?"

"Goddammit, I'm asking *you!*" barked Cleave. "Ken's mad as hell, and I don't blame him—that girl of his was shattered!"

Girl. The word caught in Jess's beleaguered mind. He remembered the way Libby had responded to him, meeting his passion with her own, welcoming the greed he'd shown at her breasts. Had it not been for the arrival of his father and brother, he would have possessed her completely within minutes. "She's no 'girl,'" he said, still aching to bury himself in the depths of her.

The senator swore roundly. "What did you say to her, Jess?" he pressed, once the spate of unpoliticianly profanity had passed.

Jess lowered his head. He'd meant the things he'd said to Libby, and he couldn't, in all honesty, have taken them back. But he knew some of what she'd been through in New York, her trysts with Stacey notwithstanding, and he was ashamed of the way he'd goaded her. She had come home to heal—the look in her eyes had told him that much—and instead of respecting that, he had made things more difficult for her.

Never one to be thwarted by silence, no matter how eloquent, Senator Barlowe persisted. "Dammit, Jess, I might expect this kind of thing from Stacey, but I thought you had more sense! You were harassing Libby about these blasted rumors your brother has been spreading, weren't you?"

Jess sighed, set aside the drink he had yet to take a sip from, and faced his angry father. "Yes," he said.

"Why?"

Stubbornly, Jess refused to answer. He took an interest in the imposing oak desk where his father sat, the heavy draperies that kept out the sun, the carved ivory of the fireplace.

"All right, mulehead," Cleave muttered furiously, "don't talk! Don't explain! And don't go near Ken Kincaid's daughter again, damn you. That man's the best foreman I've ever had and if he gets riled and quits because of you, Jess, you and I are going to come to time!"

Jess almost smiled, though he didn't quite dare. Not too many years before the phrase "come to time," when used by his father, had presaged a session in the woodshed. He wondered what it meant now that he was thirty-three years old, a member of the Montana State Bar Association, and a full partner in the family corporation. "I care about Cathy," he said evenly. "What was I supposed to do—stand by and watch Libby and Stace grind her up into emotional hamburger?"

Cleave gave a heavy sigh and sank into the richly upholstered swivel chair behind his desk. "I love Cathy too," he said at length, "but Stacey's behind this whole mess, not Libby. Dammit, that woman has been through hell from what

Ken says—she was married to a man who slept in every bed but his own, and she had to watch her nine-year-old stepson die by inches. Now she comes home looking for a little peace, and what does she get? Trouble!"

Jess lowered his head, turned away—ostensibly to take up his glass of Scotch. He'd known about the bad marriage—Ken had cussed the day Aaron Strand was born often enough—but he hadn't heard about the little boy. My God, he hadn't known about the boy.

"Maybe Strand couldn't sleep in his own bed," he said, urged on by some ugliness that had surfaced inside him since Libby's return. "Maybe Stacey was already in it."

"Enough!" boomed the senator in a voice that had made presidents tremble in their shoes. "I like Libby and I'm not going to listen to any more of this, either from you or from your brother! Do I make myself clear?"

"Abundantly clear," replied Jess, realizing that the Scotch was in his hand now and feeling honor-bound to take at least one gulp of the stuff. The taste was reminiscent of scorched rubber, but since the liquor seemed to quiet the raging demons in his mind, he finished the drink and poured another.

He fully intended to get drunk. It was something he hadn't done since high school, but it suddenly seemed appealing. Maybe he would stop hardening every time he thought of Libby, stop craving her.

Too, after the things he'd said to her that afternoon by the pond, he didn't want to remain sober any longer than necessary. "What did you mean," he ventured, after downing his fourth drink, "when you said Libby had to watch her stepson die?"

Papers rustled at the big desk behind him. "Stacey says the child had leukemia."

Jess poured another drink and closed his eyes. *Oh, Libby,*

he thought, *I'm sorry. My God, I'm sorry.* "I guess Stacey would know," he said aloud, with bitterness.

There was a short, thunderous silence. Jess expected his father to explode into one of his famous tirades, was genuinely surprised when the man sighed instead. Still, his words dropped on Jess's mind like a bomb.

"The firewater isn't going to change the fact that you love Libby Kincaid, Jess," he said reasonably. "Making her life and your own miserable isn't going to change it either."

Love Libby Kincaid? Impossible. The strange needs possessing him now were rooted in his libido, not his heart. Once he'd had her—and have her he would, or go crazy—her hold on him would be broken. "I've never loved a woman in my life," he said.

"Fool. You've loved one woman—Libby—since you were seven years old. Exactly seven years old, in fact."

Jess turned, studying his father quizzically. "What the hell are you talking about?"

"Your seventh birthday," recalled Cleave, his eyes far away. "Your mother and I gave you a pony. First time you saw Libby Kincaid, you were out of that saddle and helping her into it."

The memory burst, full-blown, into Jess's mind. A pinto pony. The new foreman arriving. The little girl with dark blue eyes and hair the color of winter moonlight.

He'd spent the whole afternoon squiring Libby around the yard, content to walk while she rode.

"What do you suppose Ken would say if I went over there and asked to see his daughter?" Jess asked.

"I imagine he'd shoot you, after today."

"I imagine he would. But I think I'll risk it."

"You've made enough trouble for one day," argued Cleave,

taking obvious note of his son's inebriated state. "Libby needs time, Jess. She needs to be close to Ken. If you're smart, you'll leave her alone until she has a chance to get her emotional bearings again."

Jess didn't want his father to be right, not in this instance, anyway, but he knew that he was. Much as he wanted to go to Libby and try to make things right, the fact was that he was the last person in the world she needed or wanted to see.

"Better?"

Libby smiled at Ken as she came into the kitchen, freshly showered and wrapped in the cozy, familiar chenille robe she'd found in the back of her closet. "Lots better," she answered softly.

Her father was standing at the kitchen stove stirring something in the blackened cast-iron skillet.

Libby scuffled to the table and sat down. It was good to be home, so good. Why hadn't she come sooner? "Whatever you're cooking there smells good," she said.

Ken beamed. In his jeans and his western shirt, he looked out of place at that stove. He should, Libby decided fancifully, have been crouching at some campfire on the range, stirring beans in a blue enamel pot. "This here's my world-famous red-devil sauce," he grinned, "for which I am known and respected."

Libby laughed, and tears of homecoming filled her eyes. She went to her father and hugged him, needing to be a little girl again, just for a moment.

3

Libby nearly choked on her first taste of Ken's taco sauce. "Did you say you were known and respected for this stuff, or known and feared?"

Ken chuckled roguishly at her tear-polished eyes and flaming face. "My calling it 'red devil' should have been a clue, dumplin'."

Libby muttered an exclamation and perversely took another bite from her bulging taco. "From now on," she said, chewing, "I'll do the cooking around this spread."

Her father laughed again and tapped one temple with a calloused index finger, his pale blue eyes twinkling.

"You deliberately tricked me!" cried Libby.

He grinned and shrugged. "Code of the West, sweetheart. Grouse about the chow, and presto—you're the cook!"

"Actually," ventured Libby with cultivated innocence, "this sauce isn't too bad."

"Too late," laughed Ken. "You already broke the code."

Libby lowered her taco to her plate and lifted both hands in a gesture of concession. "All right, all right—but have a little pity on me, will you? I've been living among dudes!"

"That's no excuse."

Libby shrugged and took up her taco again. "I tried. Have

you been doing your own cooking and cleaning all this time?"

Ken shook his head and sat back in his chair, his thumbs hooked behind his belt buckle. "Nope. The Barlowes' housekeeper sends her crew down here once in a while."

"What about the food?"

"I eat with the boys most of the time, over at the cook shack." He rose, went to fill two mugs from the coffeepot on the stove. When he turned around again, his face was serious. "Libby, what happened today? What upset you like that?"

Libby averted her eyes. "I don't know," she lied lamely.

"Dammit, you *do* know. You fainted, Libby. When Jess carried you in here, I—"

"I know," Libby broke in gently. "You were scared. I'm sorry."

Carefully, as though he feared he might drop them, Ken set the cups of steaming coffee on the table. "What happened?" he persisted as he sat down in his chair again.

Libby swallowed hard, but the lump that had risen in her throat wouldn't go down. Knowing that this conversation couldn't be avoided forever, she managed to reply, "It's complicated. Basically, it comes down to the fact that Stacey's been telling those lies."

"And?"

"And Jess believes him. He said…he said some things to me and…well, it must have created some kind of emotional overload. I just gave out."

Ken turned his mug idly between his thumb and index finger, causing the liquid to spill over and make a coffee stain on the tablecloth. "Tell me about Jonathan, Libby," he said in a low, gentle voice.

The tears that sprang into Libby's eyes were not related to the tang of her father's red-devil taco sauce. "He died," she choked miserably.

"I know that. You called me the night it happened, remember? I guess what I'm really asking you is why you didn't want me to fly back there and help you sort things out."

Libby lowered her head. Jonathan hadn't been her son, he'd been Aaron's, by a previous marriage. But the loss of the child was a raw void within her, even though months had passed. "I didn't want you to get a firsthand look at my marriage," she admitted with great difficulty—and the shame she couldn't seem to shake.

"Why not, Libby?"

The sound Libby made might have been either a laugh or a sob. "Because it was terrible," she answered.

"From the first?"

She forced herself to meet her father's steady gaze, knew that he had guessed a lot about her marriage from her rare phone calls and even rarer letters. "Almost," she replied sadly.

"Tell me."

Libby didn't want to think about Aaron, let alone talk about him to this man who wouldn't understand so many things. "He had…he had lovers."

Ken didn't seem surprised. Had he guessed that, too? "Go on."

"I can't!"

"Yes, you can. If it's too much for you right now, I won't press you. But the sooner you talk this out, Libby, the better off you're going to be."

She realized that her hands were clenched in her lap and tried to relax them. There was still a white mark on her finger where Aaron's ostentatious wedding ring had been. "He didn't care," she mourned in a soft, distracted whisper. "He honestly didn't care…"

"About you?"

"About Jonathan. Dad, he didn't care about his own son!"

"How so, sweetheart?"

Libby dashed away tears with the back of one hand. "Th-things were bad between Aaron and me b-before we found out that Jonathan was sick. After the doctors told us, it was a lot worse."

"I don't follow you, Libby."

"Dad, Aaron wouldn't have anything to do with Jonathan from the moment we knew he was dying. He wasn't there for any of the tests and he never once came to visit at the hospital. Dad, that little boy cried for his father, and Aaron wouldn't come to him!"

"Did you talk to Aaron?"

Remembered frustration made Libby's cheeks pound with color. "I *pleaded* with him, Dad. All he'd say was, 'I can't handle this.'"

"It would be a hell of a thing to deal with, Lib. Maybe you're being too hard on the man."

"Too hard? *Too hard?* Jonathan was terrified, Dad, and he was in pain—constant pain. All he asked was that his own father be strong for him!"

"What about the boy's mother? Did she come to the hospital?"

"Ellen died when Jonathan was a baby."

Ken sighed, framing a question he was obviously reluctant to ask. "Did you ever love Aaron Strand, Libby?"

Libby remembered the early infatuation, the excitement that had never deepened into real love and had quickly been quelled by the realities of marriage to a man who was funda-

mentally self-centered. She tried, but she couldn't even re-
call her ex-husband's face clearly—all she could see in her
mind was a pair of jade-green eyes, dark hair. Jess. "No," she
finally said. "I thought I did when I married him, though."

Ken stood up suddenly, took the coffeepot from its back
burner on the stove, refilled both their cups. "I don't like asking you this, but—"

"No, Dad," Libby broke in firmly, anticipating the question all too well, "I don't love Stacey!"

"You're sure about that?"

The truth was that Libby *hadn't* been sure, not entirely.
But that ill-advised episode with Jess at the end of the
swimming dock had brought everything into clear per-
spective. Just remembering how willingly she had submitted to him made her throb with embarrassment. "I'm sure,"
she said.

Ken's strong hand came across the table to close over
hers. "You're home now," he reminded her, "and things are
going to get better, Libby. I promise you that."

Libby sniffled inelegantly. "Know something, cowboy? I
love you very much."

"Bet you say that to all your fathers," Ken quipped. "You
planning to work on your comic strip tomorrow?"

The change of subject was welcome. "I'm six or eight
weeks ahead of schedule on that, and the mechanicals for the
book aren't due till fall. I think I'll go riding instead, if I can
get Cathy to go with me."

"What's a 'mechanical'?"

Libby smiled, feeling sheltered by the love of this strong
and steady man facing her. "It's the finished drawing that I
turn in, along with the instructions for the colorist."

"You don't do the colors?" Ken seemed surprised at that,

knowing, as he did, her love for vivid shades and subtle hues alike.

"No, I just do the panels and the lettering." It was good to talk about work, to think about work. Disdainful as he had been about her career, it was the one thing Aaron had not been able to spoil for her.

Nobody's fool, Ken drew her out on the subject as much as he could, and she found herself chattering on and on about cartooning and even her secret hope to branch out into portraits one day.

They talked, father and daughter, far into the night.

"You deserve this," Jess Barlowe said to his reflection in the bathroom mirror. A first-class hangover pounded in his head and roiled in his stomach, and his face looked drawn, as though he'd been hibernating like one of the bears that sometimes troubled the range stock.

Grimly he began to shave, and as he wielded his disposable razor, he wondered if Libby was awake yet. Should he stop at Ken's and talk to her before going on to the main house to spend a day with the corporation accountants?

Jess wanted to go to Libby, to tell her that he was sorry for baiting her, to try to get their complex relationship—if it *was* a relationship—onto some kind of sane ground. However, all his instincts told him that his father had been right the day before: Libby needed time.

His thoughts strayed to Libby's stepson. What would it be like to sit by a hospital bed, day after day, watching a child suffer and not being able to help?

Jess shuddered. It was hard to imagine the horror of something like that. At least Libby had had her husband to share the nightmare.

He frowned as he nicked his chin with the razor, blotted the small wound with tissue paper. If Libby had had her husband during that impossible time, why had she needed Stacey?

Stacey. Now, there was someone he could talk to. Granted, Jess had not been on the best of terms with his older brother of late, but the man had a firsthand knowledge of what was happening inside Libby Kincaid, and that was reason enough to approach him.

Feeling better for having a plan, Jess finished his ablutions and got dressed. Normally he spent his days on the range with Ken and the ranch hands, but today, because of his meeting with the accountants, he forwent his customary blue jeans and cotton workshirt for a tailored three-piece suit. He was still struggling with his tie as he made his way down the broad redwood steps that led from the loftlike second floor of his house to the living room.

Here there was a massive fireplace of white limestone, taking up the whole of one wall. The floors were polished oak and boasted a number of brightly colored Indian rugs. Two easy chairs and a deep sofa faced the hearth, and Jess's cluttered desk looked out over the ranchland and the glacial mountains beyond.

Striding toward the front door, in exasperation he gave up his efforts to get the tie right. He was glad he didn't have Stacey's job; not for him the dull task of overseeing the family's nationwide chain of steak-house franchises.

He smiled. Stacey liked playing the dude, doing television commercials, traveling all over the country.

And taking Libby Kincaid to bed.

Jess stalked across the front lawn to the carport and climbed behind the wheel of the station wagon he'd driven

since law school. One of these times, he was going to have
to get another car—something with a little flash, like Stacey's
Ferrari.

Stacey, Stacey. He hadn't even seen his brother yet, and
already he was sick of him.

The station wagon's engine made a grinding sound and
then huffed to life. Jess patted the dusty dashboard affection-
ately and grinned. A car was a car was a car, he reflected as
he backed the notorious wreck out of his driveway. The func-
tion of a car was to transport people, not impress them.

Five minutes later, Jess's station wagon chortled to an
asthmatic stop beside his brother's ice-blue Ferrari. He
looked up at the modernistic two-story house that had been
the senator's wedding gift to Stacey and Cathy and wondered
if Libby would be impressed by the place.

He scowled as he made his way up the curving white-stone
walk. What the hell did he care if Libby was impressed?

Irritated, he jabbed one finger at the special doorbell that
would turn on a series of blinking lights inside the house.
The system had been his own idea, meant to make life easier for Cathy.

His sister-in-law came to the door and smiled at him somewhat wanly, speaking with her hands. "Good morning."

Jess nodded, smiled. The haunted look in the depths of
Cathy's eyes made him angry all over again. "Is Stacey
here?" he signed, stepping into the house.

Cathy caught his hand in her own and led him through the
cavernous living room and the formal dining room beyond.
Stacey was in the kitchen, looking more at home in a three-
piece suit than Jess ever had.

"You," Stacey said tonelessly, setting down the English
muffin he'd been slathering with honey.

Cathy offered coffee and left the room when it was politely declined. Distractedly Jess reflected on the fact that her life had to be boring as hell, centering on Stacey the way it did.

"I want to talk to you," Jess said, scraping back a chrome-and-plastic chair to sit down at the table.

Stacey arched one eyebrow. "I hope it's quick—I'm leaving for the airport in a few minutes. I've got some business to take care of in Kansas City."

Jess was impatient. "What kind of man is Libby's ex-husband?" he asked.

Stacey took up his coffee. "Why do you want to know?"

"I just do. Do I have to have him checked out, or are you going to tell me?"

"He's a bastard," said Stacey, not quite meeting his brother's eyes.

"Rich?"

"Oh, yes. His family is old-money."

"What does he do?"

"Do?"

"Yeah. Does he work, or does he just stand around being rich?"

"He runs the family advertising agency; I think he has a lot of control over their other financial interests too."

Jess sensed that Stacey was hedging, wondered why. "Any bad habits?"

Stacey was gazing at the toaster now, in a fixed way, as though he expected something alarming to pop out of it. "The man has his share of vices."

Annoyed now, Jess got up, helped himself to the cup of coffee he had refused earlier, sat down again. "Pulling porcupine quills out of a dog's nose would be easier than getting answers out of you. When you say he has vices, do you mean women?"

Stacey swallowed, looked away. "To put it mildly," he said.

Jess settled back in his chair. "What the hell do you mean by that?"

"I mean that he not only liked to run around with other women, he liked to flaunt the fact. The worse he could make Libby feel about herself, the happier he was."

"Jesus," Jess breathed. "What else?" he pressed, sensing, from Stacey's expression, that there was more.

"He was impotent with Libby."

"Why did she stay? Why in God's name did she stay?" Jess mused distractedly, as much to himself as to his brother.

A cautious but smug light flickered in Stacey's topaz eyes. "She had me," he said evenly. "Besides, Jonathan was sick by that time and she felt she had to stay in the marriage for his sake."

The spacious sun-filled kitchen seemed to buckle and shift around Jess. "Why didn't she tell Ken, at least?"

"What would have been the point in that, Jess? He couldn't have made the boy well again or transformed Aaron Strand into a devoted husband."

The things Libby must have endured—the shame, the loneliness, the humiliation and grief, washed over Jess in a dismal, crushing wave. No wonder she had reached out to Stacey the way she had. No wonder. "Thanks," he said gruffly, standing up to leave.

"Jess?"

He paused in the kitchen doorway, his hands clasping the woodwork, his shoulders aching with tension. "What?"

"Don't worry about Libby. I'll take care of her."

Jess felt a despairing sort of anger course through him. "What about Cathy?" he asked, without turning around. "Who is going to take care of her?"

"You've always—"

Jess whirled suddenly, staring at his brother, almost hating him. "I've always *what?*"

"Cared for her." Stacey shrugged, looking only mildly unsettled. "Protected her…"

"Are you suggesting that I sweep up the pieces after you shatter her?" demanded Jess in a dangerous rasp.

Stacey only shrugged again.

Because he feared that he would do his brother lasting harm if he stayed another moment, Jess stormed out of the house. Cathy, dressed in old jeans, boots and a cotton blouse, was waiting beside the station wagon. The pallor in her face told Jess that she knew much more about the state of her marriage than he would have hoped.

Her hands trembled a little as she spoke with them. "I'm scared, Jess."

He drew her into his arms, held her. "I know, baby," he said, even though he knew she couldn't hear him or see his lips. "I know."

Libby opened her eyes, yawned and stretched. The smells of sunshine and fresh air swept into her bedroom through the open window, ruffling pink eyelet curtains and reminding her that she was home again. She tossed back the covers on the bed she had once shared with Cathy and got up, sleepily making her way into the bathroom and starting the water for a shower.

As she took off her short cotton nightshirt, she looked down at herself and remembered the raging sensations Jess Barlowe had ignited in her the day before. She had been stupid and self-indulgent to let that happen, but after several years of celibacy, she supposed it was natural that her passions had been stirred so easily—especially by a man like Jess.

As Libby showered, she felt renewed. Aaron's flagrant infidelities had been painful for her, and they had seriously damaged her self-esteem in the bargain.

Now, even though she had made a fool of herself by being wanton with a man who could barely tolerate her, many of Libby's doubts about herself as a woman had been eased, if not routed. She was not as useless and undesirable as Aaron had made her feel. She had caused Jess Barlowe to want her, hadn't she?

Big deal, she told the image in her mirror as she brushed her teeth. *How do you know Jess wasn't out to prove that his original opinion of you was on target?*

Deflated by this very real possibility, Libby combed her hair, applied the customary lip gloss and light touch of mascara and went back to her room to dress. From her suitcases she selected a short-sleeved turquoise pullover shirt and a pair of trim jeans. Remembering her intention to find Cathy and persuade her to go riding, she ferreted through her closet until she found the worn boots she'd left behind before moving to New York, pulling them on over a pair of thick socks.

Looking down at those disreputable old boots, Libby imagined the scorn they would engender in Aaron's jet-set crowd and laughed. Problems or no problems, Jess or no Jess, it was good to be home.

Not surprisingly, the kitchen was empty. Ken had probably left the house before dawn, but there was coffee on the stove and fruit in the refrigerator, so Libby helped herself to a pear and sat down to eat.

The telephone rang just as she was finishing her second cup of coffee, and Libby answered cheerfully, thinking that the caller would be Ken or the housekeeper at the main house, relaying some message for Cathy.

She was back at the table, the receiver pressed to her ear, before Aaron spoke.

"When are you coming home?"

"Home?" echoed Libby stupidly, off-balance, unable to believe that he'd actually asked such a question. "I *am* home, Aaron."

"Enough," he replied. "You've made your point, exhibited your righteous indignation. Now you've got to get back here because I need you."

Libby wanted to hang up, but it seemed a very long way from her chair to the wall, where the rest of the telephone was. "Aaron, we are divorced," she reminded him calmly, "and I am never coming back."

"You have to," he answered, without missing a beat. "It's crucial."

"Why? What happened to all your…friends?"

Aaron sighed. "You remember Betty, don't you? Miss November? Well, Betty and I had a small disagreement, as it happens, and she went to my family. I am, shall we say, exposed as something less than an ideal spouse.

"In any case, my grandmother believes that a man who cannot run his family—she was in Paris when we divorced, darling—cannot run a company, either. I have six months to bring you back into the fold and start an heir, or the whole shooting match goes to my cousin."

Libby was too stunned to speak or even move; she simply stood in the middle of her father's kitchen, trying to absorb what Aaron was saying.

"That," Aaron went on blithely, "is where you come in, sweetheart. You come back, we smile a lot and make a baby, my grandmother's ruffled feathers are smoothed. It's as simple as that."

Sickness boiled into Libby's throat. "I don't believe this!" she whispered.

"You don't believe what, darling? That I can make a baby? May I point out that I sired Jonathan, of whom you were so cloyingly fond?"

Libby swallowed. "Get Miss November pregnant," she managed to suggest. And then she added distractedly, more to herself than Aaron, "I think I'm going to be sick."

"Don't tell me that I've been beaten to the proverbial draw," Aaron remarked in that brutally smooth, caustic way of his. "Did the steak-house king already do the deed?"

"You are disgusting!"

"Yes, but very practical. If I don't hand my grandmother an heir, whether it's mine or the issue of that softheaded cowboy, I stand to lose millions of dollars."

Libby managed to stand up. A few steps, just a few, and she could hang up the telephone, shut out Aaron's voice and his ugly suggestions. "Do you really think that I would turn any child of mine over to someone like you?"

"There is a child, then," he retorted smoothly.

"No!" Five steps to the wall, six at most.

"Be reasonable, sweetness. We're discussing an empire here. If you don't come back and attend to your wifely duties, I'll have to visit that godforsaken ranch and try to persuade you."

"I am not your wife!" screamed Libby. One step. One step and a reach.

"Dear heart, I don't find the idea any more appealing than you do, but there isn't any other way, is there? My grandmother likes you—sees you as sturdy peasant stock—and she wants the baby to be yours."

At last. The wall was close and Libby slammed the receiver into place. Then, dazed, she stumbled back to her chair and fell into it, lowering her head to her arms. She cried hard, for herself, for Jonathan.

"Libby?"

It was the last voice she would have wanted to hear, except for Aaron's. "Go away, Stacey!" she hissed.

Instead of complying, Stacey laid a gentle hand on her shoulder. "What happened, Libby?" he asked softly. "Who was that on the phone?"

Fresh horror washed over Libby at the things Aaron had requested, mixed with anger and revulsion. God, how self-centered and insensitive that man was! And what gall he had, suggesting that she return to that disaster of a marriage, like some unquestioning brood mare, to produce a baby on order!

She gave a shuddering cry and motioned Stacey away with a frantic motion of her arm.

He only drew her up out of the chair and turned her so that he could hold her. She hadn't the strength to resist the intimacy and, in her half-hysterical state, he seemed to be the old Stacey, the strong big brother.

Stacey's hand came to the back of her head, tangling in her freshly washed hair, pressing her to his shoulder. "Tell me what happened," he urged, just as he had when Libby was a child with a skinned knee or a bee sting.

From habit, she allowed herself to be comforted. For so long there had been no one to confide in except Stacey, and it seemed natural to lean on him now. "Aaron…Aaron called. He wanted me to have his…his baby!"

Before Stacey could respond to that, the door separating

the kitchen from the living room swung open. Instinctively Libby drew back from the man who held her.

Jess towered in the doorway, pale, his gaze scorching Libby's flushed, tear-streaked face. "You know," he began in a voice that was no less terrible for being soft, "I almost believed you. I almost had myself convinced that you were above anything this shabby."

"Wait—you don't understand…"

Jess smiled a slow, vicious smile—a smile that took in his startled brother as well as Libby. "Don't I? Oh, princess, I wish I didn't." The searing jade gaze sliced menacingly to Stacey's face. "And it seems I'm going to be an uncle. Tell me, brother—what does that make Cathy?"

To Libby's horror, Stacey said nothing to refute what was obviously a gross misunderstanding. He simply pulled her back into his arms, and her struggle was virtually imperceptible because of his strength.

"Let me go!" she pleaded, frantic.

Stacey released her, but only grudgingly. "I've got a plane to catch," he said.

Libby was incredulous. "Tell him! Tell Jess that he's wrong," she cried, reaching out for Stacey's arm, trying to detain him.

But Stacey simply pulled free and left by the back door.

There was a long, pulsing silence, during which both Libby and Jess seemed to be frozen. He was the first to thaw.

"I know you were hurt, Libby," he said. "Badly hurt. But that didn't give you the right to do something like this to Cathy."

It infuriated Libby that this man's good opinion was so important to her, but it was, and there was no changing that. "Jess, I didn't do anything to Cathy. Please listen to me."

He folded his strong arms and rested against the door jamb with an ease that Libby knew was totally feigned. "I'm listening," he said, and the words had a flippant note.

Libby ignored fresh anger. "I am not expecting Stacey's baby, and this wasn't a romantic tryst. I don't even know why he came here. I was on the phone with Aaron and he—"

A muscle in Jess's neck corded, relaxed again. "I hope you're not going to tell me that your former husband made you pregnant, Libby. That seems unlikely."

Frustration pounded in Libby's temples and tightened the already constricted muscles in her throat. "I am not pregnant!" she choked out. "And if you are going to eavesdrop, Jess Barlowe, you could at least pay attention! Aaron wanted me to come back to New York and have his baby so that he would have an heir to present to his grandmother!"

"You didn't agree to that?"

"Of course I didn't agree! What kind of monster do you think I am?"

Jess shrugged with a nonchalance that was belied by the leaping green fire in his eyes. "I don't know, princess, but rest assured—I intend to find out."

"I have a better idea!" Libby flared. "Why don't you just leave me the hell alone?"

"In theory that's brilliant," he fired back, "but there is one problem: I want you."

Involuntarily Libby remembered the kisses and caresses exchanged by the pond the day before, relived them. Hot color poured into her face. "Am I supposed to be honored?"

"No," Jess replied flatly, "you're supposed to be kept so busy that you won't have time to screw up Cathy's life any more than you already have."

If Libby could have moved, she would have rushed across

that room and slapped Jess Barlowe senseless. Since she couldn't get her muscles to respond to the orders of her mind, she was forced to watch in stricken silence as he gave her a smoldering assessment with his eyes, executed a half salute and left the house.

4

When the telephone rang again, immediately after Jess's exit from the kitchen, Libby was almost afraid to answer it. It would be like Aaron to persist, to use pressure to get what he wanted.

On the other hand, the call might be from someone else, and it could be important.

"Hello?" Libby dared, with resolve.

"Ms. Kincaid?" asked a cheerful feminine voice. "This is Marion Bradshaw, and I'm calling for Mrs. Barlowe. She'd like you to meet her at the main house if you can, and she says to dress for riding."

Libby looked down at her jeans and boots and smiled. In one way, at least, she and Cathy were still on the same wavelength. "Please tell her that I'll be there as soon as I can."

There was a brief pause at the other end of the line, followed by, "Mrs. Barlowe wants me to ask if you have a car down there. If not, she'll come and pick you up in a few minutes."

Though there was no car at her disposal, Libby declined the offer. The walk to the main ranch house would give her a chance to think, to prepare herself to face her cousin again.

As Libby started out, striding along the winding tree-lined road, she ached to think that she and Cathy had come to this. Fresh anger at Stacey quickened her step.

For a moment she was mad at Cathy too. How could she believe such a thing, after all they'd been through together? How?

Firmly Libby brought her ire under control. *You don't get mad at a handicapped person*, she scolded herself.

The sun was already high and hot in the domelike sky, and Libby smiled. It was warm for spring, and wasn't it nice to look up and see clouds and mountaintops instead of tall buildings and smog?

Finally the main house came into view. It was a rambling structure of red brick, and its many windows glistened in the bright sunshine. A porch with marble steps led up to the double doors, and one of them swung open even as Libby reached out to ring the bell.

Mrs. Bradshaw, the housekeeper, stepped out and enfolded Libby in a delighted hug. A slender middle-aged woman with soft brown hair, Marion Bradshaw was as much a part of the Circle Bar B as Senator Barlowe himself. "Welcome home," she said warmly.

Libby smiled and returned the hug. "Thank you, Marion," she replied. "Is Cathy ready to go riding?"

"She's gone ahead to the stables—she'd like you to join her there."

Libby turned to go back down the steps but was stopped by the housekeeper. "Libby?"

She faced Marion, again, feeling wary.

"I don't believe it of you," said Mrs. Bradshaw firmly.

Libby was embarrassed, but there was no point in trying to pretend that she didn't get the woman's meaning. Probably everyone on the ranch was speculating about her supposed involvement with Stacey Barlowe. "Thank you."

"You stay right here on this ranch, Libby Kincaid," Marion Bradshaw rushed on, her own face flushed now. "Don't let Stacey or anybody else run you off."

That morning's unfortunate scene in Ken's kitchen was an indication of how difficult it would be to take the housekeeper's advice. Life on the Circle Bar B could become untenable if both Stacey and Jess didn't back off.

"I'll try," she said softly before stepping down off the porch and making her way around the side of that imposing but gracious house.

Prudently, the stables had been built a good distance away. During the walk, Libby wondered if she shouldn't leave the ranch after all. True, she needed to be there, but Jonathan's death had taught her that sometimes a person had to put her own desires aside for the good of other people.

But would leaving help, in the final analysis? Suppose Stacey did follow her, as he'd threatened to do? What would that do to Cathy?

The stables, like the house, were constructed of red brick. As Libby approached them, she saw Cathy leading two horses out into the sun—a dancing palomino gelding and the considerably less prepossessing pinto mare that had always been Libby's to ride.

Libby hesitated; it had been a long, long time since she'd ridden a horse, and the look in Cathy's eyes was cool. Distant. It was almost as though Libby were a troublesome stranger rather than her cousin and confidante.

As if to break the spell, Cathy lifted one foot to the stirrup of the Palomino's saddle and swung onto its back. Though she gave no sign of greeting, her eyes bade Libby to follow suit.

The elderly pinto was gracious while Libby struggled into the saddle and took the reins in slightly shaky hands. A moment later they were off across the open pastureland behind the stables, Cathy confident in the lead.

Libby jostled and jolted in the now unfamiliar saddle, and she felt a fleeting annoyance with Cathy for setting the brisk pace that she did. Again she berated herself for being angry with someone who couldn't hear.

Cathy rode faster and faster, stopping only when she reached the trees that trimmed the base of a wooded hill. There she turned in the saddle and flung a look back at the disgruntled Libby.

"You're out of practice," she said clearly, though her voice had the slurred meter of those who have not heard another person speak in years.

Libby, red-faced and damp with perspiration, was not surprised that Cathy had spoken aloud. She had learned to talk before the childhood illness that had made her deaf, and when she could be certain that no one else would overhear, she often spoke. It was a secret the two women kept religiously.

"Thanks a lot!" snapped Libby.

Deftly Cathy swung one trim blue-jeaned leg over the neck of her golden gelding and slid to the ground. The fancy bridle jingled musically as the animal bent its great head to graze on the spring grass. "We've got to talk, Libby."

Libby jumped from the pinto's back and the action engendered a piercing ache in the balls of her feet. "You've got that right!" she flared, forgetting for the moment her earlier resolve to respect Cathy's affliction. "Were you trying to get me killed?"

Watching Libby's lips, Cathy grinned. "Killed?" she echoed in her slow, toneless voice. "You're my cousin. That's important, isn't it? That we're cousins, I mean?"

Libby sighed. "Of course it's important."

"It implies a certain loyalty, don't you think?"

Libby braced herself. She'd known this confrontation was coming, of course, but that didn't mean she wanted it or was ready for it. "Yes," she said somewhat lamely.

"Are you having an affair with my husband?"

"No!"

"Do you want to?"

"What the hell kind of person do you think I am, Cathy?" shouted Libby, losing all restraint, flinging her arms out wide and startling the horses, who nickered and danced and tossed their heads.

"I'm trying to find that out," said Cathy in measured and droning words. Not once since the conversation began had her eyes left Libby's mouth.

"You already know," retorted her cousin.

For the first time, Cathy looked ashamed. But there was uncertainty in her expression, too, along with a great deal of pain. "It's no secret that Stacey wants you, Libby. I've been holding my breath ever since you decided to come back, waiting for him to leave me."

"Whatever problems you and Stacey have, Cathy, I didn't start them."

"What about all his visits to New York?"

Libby's shoulders slumped, and she allowed herself to sink to the fragrant spring-scented ground, where she sat cross-legged, her head down. With her hands she said, "You knew about the divorce, and about Jonathan. Stacey was only trying to help me through—we weren't lovers."

The lush grass moved as Cathy sat down too, facing Libby. There were tears shining in her large green eyes, and her lower lip trembled. Nervously she plied a blade of grass between her fingers.

"I'm sorry about your little boy," she said aloud.

Libby reached out, calmer now, and squeezed Cathy's hands with her own. "Thanks."

A lonely, haunted look rose in Cathy's eyes. "Stacey wanted us to have a baby," she confided.

"Why didn't you?"

Sudden color stained Cathy's lovely cheeks. "I'm deaf!" she cried defensively.

Libby released her cousin's hands to sign, "So what? Lots of deaf people have babies."

"Not me!" Cathy signaled back with spirited despair. "I wouldn't know when it cried!"

Libby spoke slowly, her hands falling back to her lap. "Cathy, there are solutions for that sort of problem. There are trained dogs, electronic devices—"

"Trained dogs!" scoffed Cathy, but there was more anguish in her face than anger. "What kind of woman needs a dog to help her raise her own baby?"

"A deaf woman," Libby answered firmly. "Besides, if you don't want a dog around, you could hire a nurse."

"No!"

Libby was taken aback. "Why not?" she signed after a few moments.

Cathy clearly had no intention of answering. She bolted to her feet and was back in the palomino's saddle before Libby could even rise from the ground.

After that, they rode without communicating at all. Knowing that things were far from settled between herself and her cousin, Libby tried to concentrate on the scenery. A shadow moved across the sun, however, and a feeling of impending disaster unfolded inside her.

* * *

Jess glared at the screen of the small computer his father placed so much store in and resisted a caveman urge to strike its side with his fist.

"Here," purred a soft feminine voice, and Monica Summers, the senator's curvaceous assistant, reached down to tap the keyboard in a few strategic places.

Instantly the profit-and-loss statement Jess had been trying to call up was prominently displayed on the screen.

"How did you do that?"

Monica smiled her sultry smile and pulled up a chair to sit down beside Jess. "It's a simple matter of command," she said, and somehow the words sounded wildly suggestive.

Jess's collar seemed to tighten around his throat, but he grinned, appreciating Monica's lithe, inviting body, her profusion of gleaming brown hair, her impudent mouth and soft gray eyes. Her visits to the ranch were usually brief, but the senator's term of office was almost over, and he planned to write a long book—with which Monica was slated to help. Until that project was completed, she would be around a lot.

The fact that the senior senator did not intend to campaign for reelection didn't seem to faze her—it was common knowledge that she had a campaign of her own in mind.

Monica had made it clear, time and time again, that she was available to Jess for more than an occasional dinner date and subsequent sexual skirmish. And before Libby's return, Jess had seriously considered settling down with Monica.

He didn't love her, but she was undeniably beautiful, and the promises she made with her skillfully made-up eyes were not idle ones. In addition to that, they had a lot of ordinary things in common—similar political views, a love of the outdoors, like tastes in music and books.

Now, even with Monica sitting so close to him, her perfume calling up some rather heated memories, Jess Barlowe was patently unmoved.

A shower of anger sifted through him. He *wanted* to be moved, dammit—he wanted everything to be the way it was before Libby's return. Return? It was an invasion! He thought about the little hellion day and night, whether he wanted to or not.

"What's wrong, Jess?" Monica asked softly, perceptively, her hand resting on his shoulder. "It's more than just this computer, isn't it?"

He looked away. The sensible thing to do would be to take Monica by the hand, lead her off somewhere private and make slow, ferocious love to her. Maybe that would exorcise Libby Kincaid from his mind.

He remembered passion-weighted breasts, bared to him on a swimming dock, remembered their nipples blossoming sweetly in his mouth. Libby's breasts.

"Jess?"

He forced himself to look at Monica again. "I'm sorry," he said. "Did you say something?"

Mischief danced in her charcoal eyes. "Yes. I offered you my body."

He laughed.

Instead of laughing herself, Monica gave him a gentle, discerning look. "Mrs. Bradshaw tells me that Libby Kincaid is back," she said. "Could it be that I have some competition?"

Jess cleared his throat and diplomatically fixed his attention on the computer screen. "Show me how you made this monster cough up that profit-and-loss statement," he hedged.

"Jess." The voice was cool, insistent.

He made himself meet Monica's eyes again. "I don't know

what I feel for Libby," he confessed. "She makes me mad as hell, but…"

"But," said Monica with rueful amusement, "you want her very badly, don't you?"

There was no denying that, but neither could Jess bring himself to openly admit to the curious needs that had been plaguing him since the moment he'd seen Libby again at the small airport in Kalispell.

Monica's right index finger traced the outline of his jaw, tenderly. Sensuously. "We've never agreed to be faithful to each other, Jess," she said in the silky voice that had once enthralled him. "There aren't any strings tying you to me. But that doesn't mean that I'm going to step back and let Libby Kincaid have a clear field. I want you myself."

Jess was saved from answering by the sudden appearance of his father in the study doorway.

"Oh, Monica—there you are," Cleave Barlowe said warmly. "Ready to start working on that speech now? We have to have it ready before we fly back to Washington, remember."

Gray eyes swept Jess's face in parting. "More than ready," she replied, and then she was out of her chair and walking across the study to join her employer.

Jess gave the computer an unloving look and switched it off, taking perverse pleasure in the way the little green words and numbers on the screen dissolved. "State of the art," he mocked, and then stood up and strode out of the room.

The accountants would be angry, once they returned from their coffee break, but he didn't give a damn. If he didn't do something physical, he was going to go crazy.

Back at the stables, Libby surrendered her horse to a ranch hand with relief. Already the muscles in her thighs were aching dully from the ride; by morning they would be in savage little knots.

Cathy, who probably rode almost every day, looked breezy and refreshed, and from her manner no one would have suspected that she harbored any ill feelings toward Libby. "Let's take a swim," she signed, "and then we can have lunch."

Libby would have preferred to soak in the hot tub, but her pride wouldn't allow her to say so. Unless a limp betrayed her, she wasn't going to let Cathy know how sore a simple horseback ride had left her.

"I don't have a swimming suit," she said, somewhat hopefully.

"That's okay," Cathy replied with swift hands. "It's an indoor pool, remember?"

"I hope you're not suggesting that we swim naked," Libby argued aloud.

Cathy's eyes danced. "Why not?" she signed impishly. "No one would see us."

"Are you kidding?" Libby retorted, waving one arm toward the long, wide driveway. "Look at all these cars! There are *people* in that house!"

"Are you so modest?" queried Cathy, one eyebrow arched.

"Yes!" replied Libby, ignoring the subtle sarcasm.

"Then we'll go back to your house and swim in the pond, like we used to."

Libby recalled the blatant way she'd offered herself to Jess Barlowe in that place and winced inwardly. The peaceful solace of that pond had probably been altered forever, and it was going to be some time before she could go there comfortably again. "It's spring, Cathy, not summer. We'd catch pneumonia! Besides, I think it's going to rain."

Cathy shrugged. "All right, all right. I'll borrow a car and we'll drive over and get your swimming suit, then come back here."

"Fine," Libby agreed with a sigh.

She was to regret the decision almost immediately. When she and Cathy reached the house they had both grown up in, there was a florist's truck parked out front.

On the porch stood an affable young man, a long, narrow box in his hands. "Hi, Libby," he said.

Libby recognized Phil Reynolds, who had been her classmate in high school. *Go away, Phil,* she thought, even as she smiled and greeted him.

Cathy's attention was riveted on the silver box he carried, and there was a worried expression on her face.

Phil approached, beaming. "I didn't even know you were back until we got this order this morning. Aren't you coming into town at all? We got a new high school..."

Simmonsville, a dried-up little community just beyond the south border of the Circle Bar B, hadn't even entered Libby's thoughts until she'd seen Phil Reynolds. She ignored his question and stared at the box he held out to her as if it might contain something squirmy and vile.

"Wh-who sent these?" she managed, all too conscious of the suspicious way Cathy was looking at her.

"See for yourself," Phil said brightly, and then he got back into his truck and left.

Libby took the card from beneath the red ribbon that bound the box and opened it with trembling fingers. The flowers couldn't be from Stacey, please God, they couldn't!

The card was typewritten. *Don't be stubborn, sweetness,* the message read. *Regards, Aaron.*

For a moment Libby was too relieved to be angry.

"Aaron," she repeated. Then she lifted the lid from the box and saw the dozen pink rosebuds inside.

For one crazy moment she was back in Jonathan's hospital room. There had been roses there, too—along with mums and violets and carnations. Aaron and his family had sent costly bouquets and elaborate toys, but not one of them had come to visit.

Libby heard the echo of Jonathan's purposefully cheerful voice. *Daddy must be busy,* he'd said.

With a cry of fury and pain, Libby flung the roses away, and they scattered over the walk in a profusion of long-stemmed delicacy. The silver box lay with them, catching the waning sunlight.

Cathy knelt and began gathering up the discarded flowers, placing them gently back in their carton. Once or twice she glanced up at Libby's livid face in bewilderment, but she asked no questions and made no comments.

Libby turned away and bounded into the house. By the time she had found a swimming suit and come back downstairs again, Cathy was arranging the rosebuds in a cut-glass vase at the kitchen sink.

She met Libby's angry gaze and held up one hand to stay the inevitable outburst. "They're beautiful, Libby," she said in a barely audible voice. "You can't throw away something that's beautiful."

"Watch me!" snapped Libby.

Cathy stepped between her cousin and the lush bouquet. "Libby, at least let me give them to Mrs. Bradshaw," she pleaded aloud. "Please?"

Glumly Libby nodded. She supposed she should be grateful that the roses hadn't been sent by Stacey in a fit of ardor, and they *were* too lovely to waste, even if she herself couldn't bear the sight of them.

Libby remembered the words on Aaron's card as she and Cathy drove back to the main house. *Don't be stubborn.* A tremor of dread flitted up and down her spine.

Aaron hadn't been serious when he'd threatened to come to the ranch and "persuade" her to return to New York with him, had he? She shivered.

Surely even Aaron wouldn't have the gall to do that, she tried to reassure herself. After all, he had never come to the apartment she'd taken after Jonathan's death, never so much as called. Even when the divorce had been granted, he had avoided her by sending his lawyer to court alone.

No. Aaron wouldn't actually come to the Circle Bar B. He might call, he might even send more flowers, just to antagonize her, but he wouldn't come in person. Despite his dismissal of Stacey as a "softheaded cowboy," he was afraid of him.

Cathy was drawing the car to a stop in front of the main house by the time Libby was able to recover herself. To allay the concern in her cousin's eyes, she carried the vase of pink roses into the kitchen and presented them to Mrs. Bradshaw, who was puzzled but clearly pleased.

Inside the gigantic, elegantly tiled room that housed the swimming pool and the spacious hot tub, Libby eyed the latter with longing. Thus, it was a moment before she realized that the pool was already occupied.

Jess was doing a furious racing crawl from one side of the deep end to the other, his tanned, muscular arms cutting through the blue water with a force that said he was trying to work out some fierce inner conflict. Watching him admiringly from the poolside, her slender legs dangling into the water, was a pretty dark-haired woman with beautiful gray eyes.

The woman greeted Cathy with an easy gesture of her hands, though her eyes were fixed on Libby, seeming to assess her in a thorough, if offhand, fashion.

"I'm Monica Summers," she said, as Jess, apparently oblivious of everything other than the furious course he was following through the water, executed an impressive somersault turn at the poolside and raced back the other way.

Monica Summers. The name was familiar to Libby, and so, vaguely, was the perfect fashion-model face.

Of course. Monica was Senator Barlowe's chief assistant. Libby had never actually met the woman, but she had seen her on television newscasts and Ken had mentioned her in passing, on occasion, over long-distance telephone.

"Hello," Libby said. "I'm—"

The gray eyes sparkled. "I know," Monica broke in smoothly. "You're Libby Kincaid. I enjoy your cartoons very much."

Libby felt about as sophisticated, compared to this woman, as a Girl Scout selling cookies door-to-door. And Monica's subtle emphasis on the word "cartoons" had made her feel defensive.

All the same, Libby thanked her and forced herself not to watch Jess's magnificent body moving through the bright blue water of the pool. It didn't bother her that Jess and Monica had been alone in this strangely sensual setting. It didn't.

Cathy had moved away, anxious for her swim.

"I'm sorry if we interrupted something," Libby said, and hated herself instantly for betraying her interest.

Monica smiled. Clearly she had not been in swimming herself, for her expensive black swimsuit was dry, and so was her long, lush hair. Her makeup, of course, was perfect. "There are always interruptions," she said, and then she turned away to take up her adoring-spectator position again, her gaze following the play of the powerful muscles in Jess's naked back.

My thighs are too fat, mourned Libby, in petulant despair. She took a seat on a lounge far removed from Jess and his lovely friend and tried to pretend an interest in Cathy's graceful backstroke.

Was Jess intimate with Monica Summers? It certainly seemed so, and Libby couldn't understand, for the life of her, why she was so brutally surprised by the knowledge. After all, Jess was a handsome, healthy man, well beyond the age of handholding and fantasies-from-afar. Had she really ever believed that he had just been existing on this ranch in some sort of suspended animation?

Cathy roused her from her dismal reflection by flinging a stream of water at her with both hands. Instantly Libby was drenched and stung to an annoyance out of all proportion to the offense. Surprising even herself, she stomped over to the hot tub, flipped the switch that would make the water bubble and churn, and after hurling one scorching look at her unrepenting cousin, slid into the enormous tile-lined tub.

The heat and motion of the water were welcome balm to Libby's muscles, if not to her spirit. She had no right to care who Jess Barlowe slept with, no right at all. It wasn't as though she had ever had any claim on his affections.

Settling herself on a submerged bench, Libby tilted her head back, closed her eyes, and tried to pretend that she was alone in that massive room with its sloping glass roof, lush plants and lounges.

The fact that she was sexually attracted to Jess Barlowe was undeniable, but it was just a physical phenomenon, certainly. It would pass.

All she had to do to accelerate the process was allow herself to remember how very demeaning Aaron's lovemaking had been. And remember she did.

After Libby had caught her husband with the first of his lovers, she had moved out of his bedroom permanently, remaining in his house only because Jonathan, still at home then, had needed her so much.

Before her brutal awakening, however, she had tried hard to make the rapidly failing marriage work. Even then, bedtime had been a horror.

Libby's skin prickled as she recalled the way Aaron would ignore her for long weeks and then pounce on her with a vicious and alarming sort of determination, tearing her clothes, sometimes bruising her.

In retrospect, Libby realized that Aaron must have been trying to prove something to himself concerning his identity as a man, but at the time she had known only that sex, much touted in books and movies, was something to be feared.

Not once had Libby achieved any sort of satisfaction with Aaron—she had only endured. Now, painfully conscious of the blatantly masculine, near-naked cowboy swimming in the pool nearby, Libby wondered if lovemaking would be different with Jess.

The way that her body had blossomed beneath his seemed adequate proof that it would be different indeed, but there was always the possibility that she would be disappointed in the ultimate act. Probably she had been aroused only because Jess had taken the time to offer her at least a taste of pleasure. Aaron had never done that, never shown any sensitivity at all.

Shutting out all sight and sound, Libby mentally decried her lack of experience. If only she'd been with even one man besides Aaron, she would have had some frame of reference, some inkling of whether or not the soaring releases she'd read about really existed.

The knowledge that so many people thought she had been carrying on a torrid affair with Stacey brought a wry smile to her lips. If only they knew.

"What are you smiling about?"

The voice jolted Libby back to the here and now with a thump. Jess had joined her in the hot tub at some point; indeed, he was standing only inches away.

Startled, Libby stared at him for a moment, then looked wildly around for Cathy and the elegant Ms. Summers.

"They went in to have lunch," Jess informed her, his eyes twinkling. Beads of water sparkled in the dark down that matted his muscular chest, and his hair had been towel-rubbed into an appealing disarray.

"I'll join them," said Libby in a frantic whisper, but the simple mechanics of turning away and climbing out of the hot tub eluded her.

Smelling pleasantly of chlorine, Jess came nearer. "Don't go," he said softly. "Lunch will wait."

Anger at Cathy surged through Libby. Why had she gone off and left her here?

Jess seemed to read the question in her face, and it made him laugh. The sound was soft—sensuously, wholly male. Overhead, spring thunder crashed in a gray sky.

Libby trembled, pressing back against the edge of the hot tub with such force that her shoulder blades ached. "Stay away from me," she breathed.

"Not on your life," he answered, and then he was so near that she could feel the hard length of his thighs against her own. The soft dark hair on his chest tickled her bare shoulders and the suddenly alive flesh above her swimsuit top. "I intend to finish what we started yesterday beside the pond."

Libby gasped as his moist lips came down to taste hers, to tame and finally part them for a tender invasion. Her hands went up, of their own accord, to rest on his hips.

He was naked. The discovery rocked Libby, made her try to twist away from him, but his kiss deepened and subdued her struggles. With his hands, he lifted her legs, draped them around the rock-hard hips she had just explored.

The imposing, heated length of his desire, now pressed intimately against her, was powerful proof that he meant to take her.

5

Libby felt as though her body had dissolved, become part of the warm, bubbling water filling the hot tub. When Jess drew back from his soft conquering of her mouth, his hands rose gently to draw down the modest top of her swimsuit, revealing the pulsing fullness of her breasts to his gaze.

It was not in Libby to protest: she was transfixed, caught up in primal responses that had no relation to good sense or even sanity. She let her head fall back, saw through the transparent ceiling that gray clouds had darkened the sky, promising a storm that wouldn't begin to rival the one brewing inside Libby herself.

Jess bent his head, nipped at one exposed, aching nipple with cautious teeth.

Libby drew in a sharp breath as a shaft of searing pleasure went through her, so powerful that she was nearly convulsed by it. A soft moan escaped her, and she tilted her head even further back, so that her breasts were still more vulnerable to the plundering of his mouth.

Inside Libby's swirling mind, a steady voice chanted a litany of logic: she was behaving in a wanton way—Jess didn't really care for her, he was only trying to prove that he could conquer her whenever he desired—this place was not private, and there was a very real danger that someone would walk in at any moment and see what was happening.

Thunder reverberated in the sky, shaking heaven and earth. And none of the arguments Libby's reason was offering had any effect on her rising need to join herself with this impossible, overbearing man feasting so brazenly on her breast.

With an unerring hand, Jess found the crux of her passion, and through the fabric of her swimsuit he stroked it to a wanting Libby had never experienced before. Then, still greedy at the nipple he was attending, he deftly worked aside the bit of cloth separating Libby's womanhood from total exposure.

She gasped as he caught the hidden nubbin between his fingers and began, rhythmically, to soothe it. Or was he tormenting it? Libby didn't know, didn't care.

Jess left her breast to nibble at her earlobe, chuckled hoarsely when the tender invasion of his fingers elicited a throaty cry of welcome.

"Go with it, Libby," he whispered. "Let it carry you high... higher..."

Libby was already soaring, sightless, mindless, conscious only of the fiery marauding of his fingers and the strange force inside her that was building toward something she had only imagined before. "Oh," she gasped as he worked this new and fierce magic. "Oh, Jess..."

Mercilessly he intensified her pleasure by whispering outrageously erotic promises, by pressing her legs wide of each other with one knee, by caressing her breast with his other hand.

A savage trembling began deep within Libby, causing her breath to quicken to a soft, lusty whine.

"Meet it, Libby," Jess urged. "Rise to meet it."

Suddenly Libby's entire being buckled in some ancient, inescapable response. The thunder in the distant skies covered her final cry of release, and she convulsed again and again, helpless in the throes of her body's savage victory.

When at last the ferocious clenching and unclenching had ceased, Libby's reason gradually returned. Forcing wide eyes to Jess's face, she saw no demand there, no mockery or revulsion. Instead, he was grinning at her, as pleased as if he'd been sated himself.

Wild embarrassment surged through Libby in the wake of her passion. She tried to avert her face, but Jess caught her chin in his hand and made her look at him.

"Don't," he said gruffly. "Don't look that way. It wasn't wrong, Libby."

His ability to read her thoughts so easily was as unsettling as the knowledge that she'd just allowed this man unconscionable liberties in a hot tub. "I suppose you think…I suppose you want…"

Jess withdrew his conquering hand, tugged her swimsuit back into place. "I think you're beautiful," he supplied, "and I want you—that's true. But for now, watching you respond like that was enough."

Libby blushed again. She was still confused by the power of her release, and she had expected Jess to demand his own satisfaction. She was stunned that he could give such fierce fulfillment and ask nothing for himself.

"You've never been with any man besides your husband, have you, Libby?"

The outrageous bluntness of that question solidified Libby's jellylike muscles, and she reached furiously for one of the towels Mrs. Bradshaw had set nearby on a low shelf. "I've been with a thousand men!" she snapped in a harsh whisper. "Why, one word from any man, and I let him…I let him…"

Jess grinned again. "You've never had a climax before," he observed.

How could he guess a thing like that? It was uncanny. Libby knew that the hot color in her face belied her sharp answer. "Of course I have! I've been married—did you think I was celibate?"

The rapid-fire hysteria of her words only served to amuse Jess, it seemed. "We both know, Libby Kincaid, that you are, for all practical intents and purposes, a virgin. You may have lain beneath that ex-husband of yours and wished to God that he would leave you alone, but until a few minutes ago you had never even guessed what it means to be a woman."

Libby wouldn't have thought it possible to be as murderously angry as she was at that moment. "Why, you arrogant, *insufferable*…"

He caught her hand at the wrist before it could make the intended contact with his face. "You haven't seen anything yet, princess," he vowed with gentle force. "When I take you to bed—and I assure you that I will—I'll prove that everything I've said is true."

While Libby herself was outraged, her traitorous body yearned to lie in his bed, bend to his will. Having reached the edges of passion, it wanted to go beyond, into the molten core. "You egotistical bastard!" Libby hissed, breaking away from him to lift herself out of the hot tub and land on its edge with an inelegant, squishy plop, "You act as if you'd invented sex!"

"As far as you're concerned, little virgin, I did. But have no fear—I intend to deflower you at the first opportunity."

Libby stood up, wrapped her shaky, nerveless form in a towel the size of a bedsheet. "Go to hell!"

Jess rose out of the water, not the least bit self-conscious of his nakedness. The magnitude of his desire for her was all too obvious.

"The next few hours will be just that," he said, reaching for a towel of his own. Naturally, the one he selected barely covered him.

Speechless, Libby imagined the thrust of his manhood, imagined her back arching to receive him, imagined a savage renewal of the passion she had felt only minutes before.

Jess gave her an amused sidelong glance, as though he knew what she was thinking, and intoned, "Don't worry, princess. I'll court you if that's what you want. But I'll have you, too. And thoroughly."

Having made this incredible vow, he calmly walked out of the room, leaving Libby alone with a clamoring flock of strange emotions and unmet needs.

The moment Jess was gone, she stumbled to the nearest lounge chair and sank onto it, her knees too weak to support her. *Well, Kincaid,* she reflected wryly, *now you know. Satisfied?*

Libby winced at the last word. Though she might have wished otherwise, given the identity of the man involved, she was just that.

With carefully maintained dignity, Jess Barlowe strode into the shower room adjoining the pool and wrenched on one spigot. As he stepped under the biting, sleetlike spray, he gritted his teeth.

Gradually his body stopped screaming and the stubborn evidence of his passion faded. With relief, Jess dived out of the shower stall and grabbed a fresh towel.

A hoarse chuckle escaped him as he dried himself with

brisk motions. Good God, if he didn't have Libby Kincaid soon, he was going to die of pneumonia. A man could stand only so many plunges into icy ponds, only so many cold showers.

A spare set of clothes—jeans and a white pullover shirt—awaited Jess in a cupboard. He donned them quickly, casting one disdainful look at the three-piece suit he had shed earlier. His circulation restored, to some degree at least, he toweled his hair and then combed it with the splayed fingers of his left hand.

A sweet anguish swept through him as he remembered the magic he had glimpsed in Libby's beautiful face during that moment of full surrender. *My father was right,* Jess thought as he pulled on socks and old, comfortable boots. *I love you, Libby Kincaid. I love you.*

Jess was not surprised to find that Libby wasn't with Cathy and Monica in the kitchen—she had probably made some excuse to get out of joining them for lunch and gone off to gather her thoughts. God knew, she had to be every bit as undone and confused as he was.

Mostly to avoid the sad speculation in Monica's eyes, Jess glanced toward the kitchen windows. They were already sheeted with rain.

A crash of thunder jolted him out of the strange inertia that had possessed him. He glanced at Cathy, saw an impish light dancing in her eyes.

"You can catch her if you hurry," she signed, cocking her head to one side and grinning at him.

Did she know what had happened in the hot tub? Some of the heat lingering in Jess's loins rose to his face as he bolted out of the room and through the rest of the house.

The station wagon, an eyesore among the other cars

parked in front of the house, patently refused to start. Annoyed, Jess "borrowed" Monica's sleek green Porsche without a moment's hesitation, and his aggravation grew as he left the driveway and pulled out onto the main road.

What the hell did Libby think she was doing, walking in this rain? And why had Cathy let her go?

He found Libby near the mailboxes, slogging despondently along, soaked to the skin.

"Get in!" he barked, furious in his concern.

Libby lifted her chin and kept walking. Her turquoise shirt was plastered to her chest, revealing the outlines of her bra, and her hair hung in dripping tendrils.

"Now!" Jess roared through the window he had rolled down halfway.

She stopped, faced him with indigo fury sparking in her eyes. "Why?" she yelled over the combined roars of the deluge and Monica's car engine. "Is it time to teach me what it means to be a woman?"

"How the hell would I know what it means to be a woman?" he shouted back. "Get in this car!"

Libby told him to do something that was anatomically impossible and then went splashing off down the road again, ignoring the driving rain.

Rasping a swearword, Jess slipped the Porsche out of gear and wrenched the emergency brake into place. Then he shoved open the door and bounded through the downpour to catch up with Libby, grasp her by the shoulders and whirl her around to face him.

"If you don't get your backside into that car *right now,*" he bellowed, "I swear to God I'll *throw* you in!"

She assessed the Porsche. "Monica's car?"

Furious, Jess nodded. Christ, it was raining so hard tha

his clothes were already saturated and she was standing there talking details!

An evil smile curved Libby's lips and she stalked toward the automobile, purposely stepping in every mud puddle along the way. Jess could have sworn that she enjoyed sinking, sopping wet, onto the heretofore spotless suede seat.

"Home, James," she said smugly, folding her arms and grinding her mud-caked boots into the lush carpeting on the floorboard.

Jess had no intention of taking Libby to Ken's place, but he said nothing. Envisioning her lying in some hospital bed, wasted away by a case of rain-induced pneumonia, he ground the car savagely back into gear and gunned the engine.

When they didn't take the road Libby expected, the smug look faded from her face and she stared at Jess with wide, wary eyes. "Wait a minute…"

Jess flung an impudent grin at her and saluted with one hand. "Yes?" he drawled, deliberately baiting her.

"Where are we going?"

"My place," he answered, still angry. "It's the classic situation, isn't it? I'll insist you get out of those wet clothes, then I'll toss you one of my bathrobes and pour brandy for us both. After that, lady, I'll make mad love to you."

Libby paled, though there was a defiant light in her eyes. "On a fur rug in front of your fireplace, no doubt!"

"No doubt," Jess snapped, wondering why he found it impossible to deal with this woman in a sane and reasonable way. It would be so much simpler just to tell her straight out that he loved her, that he needed her. But he couldn't quite bring himself to do that, not just yet, and he was still mad as hell that she would walk in the pouring rain like that.

"Suppose I tell you that I don't want you to 'make mad

love' to me, as you so crudely put it? Suppose I tell you that I won't give in to you until the first Tuesday after doomsday, if then, brandy and fur rugs notwithstanding?"

"The way you didn't give in in the hot tub?" he gibed, scowling.

Libby blushed. "That was different!"

"How so?"

"You...you *cornered* me, that's how."

His next words were out of his mouth before he could call them back. "I know about your ex-husband, Libby."

She winced, fixed her attention on the overworked windshield wipers. "What does he have to do with anything?"

Jess shifted to a lower gear as he reached the road leading to his house and turned onto it. "Stacey told me about the women."

The high color drained from Libby's face and she would not look at him. She appeared ready, in fact, to thrust open the door on her side of the car and leap out. "I don't want to talk about this," she said after an interval long enough to bring them to Jess's driveway.

"Why not, Libby?" he asked, and his voice was gentle, if a bit gruff.

One tear rolled over the wet sheen on her defiant rain-polished face, and Libby's chin jutted out in a way that was familiar to him, at once maddening and appealing. "Why do you want to talk about Aaron?" she countered in low, ragged tones. "So you can sit there and feel superior?"

"You know better."

She glared at him, her bruised heart in her eyes, and Jess ached for her. She'd been through so much, and he wished that he could have taken that visible, pounding pain from inside her and borne it himself.

"I don't know better, Jess," she said quietly. "We haven't exactly been kindred spirits, you and I. For all I know, you just want to torture me. To throw all my mistakes in my face and watch me squirm."

Jess's hands tightened on the steering wheel. It took great effort to reach down and shut off the Porsche's engine. "It's cold out here," he said evenly, "and we're both wet to the skin. Let's go inside."

"You won't take me home?" Her voice was small.

He sighed. "Do you want me to?"

Libby considered, lowered her head. "No," she said after a long time.

The inside of Jess's house was spacious and uncluttered. There were skylights in the ceiling and the second floor appeared to be a loft of some sort. Lifting her eyes to the railing above, Libby imagined that his bed was just beyond it and blushed.

Jess seemed to be ignoring her; he was busy with newspaper and kindling at the hearth. She watched the play of the muscles in his back in weary fascination, longing to feel them beneath her hands.

The knowledge that she loved Jess Barlowe, budding in her subconscious mind since her arrival in Montana, suddenly burst into full flower. But was the feeling really new?

If Libby were to be honest with herself—and she tried to be, always—she had to admit that the chances were good that she had loved Jess for a very long time.

He turned, rose from his crouching position, a small fire blazing and crackling behind him. "How do you like my house?" he asked with a half smile.

Between her newly recognized feelings for this man and

the way his jade eyes seemed to see through all her reserve to the hurt and confusion hidden beneath, Libby felt very vulnerable. Trusting in an old trick that had always worked in the past, she looked around in search of something to be angry about.

The skylights, the loft, the view of the mountains from the windows beyond his desk—all of it was appealing. Masculine. Quietly romantic.

"Perfect quarters for a wealthy and irresponsible playboy," she threw out in desperation.

Jess stiffened momentarily, but then an easy grin creased his face. "I think that was a shot, but I'm not going to fire back, Libby, so you might as well relax."

Relax? Was the man insane? Half an hour before, he had blithely brought her to climax in a hot tub, for God's sake, and now they were alone, the condition of their clothes necessitating that they risk further intimacies by stripping them off, taking showers. If they couldn't fight, what *were* they going to do?

Before Libby could think of anything to say in reply, Jess gestured toward the broad redwood stairs leading up to the loft. "The bathroom is up there," he said. "Take a shower. You'll find a robe hanging on the inside of the door." With that, he turned away to crouch before the fire again and add wood.

Because she was cold and there seemed to be no other options, Libby climbed the stairs. It wasn't until she reached the loft that her teeth began to chatter.

There she saw Jess's wide unmade bed. It was banked by a line of floor-to-ceiling windows, giving the impression that the room was open to the outdoors, and the wrinkled sheets probably still bore that subtle, clean scent that was Jess's alone...

Libby took herself in hand, wrenched her attention away from the bed. There was a glass-fronted wood-burning stove in one corner of the large room, and a long bookshelf on the other side was crammed with everything from paperback mysteries to volumes on veterinary medicine.

Libby made her way into the adjoining bathroom and kicked off her muddy boots, peeled away her jeans and shirt, her sodden underwear and socks. Goosebumps leapt out all over her body, and they weren't entirely related to the chill.

The bathtub was enormous, and like the bed, it was framed by tall uncurtained windows. Bathing here would be like bathing in the high limbs of a tree, so sweeping was the view of mountains and grassland beyond the glass.

Trembling a little, Libby knelt to turn on the polished brass spigots and fill the deep tub. The water felt good against her chilled flesh, and she was submerged to her chin before she remembered that she had meant to take a quick shower, not a lingering, dreamy bath.

Libby couldn't help drawing a psychological parallel between this tub and the larger one at the main house, where she had made such a fool of herself. Was there some mysterious significance in the fact that she'd chosen the bathtub over the double-wide shower stall on the other side of the room?

Now you're really getting crazy, Kincaid, she said to herself, settling back to soak.

Somewhere in the house, a telephone rang, was swiftly answered.

Libby relaxed in the big tub and tried to still her roiling thoughts and emotions. She would not consider what might happen later. For now, she wanted to be comforted, pampered. Deliciously warm.

She heard the click of boot heels on the stairs, though, and sat bolt upright in the water. A sense of sweet alarm raced through her system. Jess wouldn't come in, actually *come in*, would he?

Of course he would! Why would a bathroom door stop a man who would make such brazen advances in a hot tub?

With frantic eyes Libby sought the towel shelf. It was entirely too far away, and so was the heavy blue-and-white velour robe hanging on the inside of the door. She sank into the bathwater until it tickled her lower lip, squeezed her eyes shut and waited.

"Lib?"

"Wh-what?" she managed. He was just beyond that heavy wooden panel, and Libby found herself hoping...

Hoping what? That Jess would walk in, or that he would stay out? She honestly didn't know.

"That was Ken on the phone," Jess answered, making no effort to open the door. "I told him you were here and that I'd bring you home after the rain lets up."

Libby reddened, there in the privacy of that unique bathroom, imagining the thoughts that were probably going through her father's mind. "Wh-what did he say?"

Jess chuckled, and the sound was low, rich. "Let me put it this way: I don't think he's going to rush over here and defend your virtue."

Libby was at once pleased and disappointed. Wasn't a father *supposed* to protect his daughter from persuasive lechers like Jess Barlowe?

"Oh," she said, her voice sounding foolish and uncertain. "D-do you want me to hurry? S-so you can take a shower, I mean?"

"Take your time," he said offhandedly. "There's another bathroom downstairs—I can shower there."

Having imparted this conversely comforting and disenchanting information, Jess began opening and closing drawers. Seconds later, Libby again heard his footsteps on the stairs.

Despite the fact that she would have preferred to lounge in that wonderful bathtub for the rest of the day, Libby shot out of the water and raced to the towel bar. This was her chance to get dried off and dressed in something before Jess could incite her to further scandalous behavior.

She was wrapped in his blue-and-white bathrobe, the belt securely tied, and cuddled under a knitted afghan by the time Jess joined her in the living room, looking reprehensibly handsome in fresh jeans and a green turtleneck sweater. His hair, like her own, was still damp, and there was a smile in his eyes, probably inspired by the way she was trying to burrow deeper into her corner of the couch.

"There isn't any brandy after all," he said with a helpless gesture of his hands. "Will you settle for chicken soup?"

Libby would have agreed to anything that would get Jess out of that room, even for a few minutes, and he would have to go to the kitchen for soup, wouldn't he? Unable to speak, she nodded.

She tried to concentrate on the leaping flames in the fireplace, but she could hear the soft thump of cupboard doors, the running of tapwater, the singular whir of a microwave oven. The sharp *ting* of the appliance's timer bell made her flinch.

Too soon, Jess returned, carrying two mugs full of steaming soup. He extended one to Libby and, to her eternal gratitude, settled in a chair nearby instead of on the couch beside her.

Outside, the rain came down in torrents, making a musical, pelting sound on the skylights, sliding down the windows in sheets. The fire snapped and threw out sparks, as if to mock the storm that could not reach it.

Jess took a sip of the hot soup and grinned. "This doesn't exactly fit the scenario I outlined in the car," he said, lifting his cup.

"You got everything else right," Libby quipped, referring to the bath she'd taken and the fact that she was wearing his robe. Instantly she realized how badly she'd slipped, but it was too late to call back her words, and the ironic arch of Jess's brow and the smile on his lips indicated that he wasn't going to let the comment pass.

"Everything?" he teased. "There isn't any fur rug, either."

Libby's cheekbones burned. Unable to say anything, she lowered her eyes and watched the tiny noodles colliding in her mug of soup.

"I'm sorry," Jess said softly.

She swallowed hard and met his eyes. He did look contrite, and there was nothing threatening in his manner. Because of that, Libby dared to ask, "Do you really mean to…to make love to me?"

"Only if you want me to," he replied. "You must know that I wouldn't force you, Libby."

She sensed that he meant this and relaxed a little. Sooner or later, she was going to have to accept the fact that all men didn't behave in the callous and hurtful way that Aaron had. "You believe me now—don't you? About Stacey, I mean?"

If that off-the-wall question had surprised or nettled Jess, he gave no indication of it. He simply nodded.

Some crazy bravery, carrying her forward like a reckless tide, made Libby put aside her carefully built reserve and blurt out, "Do you think I'm a fool, Jess?"

Jess gaped at her, the mug of soup forgotten in his hands. "A fool?"

Libby lowered her eyes. "I mean...well...because of Aaron."

"Why should I think anything like that?"

Thunder exploded in the world outside the small cocoon-like one that held only Libby and Jess. "He was...he..."

"He was with other women," supplied Jess quietly. Gently.

Libby nodded, managed to look up.

"And you stayed with him." He was setting down the mug, drawing nearer. Finally he crouched before her on his haunches and took the cup from her hands to set it aside. "You couldn't leave Jonathan, Libby. I understand that. Besides, why should the fact that you stuck with the marriage have any bearing on my attitude toward you?"

"I just thought..."

"What?" prodded Jess when her sentence fell away. "What did you think, Libby?"

Tears clogged her throat. "I thought that I couldn't be very desirable if my o-own husband couldn't...wouldn't..."

Jess gave a ragged sigh. "My God, Libby, you don't think that Aaron was unfaithful because of some lack in you?"

That was exactly what she'd thought, on a subliminal level at least. Another woman, a stronger, more experienced, more alluring woman, might have been able to keep her husband happy, make him want her.

Jess's hands came to Libby's shoulders, gentle and insistent. "Lib, talk to me."

"Just how terrific could I be?" she erupted suddenly, in the anguish that would be hidden no longer. "Just how desirable? My husband needed other women because he couldn't bring himself to make love to me!"

Jess drew her close, held her as the sobs she had restrained at last broke free. "That wasn't your fault, Libby," he breathed, his hand in her hair now, soothing and strong. "Oh, sweetheart, it wasn't your fault."

"Of course it was!" she wailed into the soft green knit of his sweater, the hard strength of the shoulder beneath. "If I'd been better...if I'd known how..."

"Shhh. Baby, don't. Don't do this to yourself."

Once freed, Libby's emotions seemed impossible to check. They ran as deep and wild as any river, swirling in senseless currents and eddies, causing her pride to founder.

Jess caught her trembling hands in his, squeezed them reassuringly. "Listen to me, princess," he said. "These doubts that you're having about yourself are understandable, under the circumstances, but they're not valid. You are desirable." He paused, searched her face with tender, reproving eyes. "I can swear to that."

Libby still felt broken, and she hadn't forgotten the terrible things Aaron had said to her during their marriage—that she was cold and unresponsive, that he hadn't been impotent before he'd married her. Time and time again he had held up Jonathan as proof that he had been virile with his first wife, taken cruel pleasure in pointing out that none of his many girlfriends found him wanting.

Wrenching herself back to the less traumatic present, Libby blurted out, "Make love to me, Jess. Let me prove to myself—"

"No," he said with cold, flat finality. And then he released her hands, stood up and turned away as if in disgust.

6

"I thought you wanted me," Libby said in a small, broken voice.

Jess's broad back stiffened, and he did not turn around to face her. "I do."

"Then, why...?"

He went to the fireplace, took up a poker, stoked the blazing logs within to burn faster, hotter. "When I make love to you, Libby, it won't be because either one of us wants to prove anything."

Libby lowered her head, ashamed. As if to scold her, the wind and rain lashed at the windows and the lightning flashed, filling the room with its eerie blue-gold light. She began to cry again, this time softly, wretchedly.

And Jess came to her, lifted her easily into his arms. Without a word, he carried her up the stairs, across the storm-shadowed loft room to the bed. After pulling back the covers with one hand, he lowered her to the sheets. "Rest," he said, tucking the blankets around her.

Libby gaped at him, amazed and stricken. She couldn't help thinking that he wouldn't have tucked Monica Summers into bed this way, kissed *her* forehead as though she were some overwrought child needing a nap.

"I don't want to rest," Libby said, insulted. And her hands moved to pull the covers down.

Jess stopped her by clasping her wrists. A muscle knotted in his jaw, and his jade-green eyes flashed, their light as elemental as that of the electrical storm outside. "Don't Libby. Don't tempt me."

She *had* been tempting him—if he hadn't stopped her when he did, she would have opened the robe, wantonly displayed her breasts. Now, she was mortally embarrassed. What on earth was making her act this way?

"I'm sorry," she whispered. "I don't know what's the matter with me."

Jess sat down on the edge of the bed, his magnificent face etched in shadows, his expression unreadable. "Do we have to go into that again, princess? Nothing is wrong with you."

"But—"

Jess laid one index finger to her lips to silence her. "It would be wrong if we made love now, Libby—don't you see that? Afterward, you'd be telling yourself what a creep I was for taking advantage of you when you were so vulnerable."

His logic was unassailable. To lighten the mood, Libby summoned up a shaky grin. "Some playboy you are. Chicken soup. Patience. Have you no passion?"

He laughed. "More than I know what to do with," he said, standing up, walking away from the bed. At the top of the stairs he paused. "Am I crazy?"

Libby didn't answer. Smiling, she snuggled down under the covers—she was just a bit tired—and placidly watched the natural light show beyond the windows. Maybe later there would be fireworks of another sort.

Downstairs, Jess resisted a fundamental urge to beat his

head against the wall. Libby Kincaid was up there in his bed, for God's sake, warm and lush and wanting him.

He ached to go back up the stairs and finish what they'd begun that morning in the hot tub. He couldn't, of course, because Libby was in no condition, emotionally, for that kind of heavy scene. If he did the wrong thing, said the wrong thing, she could break, and the pieces might not fit together again.

In a fit of neatness, Jess gathered up the cups of cold chicken soup and carried them into the kitchen. There he dumped their contents into the sink, rinsed them, and stacked them neatly in the dishwasher.

The task was done too quickly. What could he do? He didn't like the idea of leaving Libby alone, but he didn't dare go near her again, either. The scent of her, the soft disarray of her hair, the way her breasts seemed to draw at his mouth and the palms of his hands—all those things combined to make his grasp on reason tenuous.

Jess groaned, lifted his eyes to the ceiling and wondered if he was going to have to endure another ice-cold shower. The telephone rang, startling him, and he reached for it quickly. Libby might already be asleep, and he didn't want her to be disturbed.

"Hello?"

"Jess?" Monica's voice was calm, but there was an undercurrent of cold fury. "Did you take my car?"

He sighed, leaning back against the kitchen counter. "Yeah. Sorry. I should have called you before this, but—"

"But you were busy."

Jess flinched. Exactly what could he say to that? "Monica—"

"Never mind, Jess." She sighed the words. "I didn't have

any right to say that. And if you helped yourself to my car, you must have had a good reason."

Why the hell did she have to be so reasonable? Why didn't Monica yell at him or something, so that he could get mad in good conscience and stop feeling like such an idiot? "I'm afraid the seats are a little muddy," he said.

"Muddy? Oh, yes—the rain. Was Libby okay?"

Again Jess's gaze lifted to the ceiling. Libby was not okay, thanks to him and Stacey and her charming ex-husband. But then, Monica was just making polite conversation, not asking for an in-depth account of Libby's emotional state. "She was drenched."

"So you brought her there, got her out of her wet clothes, built a fire—"

The anger Jess had wished for was suddenly there. "Monica."

She drew in a sharp breath. "All right, all right—I'm sorry. I take it our dinner date is off?"

"Yeah," Jess answered, turning the phone cord between his fingers. "I guess it is."

Monica was nothing if not persistent—probably that quality accounted for her impressive success in political circles. "Tomorrow night?"

Jess sighed. "I don't know."

There was a short, uncomfortable silence. "We'll talk later," Monica finally said brightly. "Listen, is it okay if I send somebody over there to get my car?"

"I'll bring it to you," Jess said. It was, after stealing it, the least he could do. He'd check first, to make sure that Libby really was sleeping, and with luck, he could be back before she woke up.

"Thanks," sang Monica in parting.

Jess hung up the phone and climbed the stairs, pausing at the edge of the bedroom. He dared go no further, wanting that rumple-haired little hellion the way he did. "Libby?"

When there was no answer, Jess turned and went back down the stairs again, almost grateful that he had somewhere to go, something to do.

Monica hid her annoyance well as she inspected the muddy splotches on her car's upholstery. Overhead, the incessant rain pummeled the garage roof.

"I'm sorry," Jess said. It seemed that he was always apologizing for one thing or another lately. "My station wagon wouldn't start, and I was in a hurry…"

Monica allowed a flicker of anger to show in her gray eyes. "Right. When there is a damsel to be rescued, a knight has to grab the first available charger."

Having no answer for that, Jess shrugged. "I'll have your car cleaned," he offered when the silence grew too long, and then he turned to walk back out of the garage and down the driveway to his own car, which refused to start.

He got out and slammed the door. "Damn!" he bellowed, kicking yet another dent into the fender.

"Problems?"

Jess hadn't been aware of Ken until that moment, hadn't noticed the familiar truck parked nearby. "It would take all day to list them," he replied ruefully.

Ken grinned a typical sideways grin, and his blue eyes twinkled. He seemed oblivious of the rain pouring off the brim of his ancient hat and soaking through his denim jacket and jeans. "I think maybe my daughter might be at the top of the list. Is she all right?"

"She's…" Jess faltered, suddenly feeling like a high-school kid. "She's sleeping."

Ken laughed. "Must have been real hard to say that," he observed, "me being her daddy and all."

"It isn't...I didn't..."

Again Ken laughed. "Maybe you should," he said.

Jess was shocked—so shocked that he was speechless.

"Take my truck if you need it," Ken offered calmly, his hand coming to rest on Jess's shoulder. "I'll get a ride home from somebody here. And, Jess?"

"What?"

"Don't hurt Libby. She's had enough trouble and grief as it is."

"I know that," Jess replied, as the rain plastered his hair to his neck and forehead and made his clothes cling to his flesh in sodden, clammy patches. "I swear I won't hurt her."

"That's good enough for me," replied Libby's father, and then he pried the truck keys out of his pocket and tossed them to Jess.

"Ken..."

The foreman paused, looking back, his eyes wise and patient. How the hell was Jess going to ask this man what he had to ask, for Libby's sake?

"Spit it out, son," Ken urged. "I'm getting wet."

"Clothes—she was...Libby was caught in the rain, and she needs dry clothes."

Ken chuckled and shrugged his shoulders. "Stop at our place and get some of her things then," he said indulgently.

Jess was suddenly as confused by this man as he was by his daughter. What the hell was Ken doing, standing there taking this whole thing so calmly? Didn't it bother him, knowing what might happen when Jess got back to that house?

"See ya," said Ken in parting.

Completely confused, Jess got into Ken's truck and drove away. It wasn't until he'd gotten a set of dry clothes for Libby and reached his own house again that he understood. Ken trusted him.

Jess let his forehead rest on the truck's steering wheel and groaned. He couldn't stand another cold shower, dammit. He just couldn't.

But Ken trusted him. Libby was lying upstairs in his bed, and even if she was, by some miracle, ready to handle what was destined to happen, Jess couldn't make love to her. To do so would be to betray a man who had, in so many ways, been as much a father to him as Cleave Barlowe had.

The problem was that Jess couldn't think of Libby as a sister.

Jess sat glumly at the little table in the kitchen, making patterns in his omelet with a fork. Tiring of that, he flung Libby a beleaguered look and sneezed.

She felt a surge of tenderness. "Aren't you hungry?"

He shook his head. "Libby…"

It took all of her forbearance not to stand up, round the table, and touch Jess's forehead to see if he had a fever. "What?" she prompted softly.

"I think I should take you home."

Libby was hurt, but she smiled brightly. "Well, it *has* stopped raining," she reasoned.

"And I've got your dad's truck," added Jess.

"Um-hmm. Thanks for stopping and getting my clothes, by the way."

Outside, the wind howled and the night was dark. Jess gave the jeans and loose pink sweater he had picked up for Libby a distracted look and sneezed again. "You're welcome."

"And you, my friend, are sick."

Jess shook his head, went to the counter to pour coffee from the coffeemaker there. "Want some?" he asked, lifting the glass pot.

Libby declined. "Were you taking another shower when I got up?" she ventured cautiously. The peace between them, for all its sweet glow, was still new and fragile.

Libby would have sworn that he winced, and his face was unreadable. "I'm a clean person," he said, averting his eyes.

Libby bit the inside of her lower lip, suddenly possessed by an untimely urge to laugh. Jess had been shivering when he came out of that bathroom and unexpectedly encountered his newly awakened houseguest.

"Right," she said.

Jess sneezed again, violently. Somehow, the sound unchained Libby's amusement and she shrieked with laughter.

"What is so goddamn funny?" Jess demanded, setting his coffee cup down with an irritated thump and scowling.

"N-nothing," cried Libby.

Suddenly Jess was laughing too. He pulled Libby out of her chair and into his arms, and she deliberately pressed herself close to him, delighting in the evidence of his desire, in the scent and substance and strength of him.

She almost said that she loved him.

"You wanted my body!" she accused instead, teasing.

Jess groaned and tilted his head back, ostensibly to study the ceiling. Libby saw a muscle leap beneath his chin and wanted to kiss it, but she refrained.

"You were taking a cold shower, weren't you, Jess?"

"Yes," he admitted with a martyrly sigh. "Woman, if I die of pneumonia, it will be your fault."

"On the contrary. I've done everything but throw myself at your feet, mister, and you haven't wanted any part of me."

"Wrong." Jess grinned wickedly, touching the tip of her breast with an index finger. "I want this part…" The finger trailed away, following an erotic path. "And this part…"

It took all of Libby's courage to say the words again, after his brisk rejection earlier. "Make love to me, Jess."

"My God, Libby—"

She silenced him by laying two fingers to his lips. Remembering the words he had flung at her in the Cessna the day of her arrival, she said saucily, "If it feels good, do it."

Jess gave her a mock scowl, but his arms were around her now, holding her against him. "You were a very mean little kid," he muttered, "and now you're a mean adult. Do you know what you're doing to me, Kincaid?"

Libby moved her hips slightly, delighting in the contact and the guttural groan the motion brought from Jess. "I have some vague idea, yes."

"Your father trusts me."

"My father!" Libby stared up at him, amazed. "Is that what you've been worried about? What my father will think?"

Jess shrugged, and his eyes moved away from hers. Clearly he was embarrassed. "Yes."

Libby laughed, though she was not amused. "You're not serious!"

His eyes came back to meet hers and the expression in their green depths was nothing if not serious. "Ken is my best friend," he said.

"Shall I call him up and ask for permission? Better yet, I could drive over there and get a note!"

The taunts caused Jess to draw back a little, though their thighs and hips were still touching, still piping primitive messages one to the other. "Very funny!" he snapped, and a muscle bunched in his neck, went smooth again.

Libby was quietly furious. "You're right—it isn't funny. This is my body, Jess—mine. I'm thirty-one years old and I make my own living and I *damned well* don't need my daddy's permission to go to bed with a man!"

The green eyes were twinkling with mischief. "That's a healthy attitude if I've ever heard one," he broke in. "However, before we go up those stairs, there is one more thing I want to know. Are you using me, Libby?"

"Using you?"

"Yes. Do I really mean something to you, or would any man do?"

Libby felt as though she'd just grabbed hold of a high-voltage wire; in a few spinning seconds she was hurled from pain to rage to humiliation.

Jess held her firmly. "I see the question wasn't received in the spirit in which it was intended," he said, his eyes serious now, searching her burning, defiant face. "What I meant to ask was, are we going to be making love, Libby, or just proving that you can go the whole route and respond accordingly?"

Libby met his gaze bravely, though inside she was still shaken and angry. "Why would I go to all this trouble, Jess, if I didn't want you? After all, I could have just stopped someone on the street and said, 'Excuse me, sir, but would you mind making love to me? I'd like to find out if I'm frigid or not.'"

Jess sighed heavily, but his hands were sliding up under the back of Libby's pink sweater, gently kneading the firm flesh there. The only sign that her sarcasm had rankled him was the almost imperceptible leaping of the pulsepoint beneath his right ear.

"I guess I'm having a little trouble understanding your sudden change of heart, Libby. For years you've hated my guts. Now, after confiding that your ex-husband put you through some kind of emotional wringer and left you feeling about as attractive as a sink drain, you want to share my bed."

Libby closed her eyes. The motion of his hands on her back was hypnotic, making it hard for her to breathe, let alone think. When she felt the catch of her bra give way, she shivered.

She should tell him that she loved him, that maybe, despite outward appearances, she'd always loved him, but she didn't dare. This was a man who had thought the worst of her at every turn, who had never missed a chance to get under her skin. Allowing him inside the fortress where her innermost emotions were stored could prove disastrous.

His hands came slowly around from her back to the aching roundness of her breasts, sliding easily, brazenly under the loosened bra.

"Answer me, Libby," he drawled, his voice a sleepy rumble.

She was dazed; his fingers came to play a searing symphony at her nipples, plying them, drawing at them. "I...I want you. I'm not trying to p-prove anything."

"Let me look at you, Libby."

Libby pulled the pink sweater off over her head, stood perfectly still as Jess dispensed with her bra and then stepped back a little way to admire her.

He outlined one blushing nipple with the tip of his finger, progressed to wreak the same havoc on the other. Then, with strong hands, he lifted Libby up onto a counter, so that her breasts were on a level with his face.

She gasped as he took languid, tentative suckle at one

peak, then trailed a path with the tip of his tongue to the other, conquering it with lazy ease.

She was desperate now. "Make love to me," she whispered again in broken tones.

"Make love to me, *Jess,*" he prompted, nibbling now, driving her half-wild with the need of him.

Libby swallowed hard, closed her eyes. His teeth were scraping gently at her nipple now, rousing it to obedience. "Make love to me, Jess," she repeated breathlessly.

He withdrew his mouth, cupping her in his hands, letting his thumbs do the work his lips and teeth had done before. "Open your eyes," he commanded in a hoarse rumble. "Look at me, Libby."

Dazed, her very soul spinning within her, Libby obeyed.

"Tell me," he insisted raggedly, "that you're not seeing Stacey or your misguided ex-husband. Tell me that you see *me,* Libby."

"I do, Jess."

He lifted her off the counter and into his arms, and his mouth came down on hers, cautious at first, then almost harshly demanding. Libby was electrified by the kiss, by the searching fierceness of his tongue, by the moan of need that came from somewhere deep inside him. Finally he ended the kiss, and his eyes were smiling into hers.

Feeling strangely giddy, Libby laughed. "Is this the part where you make love to me?"

"This is it," he replied, and then they were moving through the house toward the stairs. Lightning crackled and flashed above the skylights, while thunder struck a booming accompaniment.

"The earth is moving already," said Libby into the Jess-scented wool of his sweater.

Jess took the stairs two at a time. "Just wait," he replied.

In the bedroom, which was lit only by the lightning that was sundering the night sky, he set Libby on her feet. For a moment they just stood still, looking at each other. Libby felt as though she had become a part of the terrible storm that was pounding at the tall windows, and she grasped Jess's arms so that she wouldn't be blown away to the mountaintops or flung beyond the angry clouds.

"Touch me, Libby," Jess said, and somehow, even over the renewed rage of the storm, she heard him.

Cautiously she slid her hands beneath his sweater, splaying her fingers so that she could feel as much of him as possible. His chest was hard and broad and softly furred, and he groaned as she found masculine nipples and explored them.

Libby moved her hands down over his rib cage to the sides of his waist, up his warm, granite-muscled back. *I love you,* she thought, and then she bit her lower lip lest she actually say the words.

At some unspoken urging from Jess, she caught his sweater in bunched fists and drew it up over his head. Silver-blue lightning scored the sky and danced on the planes of his bare chest, his magnificent face.

Libby was drawn to him, tasting one masculine nipple with a cautious tongue, suckling the other. He moaned and tangled his fingers in her hair, pressing her close, and she knew that he was experiencing the same keen pleasure she had known.

Presently he caught her shoulders in his hands and held her at arm's length, boldly admiring her bare breasts. "Beautiful," he rasped. "So beautiful."

Libby had long been ashamed of her body, thinking it inadequate. Now, in this moment of storm and fury, she was proud of every curve and hollow, every pore and freckle. She removed her jeans and panties with graceful motions.

Jess's reaction was a low, rumbling groan, followed by a gasp of admiration. He stood still, a western Adonis, as she undid his jeans, felt the hollows of his narrow hips, the firmness of his buttocks. Within seconds he was as naked as Libby.

She caught his hands in her own, drew him toward the bed. But instead of reclining with her there, he knelt at the side, positioned Libby so that her hips rested on the edge of the mattress.

His hands moved over every part of her—her breasts, her shoulders, her flat, smooth stomach, the insides of her trembling thighs.

"Jess..."

"Shh, it's all right."

"But..." Libby's back arched and a spasm of delight racked her as he touched the curls sheltering the core of her passion, first with his fingers, then with his lips. "Oh... wait...oh, Jess, no..."

"Yes," he said, his breath warm against her. And then he parted her and took her fully into his mouth, following the instinctive rising and falling of her hips, chuckling at the soft cry she gave.

A violent shudder went through Libby's already throbbing body, and her knees moved wide of each other, shaking, made of no solid substance.

Frantic, she found his head, tangled her fingers in his hair. "Stop," she whimpered, even as she held him fast.

Jess chuckled again and then went right on consuming her, his hands catching under her knees, lifting them higher, pressing them farther apart.

Libby was writhing now, her breath harsh and burning, her vision blurred. The storm came inside the room and swept her up, up, up, beyond the splitting skies. She cried out in wonder as she collided with the moon and bounced off, to be enfolded by a waiting sun.

When she came back inside herself, Jess was beside her on the bed, soothing her with soft words, stroking away the tears that had somehow gathered on her face.

"I've never read…" she whispered stupidly. "I didn't know…"

Jess was drawing her up, so that she lay full on the bed, naked and sated at his side. "Look it up," he teased, kissing her briefly, tenderly. "I think it would be under O."

Libby laughed, and the sound was a warm, soft contrast to the tumult of the storm. "What an ego!"

With an index finger, Jess traced her lips, her chin, the moist length of her neck. Small novas flashed and flared within her as her pulsing senses began to make new demands.

When his mouth came to her breast again, Libby arched her back and whimpered. "Jess…Jess…"

He circled the straining nipple with a warm tongue. "What, babe?"

No coherent words would come to Libby's beleaguered mind. "I don't know," she managed finally. "I don't know!"

"I do," Jess answered, and then he suckled in earnest.

Powerless under the tyranny of her own body, Libby gave herself up to sensation. It seemed that no part of her was left untouched, unconquered, or unworshiped.

When at last Jess poised himself above her, strong and fully a man, his face reflected the flashing lightning that seemed to seek them both.

"I'm Jess," he warned again in a husky whisper that betrayed his own fierce need.

Libby drew him to her with quick, fevered hands. "I know," she gasped, and then she repeated his name like some crazy litany, whispering it first, sobbing it when he thrust his searing magnificence inside her.

He moved slowly at first, and the finely sculptured planes of his face showed the cost of his restraint, the conflicting force of his need. "Libby," he pleaded. "Oh, God...Libby..."

She thrust her hips upward in an instinctive, unplanned motion that shattered Jess's containment and caused his great muscular body to convulse once and then assert its dominance in a way that was at once fierce and tender. It seemed that he sought some treasure within her, so deeply did he delve, some shimmering thing that he would perish without.

His groans rose above the sound of thunder, and as his pace accelerated and his passion was unleashed, Libby moved in rhythm with him, one with him, his.

Their bodies moved faster, agile in their quest, each glistening with the sheen of sweet exertion, each straining toward the sun that, this time, would consume them both.

The tumult flung them high, tore them asunder, fused them together again. Libby sobbed in the hot glory of her release and heard an answering cry from Jess.

They clung together, struggling for breath, for a long time after the slow, treacherous descent had been made. Twice, on the way, Libby's body had paused to greedily claim what had been denied it before.

She was flushed, reckless in her triumph. "I did it," she exalted, her hands moving on the slackened muscles in Jess's back. "I did it...I responded..."

Instantly she felt those muscles go taut, and Jess's head

shot up from its resting place in the curve where her neck and shoulder met.

"What?"

Libby stiffened, knowing now, too late, how grave her mistake had been. "I mean, *we* did it…" she stumbled lamely.

But Jess was wrenching himself away from her, searching for his clothes, pulling them on. "Congratulations!" he yelled.

Libby sat up, confused, wildly afraid. Dear God, was he going to walk out now? Was he going to hate her for a few thoughtless words?

"Jess, wait!" she pleaded, clutching the sheet to her chest. "Please!"

"For what, Libby?" he snapped from the top of the stairs. "Exhibit B? Is there something else you want to prove?"

"Jess!"

But he was storming down the stairs, silent in his rage, bent on escaping her.

"Jess!" Libby cried out again in fear, tears pouring down her face, her hands aching where they grasped the covers.

The only answer was the slamming of the front door.

7

Ken Kincaid looked up from the cards in his hand as the lights flickered, went out, came on again. Damn, this was a hell of a storm—if the rain didn't let up soon, the creeks would overflow and they'd have range calves drowning right and left.

Across the table, Cleave Barlowe laid down his own hand of cards. "Quite a storm, eh?" he asked companionably. "Jess bring your truck back yet?"

"I don't need it," said Ken, still feeling uneasy.

Lightning creased the sky beyond the kitchen window, and thunder shook the old house on its sturdy foundations. Cleave grinned. "He's with Libby, then?"

"Yup," said Ken, smiling himself.

"Think they know the sky's turning itself inside out?"

There was an easing in Ken; he laughed outright. "Doubt it," he replied, looking at his cards again.

For a while the two men played the two-handed poker they had enjoyed for years, but it did seem that luck wasn't running with either one of them. Finally they gave up the effort and Cleave went home.

With his old friend gone, Ken felt apprehensive again. He went around the house making sure all the windows were closed against the rain, and wondered why one storm should bother him that way, when he'd seen a thousand and never found them anything more than a nuisance.

He was about to shut off the lamp in the front room when he saw the headlights of his own truck swing into the driveway. Seconds later, there was an anxious knock at the door.

"Jess?" Ken marveled, staring at the haggard, rain-drenched man standing on the front porch. "What the hell...?"

Jess looked as though he'd just taken a first-rate gut punch. "Could I come in?"

"That's a stupid question," retorted Ken, stepping back to admit his unexpected and obviously distraught visitor. "Is Libby okay?"

Jess's haunted eyes wouldn't quite link up with Ken's. "She's fine," he said, his hands wedged into the pockets of his jeans, his hair and sweater dripping rainwater.

Ken arched an eyebrow. "What'd you do, anyway—ride on the running board of that truck and steer from outside?"

Jess didn't answer; he didn't seem to realize that he was wet to the skin. There was a distracted look about him that made Ken ache inside.

In silence Ken led the way into the kitchen, poured a dose of straight whiskey into a mug, added strong coffee.

"You look like you've been dragged backward through a knothole," he observed when Jess was settled at the table. "What happened?"

Jess closed his hands around the mug. "I'm in love with your daughter," he said after a long time.

Ken sat down, allowed himself a cautious grin. "If you drove over here in this rain just to tell me that, friend, you got wet for nothing."

"You knew?" Jess seemed honestly surprised.

"Everybody knew. Except maybe you and Libby."

Jess downed the coffee and the potent whiskey almost in a single gulp. There was a struggle going on in his face, as though he might be fighting hard to hold himself together.

Ken rose to put more coffee into Jess's mug, along with a lot more whiskey. If ever a man needed a drink, this one did.

"Maybe you'd better put on some dry clothes," the older man ventured.

Jess only shook his head.

Ken sat back in his chair and waited. When Jess was ready to talk, he would. There was, Ken had learned, no sense in pushing before that point was reached.

"Libby's beautiful, you know," Jess remarked presently, as he started on his third drink.

Ken smiled. "Yeah. I've noticed."

Simple and ordinary though they were, the words triggered some kind of emotional reaction in Jess, broke down the barriers he had been maintaining so carefully. His face crumbled, he lowered his head to his arms, and he cried. The sobs were deep and dry and ragged.

Hurting because Jess hurt, Ken waited.

Soon enough, his patience was rewarded. Jess began to talk, brokenly at first, and then with stone-cold reason.

Ken didn't react openly to anything he said; much of what Jess told him about Libby's marriage to Aaron Strand came as no real surprise. He was wounded, all the same, for his daughter and for the devastated young man sitting across the table from him.

The level of whiskey in Ken's bottle went down as the hour grew later. Finally, when Jess was so drunk that his words started getting all tangled up with each other, Ken half led, half carried him up the stairs to Libby's room.

In the hallway, he paused, reflecting. Life was a hell of a thing, he decided. Here was Jess, sleeping fitfully in Libby's bed, all alone. And just up the hill, chances were, Libby was tossing and turning in Jess's bed, just as lonely.

Not for the first time, Ken Kincaid felt a profound desire to get them both by the hair and knock their heads together.

Libby cried until far into the night and then, exhausted, she slept. When she awakened, shocked to find herself in Jess Barlowe's bed, she saw that the world beyond the windows had been washed to a clean sparkle.

The world inside her seemed tawdry by comparison.

Her face feeling achy and swollen, Libby got out of bed, stumbled across the room to the bathroom. Jess was nowhere in the house; she would have sensed it if he were.

As Libby filled the tub with hot water, she wondered whether she was relieved that he wasn't close by, or disappointed. A little of both, she concluded as she slid into her bath and sat there in miserable reverie.

Facing Jess now would have been quite beyond her. Why, why had she said such a foolish thing, when she might have known how Jess would react? On the other hand, why had *he* made such a big deal out of a relatively innocuous remark?

More confused than ever, Libby finished her bath and climbed out to dry herself with a towel. In short order she was dressed and her hair was combed. Because she had no toothbrush—Jess had forgotten that when he picked up her things—she had to be content with rinsing her mouth.

Downstairs, Libby stood staring at the telephone, willing herself to call her father and confess that she needed a ride home. Pride wouldn't allow that, however, and she had made up her mind to walk the distance when she heard a familiar engine outside, the slam of a truck door.

Jess was back, she thought wildly. Where had he been all night? With Monica? What would she say to him?

The questions were pointless, for when Libby forced herself to go to the front door and open it, she saw her father striding up the walk, not Jess.

Fresh embarrassment stained Libby's cheeks, though there was no condemnation in Ken's weathered face, no anger in his understanding eyes. "Ride home?" he said.

Unable to speak, Libby only nodded.

"Pretty bad night?" he ventured in his concise way when they were both settled in the truck and driving away.

"Dismal," replied Libby, fixing her eyes on the red Hereford cattle grazing in the green, rain-washed distance.

"Jess isn't in very good shape either," commented Ken after an interval.

Libby's eyes were instantly trained on her father's profile. "You've seen him?"

"Seen him?" Ken laughed gruffly. "I poured him into bed at three this morning."

"He was drunk?" Libby was amazed.

"He had a nip or two."

"How is he now?"

Ken glanced at her, turned his eyes back to the rutted, winding country road ahead. "Jess is hurting," he said, and there was a finality in his tone that kept Libby from asking so much as one more question.

Jess is hurting. What the devil did that mean? Was he hung over? Had the night been as miserable for him as it had been for her?

Presently the truck came to a stop in front of the big Victorian house that had been "home" to Libby for as long as she could remember. Ken made no move to shut off the engine, and she got out without saying good-bye. For all her brave words of the night before, about not needing her father's approval, she felt estranged from him now, subdued.

After forcing down a glass of orange juice and a slice of toast in the kitchen, Libby went into the studio Cathy and her father had improvised for her and did her best to work. Even during the worst days in New York, she had been able to find solace in the mechanics of drawing her cartoon strip, forgetting her own troubles to create comical dilemmas for Liberated Lizzie.

Today was different.

The panels Libby sketched were awkward, requiring too many erasures, and even if she had been able to get the drawings right, she couldn't have come up with a funny thought for the life of her.

At midmorning, Libby decided that her career was over and paced from one end of the studio to the other, haunted by thoughts of the night before.

Jess had made it clear, in his kitchen, that he didn't want to make love just to let Libby prove that she was "normal." And what had she done? She'd *gloated*.

Shame ached in Libby's cheeks as she walked. *I did it*, she'd crowed, as though she were Edison and the first electric light had just been lit. God, how could she have been so stupid? So insensitive?

"You did have a little help, you know," she scolded herself out loud. And then she covered her face with both hands and cried. It had been partly Jess's fault, that scene—he had definitely overreacted, and on top of that, he had been unreasonable. He had stormed out without giving Libby a chance to make things right.

Still, it was all too easy to imagine how he'd felt. Used. And the truth was that, without intending to, Libby had used him.

Small, strong hands were suddenly pulling Libby's hands away from her face. Through the blur, she saw Cathy watching her, puzzled and sad.

"What's wrong?" her cousin asked. "Please, Libby, tell me what's wrong."

"Everything!" wailed Libby, who was beyond trying to maintain her dignity now.

Gently Cathy drew her close, hugged her. For a moment they were two motherless little girls again, clinging to each other because there were some pains that even Ken, with his gruff, unswerving devotion, couldn't ease.

The embrace was comforting, and after a minute or two Libby recovered enough to step back and offer Cathy a shaky smile. "I've missed you so much, Cathy," she said.

"Don't get sloppy," teased Cathy, using her face to give the toneless words expression.

Libby laughed. "What are you doing today, besides being one of the idle rich?"

Cathy tilted her head to one side. "Did you really stay with Jess last night?" she asked with swift hands.

"Aren't we blunt today?" Libby shot back, both speaking and signing. "I suppose the whole ranch is talking about it!"

Cathy nodded.

"Damn!"

"Then it's true!" exalted Cathy aloud, her eyes sparkling.

Some of Libby's earlier remorse drained away, pushed aside by feelings of anger and betrayal. "Has Jess been bragging?" she demanded, her hands on her hips, her indignation warm and thick in her throat.

"He isn't the type to do that," Cathy answered in slow, carefully formed words, "and you know it."

Libby wasn't so certain—Jess had been very angry, and his pride had been stung. Besides, the only other person who had known was Ken, and he was notoriously tight-lipped when it came to other people's business. "Who told you?" she persisted, narrowing her eyes.

"Nobody had to," Cathy answered aloud. "I was down at the stables, saddling Banjo, and one of the range crews was there—ten or twelve men, I guess. Anyway, there was a fight out front—Jess punched out one of the cowboys."

Libby could only gape.

Cathy gave the story a stirring finale. "I think Jess would have killed that guy if Ken hadn't hauled him off."

Libby found her voice. "Was Jess hurt? Cathy, did you see if he was hurt?"

Cathy grinned at her cousin's undisguised concern. "Not a scratch. He got into an argument with Ken and left."

Libby felt a strong need to find her father and ask him exactly what had happened, but she knew that the effort would be wasted. Even if she could find Ken, which was unlikely considering the size of the ranch and all the places he could be, he wouldn't explain.

Cathy was studying the messy piece of drawing paper affixed to the art board. "You're not going to work?" she signed.

"I gave up," Libby confessed. "I couldn't keep my mind on it."

"After a night with Jess Barlowe, who could?"

Libby suddenly felt challenged, defensive. She even thought that, perhaps, there was more to the deep closeness between Jess and Cathy than she had guessed. "What do you know about spending the night with Jess?" she snapped before she could stop herself.

Cathy rolled her beautiful green eyes. "*Nothing.* For better or worse, and mostly it's been better, I'm married to Jess's brother—remember?"

Libby swallowed, feeling foolish. "Where is Stacey, anyway?" she asked, more to make conversation than because she wanted to know.

The question brought a shadow of sadness to Cathy's face. "He's away on one of his business trips."

Libby sat down on her art stool, folded her hands. "Maybe you should have gone with him, Cathy. You used to do that a lot, didn't you? Maybe if you two could be alone…talk…"

The air suddenly crackled with Cathy's anger and hurt. "*He* talks!" she raged aloud. "I just move my hands!"

Libby spoke softly, gently. "You could talk to Stacey, Cathy—really talk, the way you do with me."

"No."

"Why not?"

"I know I sound like a record playing on the wrong speed, that's why!"

"Even if that were so, would it matter?" signed Libby, frowning. "Stacey knew you were deaf before he married you, for heaven's sake."

Cathy's head went down. "He must have felt sorry for me or something."

Instantly Libby was off her stool, gripping Cathy's shoulders in firm, angry hands. "He loves you!"

Tears misted the emerald-green eyes and Cathy's lower lip trembled. "No doubt that's why he intends to divorce me and marry you, Libby."

"No," insisted Libby, giving her cousin a slight shake.

"No, that isn't true. I think Stacey is confused, Cathy. Upset. Maybe it's this thing about your not wanting to have a baby. Or maybe he feels that you don't need him, you're so independent."

"Independent? Don't look now, Libby Kincaid, but *you're* the independent one! You have a career…you can hear—"

"Will you stop feeling sorry for yourself, dammit!" Libby almost screamed. "I'm so tired of hearing how you suffer! For God's sake, stop whining and fight for the man you love!"

Cathy broke free of Libby's grasp, furious, tears pouring down her face. "It's too late!" she cried. "You're here now, and it's too late!"

Libby sighed, stepped back, stricken by her own outburst and by Cathy's, too. "You're forgetting one thing," she reasoned quietly. "I'm not in love with Stacey. And it would take two of us to start anything, wouldn't it?"

Cathy went to the windows and stared out at the pond, her chin high. Knowing that her cousin needed this interval to restore her dignity and assemble her thoughts, Libby did not approach her.

Finally Cathy sniffled and turned back to offer a shaky smile. "I didn't come over here to fight with you," she said clearly. "I'm going to Kalispell, and I wanted to know if you would like to come with me."

Libby agreed readily, and after changing her clothes and leaving a quick note for Ken, she joined Cathy in the shiny blue Ferrari.

The ride to Kalispell was a fairly long one, and by the time Cathy and Libby reached the small city, they had reestablished their old, easy relationship.

They spent the day shopping, had lunch in a rustic steak

house bearing the Circle Bar B brand, and then started home again.

"Are you really going to give that to Jess?" Cathy asked, her eyes twinkling when she cast a look at the bag in Libby's lap.

"I may lose my courage." Libby frowned, wondering what had possessed her to buy a T-shirt with such an outlandish saying printed on it. She supposed she'd hoped that the gesture would penetrate the barrier between herself and Jess, enabling them to talk.

"Take my advice," said Cathy, guiding the powerful car off the highway and onto the road that led to the heart of the ranch. "Give him the shirt."

"Maybe," said Libby, looking off into the sweeping, endless blue sky. A small airplane was making a graceful descent toward the Circle Bar B landing strip.

"Who do you suppose that is?" Libby asked, catching Cathy's attention with a touch on her arm.

The question was a mistake. Cathy, who had not, of course, heard the plane's engine, scanned the sky and saw it. "Why don't we find out?"

Libby scrunched down in her seat, sorry that she had pointed out the airplane now. Suppose Stacey was aboard, returning from his business trip, and there was another uncomfortable scene at the airstrip? Suppose it was Jess, and he either yelled at Libby or, worse yet, pretended that she wasn't there?

"I'd rather go home," she muttered.

But Cathy's course was set, and the Ferrari bumped and jostled over the road to the landing strip as though it were a pickup truck.

The plane came to a smooth stop as Cathy parked at one

side of the road and got out of the car, shading her eyes with one hand, watching. Libby remained in her seat.

She had, it seemed, imagined only part of the possible scenario. The pilot was Jess, and his passenger was a wan, tight-lipped Stacey.

"Oh, God," said Libby, sinking even further into the car seat. She would have kept her face hidden in her hand forever, probably, if it hadn't been for the crisp, insistent tap at her window.

Having no other choice, she rolled the glass down and squinted into Jess Barlowe's unreadable, hard-lined face. "Come with me," he said flatly.

Libby looked through the Ferrari's windshield, saw Stacey and Cathy standing nearby, a disturbing distance between them. Cathy was glaring angrily into Stacey's face, and Stacey was casting determined looks in Libby's direction.

"They need some time alone," Jess said, his eyes linking fiercely, warningly, with Libby's as he opened the car door for her.

Anxious not to make an obviously unpleasant situation any worse, Libby gathered up her bags and her purse and got out of the car, following along behind Jess's long strides. The station wagon, which she hadn't noticed before, was parked close by.

Without looking back at Stacey and Cathy, Libby slid gratefully into the dusty front seat and closed her eyes. Not until the car was moving did she open them, and even then she couldn't quite bring herself to look at the man behind the wheel.

"That was touching," he said in a vicious rasp.

Libby stiffened in the seat, staring at Jess's rock-hard profile now. "What did you say?"

The powerful shoulders moved in an annoying shrug. "Your wanting to meet Stacey on his triumphant return."

It took Libby a moment to absorb what he was implying. When she had, she slammed him with the paper bag that contained the T-shirt she'd bought for him in Kalispell and hissed, "You bastard! I didn't know Stacey was going to be on that plane, and if I had, I certainly wouldn't have been there at all!"

"Sure," he drawled, and even though he was grinning and looking straight ahead at the road, there was contempt in his tone and a muscle pulsing at the base of his jaw.

Libby felt tears of frustration rise in her eyes. "I thought you believed me," she said.

"I thought I did too," Jess retorted with acid amusement. "But that was before you showed up at the landing strip at such an opportune moment."

"It was Cathy's idea to meet the plane!"

"Right."

The paper bag crackled as Libby lifted it, prepared to swing.

"Do that again and I'll stop this car and raise blisters on your backside," Jess warned, without so much as looking in her direction.

Libby lowered the bag back to her lap, swallowed miserably, and turned her attention to the road. She did not believe Jess's threat for one moment, but she felt childish for trying to hit him with the bag. "Cathy told me there was a fight at the stables this morning," she dared after a long time. "What happened?"

Another shrug, as insolent as the first, preceded his reply. "One of Ken's men said something I didn't like."

"Like what?"

"Like didn't it bother me to sleep with my brother's mistress."

Libby winced, sorry for pressing the point. "Oh, God," she said, and she was suddenly so tired, so broken, and so frustrated that she couldn't hold back her tears anymore. She covered her face with both hands and turned her head as far away from Jess as she could, but the effort was useless.

Jess stopped the station wagon at the side of the road, turned Libby easily toward him. Through a blur, she saw the Ferrari race past.

"Let go of me!"

Jess not only didn't let go, he pulled her close. "I'm sorry," he muttered into her hair. "God, Libby, I don't know what comes over me, what makes me say things to hurt you."

"Garden-variety hatred!" sniffled Libby, who was already forgiving him even though it was against her better judgment.

He chuckled. "No. I couldn't ever hate you, Libby."

She looked up at him, confused and hopeful. Before she could think of anything to say, however, there was a loud *pop* from beneath the hood of the station wagon, followed by a sizzle and clouds of steam.

"Goddammit!" rasped Jess.

Libby laughed, drunk on the scent of him, the closeness of him, the crazy paradox of him. "This crate doesn't exactly fit your image, you know," she taunted. "Why don't you get yourself a decent car?"

He turned from glowering at the hood of the station wagon to smile down into her face. "If I do, Kincaid, will you let me make love to you in the back seat?"

She shoved at his immovable chest with both hands, laughing again. "No, no, a thousand times no!"

Jess nibbled at her jawline, at the lobe of her ear, chuckled huskily as she tensed. "How many times no?"

"Maybe," said Libby.

Just when she thought she would surely go crazy, Jess drew back from his brazen pursuits and smiled lazily. "It is time I got a new car," he conceded, with an evil light glistening in his jade eyes. "Will you come to Kalispell and help me pick it out, Libby?"

A thrill skittered through Libby's body and flamed in her face. "I was just there," she protested, clutching at straws.

"It shouldn't…"—Jess bent, nipped at the side of her neck with gentle teeth—"take long. A couple of days at the most."

"A couple of days!"

"And nights." Jess's lips were scorching their way across the tender hollow of her throat. "Think about it, Lib. Just you and me. No Stacey. No Cathy. No problems."

Libby shivered as a knowledgeable hand closed over one of her breasts, urging, reawakening. "No p-problems?" she echoed.

Jess undid the top button of her blouse.

Libby's breath caught in her throat; she felt heat billowing up inside her, foaming out, just as it was foaming out of the station wagon's radiator. "Wh-where would we s-stay?"

Another button came undone.

Jess chuckled, his mouth on Libby's collarbone now, tasting it, doing nothing to cool the heat that was pounding within her. "How about"—the third button gave way, and Libby's bra was displaced by a gentle hand—"one of those motels…with the…vibrating beds?"

"Tacky," gasped Libby, and her eyes closed languidly and her head fell back as Jess stroked the nipple he'd just found to pebble-hard response.

"My condo, then," he said, and his lips were sliding down from her collarbone, soft, soft, over the upper rounding of her bare breast.

Libby gasped and arched her back as his lips claimed the distended, hurting peak. "Jess…oh, God…this is a p-public road!"

"Umm," Jess said, lapping at her now with the tip of his tongue. "Will you go with me, Libby?"

Wild need went through her as he stroked the insides of her thighs, forcing her blue-jeaned legs apart. And all the while he plied her nipple into a panic of need. "Yes!" she gasped finally.

Jess undid the snap of her jeans, slid his hand inside, beneath the scanty lace of her panties.

"Damn you," Libby whispered hoarsely, "s-stop that! I said I'd go—"

He told her what else she was about to do. And one glorious, soul-scoring minute later, she did.

Red in the face, still breathing heavily, Libby closed her jeans, tugged her bra back into place, buttoned her blouse. God, what if someone had come along and seen her letting Jess…letting him play with her like that?

All during the ride home, she mentally rehearsed the blistering diatribe he deserved to hear. He could just go to Kalispell by *himself,* she would tell him. If he thought for one damned minute that he was going to take her to his condo and make love to her, he was sadly mistaken, she would say.

"Be ready in half an hour," Jess told her at her father's front door.

"Okay," Libby replied.

After landing the Cessna in Kalispell and making arrangements to rent a car, which turned out to be a temperamental cousin to Jess's station wagon, they drove through the small city to an isolated tree-dense property beyond. There were at least a million stars in the sky, and as the modest car rattled over a narrow wooden bridge spanning a creek, Libby couldn't help giving in a little to the romance of it all.

Beyond the bridge, there were more trees—towering ponderosa pines, whispering, shiny-leaved birches. They stopped in the driveway of a condominium that stood apart from several others. Jess got out of the car, came around to open Libby's door for her.

"Let's get rid of the suitcases and go out for something to eat," he said.

Libby's stomach rumbled inelegantly, and Jess laughed as he caught her hand in his and drew her up the darkened walk to the front door of the condominium. "That shoots my plans for a little fun before dinner," he teased.

"There's always after," replied Libby, lifting her chin.

8

The inside of the condominium was amazingly like Jess's house on the ranch. There was a loft, for instance, this one accessible by both stairs and, of all things, a built-in ladder. Too, the general layout of the rooms was much the same.

The exceptions were that the floors were carpeted rather than bare oak, and the entire roof was made of heavy glass. *When we make love here, I'll be able to look up and see the stars,* Libby mused.

"Like it?" Jess asked, setting the suitcases down and watching her with discerning, mirthful green eyes.

Libby was uncomfortable again, doubting the wisdom of coming here now that she was faced with the realities of the situation. "Is this where you bring all your conquests?"

Jess smiled, shrugged.

"Well?" prodded Libby, annoyed because he hadn't even had the common decency to offer a denial.

He sat down on the stone ledge fronting the fireplace, wrapped his hands around one knee. "The place does happen to be something of a love nest, as a matter of fact."

Libby was stung. Dammit, how unchivalrous could one man be? "Oh," she said loftily.

"It's my father's place," Jess said, clearly delighting in her obvious curiosity and the look of relief she couldn't quite hide.

"Your father's?"

Jess grinned. "He entertains his mistress here, from time to time. In his position, he has to be discreet."

Libby was gaping now, trying to imagine the sedate, dignified Senator Barlowe cavorting with a woman beneath slanted glass roofs, climbing ladders to star-dappled lofts.

Jess's amused gaze had strayed to the ladder. "It probably puts him in mind of the good old days—climbing into the hayloft, and all that."

Libby blushed. She was still quite disturbed by that ladder, among other things. "You did ask the senator's permission to come here, didn't you?"

Jess seemed to know that she had visions of Cleave Barlowe carrying some laughing woman over the threshold and finding the place already occupied. "Yes," he assured her in a teasing tone, rising and coming toward her. "I said, 'Mind if I take Libby to your condo, dear old dad, and take her to bed?' And he said—"

"Jess!" Libby howled, in protest.

He laughed, caught her elbows in his hands, kissed her playfully, his lips sampling hers, tugging at them in soft entreaty. "My father is in Washington," he said. "Stop worrying."

Libby pulled back, her face hot, her mind spinning. "I'm hungry!"

"Umm," replied Jess, "so am I."

Why did she feel like a sixteen-year-old on the verge of big trouble? "Please…let's go now."

Jess sighed.

They went, but they were back, arms burdened with cartons of Chinese food, in less than half an hour.

While Jess set the boxes out on the coffee table, Libby went to the kitchen for plates and silverware. Scribbled on a blackboard near the sink, she saw the surprising words: "Thanks, Ken. See you next week. B."

A soft chuckle simmered up into Libby's throat and emerged as a giggle. Could it be that her father, her serious, hardworking father, had a ladyfriend who visited him here in this romantic hideaway? Tilting her head to one side, she considered, grinned again. "Naaaah!"

But Libby's grin wouldn't fade as she carried plates, forks, spoons and paper napkins back into the living room.

"What's so funny?" Jess asked, trying to hide the hunk of sweet-and-sour chicken he had just purloined from one of the steaming cartons.

"Nothing," said Libby, catching his hand and raising it to his mouth. Sheepishly he popped the tidbit of chicken onto his tongue and chewed.

"You lie," Jess replied, "but I'm too hungry to press the point."

While they ate, Libby tried to envision what sort of woman her father would be drawn to—tall, short? Quiet, talkative?

"You're mulling over more than the chow mein," accused Jess presently in a good-natured voice. "Tell me, what's going on in that gifted little head?"

Libby shrugged. "Romance."

He grinned. "That's what I like to hear."

But Libby was thinking seriously, following her thoughts through new channels. In all the years since her mother's death, just before Cathy had come to live on the ranch, she had never imagined Ken Kincaid caring about another woman. "It isn't as though he's old," she muttered, "or unattractive."

Jess set down his plate with a mockingly forceful thump. "That does it. Who are you talking about, Kincaid?" he demanded archly, his wonderful mouth twitching in the effort to suppress a grin.

She perused him with lofty disdain. "Am I correct in assuming that you are jealous?"

"Jealous as hell," came the immediate and not-so-jovial response.

Libby laughed, laid a hand on his knee. "If you must know, I was thinking about my father. I've always kept him in this neat little cubicle in my mind, marked 'Dad.' If you can believe it, it has just now occurred to me that he's a man, with a life, and maybe even a love, of his own."

Mirth danced in Jess's jade eyes, but if he knew anything about Ken's personal life, he clearly wasn't going to speak of it. "Pass the eggroll," he said diplomatically.

When the meal was over, Libby's reflections began to shift to matters nearer the situation at hand.

"I don't know what I'm doing here," she said pensively as she and Jess cleared the coffee table and started toward the kitchen with the debris. "I must be out of my mind."

Jess dropped the cartons and the crumpled napkins into the trash compactor. "Thanks a lot," he said, watching her attentively as she rinsed the plates and silverware and put them into the dishwasher.

Wearing tailored gray slacks and a lightweight teal-blue sweater, he was devastatingly attractive. Still, the look Libby gave him was a serious, questioning one. "What is it with us, Jess? What makes us behave the way we do? One minute, we're yelling at each other, or not speaking at all, and the next we're alone in a place like this."

"Chemistry?"

Libby laughed ruefully. "More like voodoo. So what kind of car are you planning to buy?"

Jess drew her to him; his fingertips were butterfly-light on the small of her back. "Car?" he echoed, as though the word were foreign.

There was a soft, quivering ache in one corner of Libby's heart. Why couldn't things always be like this between them? Why did they have to wrangle so fiercely before achieving this quiet accord? "Stop teasing me," she said softly. "We did come here to buy a car, you know."

Jess's hands pulled her blouse up and out of her slacks, made slow-moving, sensuous circles on her bare back. "Yes," he said in a throaty rumble. "A car. But there are lots of different kinds of cars, aren't there, Libby? And a decision like this can't be made in haste."

Libby closed her eyes, almost hypnotized by the slow, languid meter of his words, the depth of his voice. "N-no," she agreed.

"Definitely not," he said, his mouth almost upon hers. "It could take two—or three—days to decide."

"Ummm," agreed Libby, slipping deeper and deeper under his spell.

Jess had pressed her back against a counter, and his body formed an impassable barricade, leaning, hard and fragrant, into hers. He was tracing the length of her neck with soft, searing lips, tasting the hollow beneath her ear.

Finally he kissed her, first with tenderness, then with fervor, his tongue seeking and being granted sweet entry. This preliminary joining made Libby's whole entity pulse with an awareness of the primitive differences between his body and her own. Where she was soft and yielding, he was fiercely hard. Her nipples pouted into tiny peaks, crying out for his attention.

Seeming to sense that, Jess unbuttoned her blouse with deft, brazen fingers that felt warm against her skin. He opened the front catch on her bra, admired the pink-tipped lushness that seemed to grow richer and rounder under his gaze.

Idly he bent to kiss one peak into ferocious submission, and Libby groaned, her head falling back. Etched against the clear roof, she saw the long needles of ponderosa pines splintering the spring moonlight into shards of silver.

After almost a minute of pleasure so keen that Libby was certain she couldn't bear it, Jess turned to the other breast, kissing, suckling, nipping softly with his teeth. And all the while, he worked the opposite nipple skillfully with his fingers, putting it through delicious paces.

Libby was almost mindless by the time she felt the snap and zipper of her jeans give way, and her hands were still tangled in his dark hair as he knelt. Down came the jeans, her panties with them.

She could manage no more than a throaty gasp as his hands stroked the smooth skin of her thighs, the V of curls at their junction. She felt his breath there, warm, promising to cherish.

Libby trembled as he sought entrance with a questioning kiss, unveiled her with fingers that would not await permission.

As his tongue first touched the tenderness that had been hidden, his hands came to Libby's hips, pressing her down onto this fiery, inescapable glory. Only when she pleaded did he tug her fully into his mouth and partake of her.

Jess enjoyed Libby at his leisure, demanding her essence, showing no mercy even when she cried out and shuddered upon him in a final, soaring triumph. When her own chants of passion had ceased, she was conscious of his.

Jess still knelt before her, his every touch saying that he was worshiping, but there was sweet mastery in his manner, too. After one kiss of farewell, he gently drew her jeans and panties back into place and stood.

Libby stared at him, amazed at his power over her. He smiled at her wonder, though there was a spark of that same emotion deep in his eyes, and then lifted her off her feet and into his arms.

Say "I love you," Libby thought with prayerful fervor.

"I need you," he said instead.

And, for the moment, it was enough.

Stars peeked through the endlessly varied patterns the fallen pine needles made on the glass roof, as if to see and assess the glory that glowed beneath. Libby preened under their celestial jealousy and cuddled closer to Jess's hard, sheet-entangled frame.

"Why didn't you ever marry, Jess?" she asked, tracing a soft path across his chest with her fingers.

The mattress shifted as he moved to put one arm around Libby and draw her nearer still. "I don't know. It always seemed that marriage could wait."

"Didn't you even come close?"

Jess sighed, his fingers moving idly in her hair. "A couple of times I seriously considered it, yes. I guess it bothered me, subliminally, that I was looking these women over as though they were livestock or something. This one would have beautiful children, that one would like living on the ranch—that sort of thing."

"I see."

Jess stiffened slightly beneath the patterns she was making in the soft swirls of hair on his chest, and she felt the question coming long before he uttered it.

"What attracted you to Aaron Strand?"

Libby had been pondering that mystery herself, ever since her marriage to Aaron had begun to dissolve. Now, suddenly, she was certain that she understood. Weak though he might be, Aaron Strand was tall, dark-haired, broad in the shoulders. He had given the impression of strength and self-assurance, qualities that any woman would find appealing.

"I guess I thought he was strong, like Dad," she said, because she couldn't quite amend the sentence to a full truth and admit that she had probably superimposed Jess's image over Aaron's in the first place.

"Ummm," said Jess noncommittally.

"Of course, he is actually very weak."

Jess offered no comment.

"I guess my mistake," Libby went on quietly, "was in seeing myself through Aaron's eyes. He made me feel so worthless…"

"Maybe that made him feel better about himself."

"Maybe. But I still hate him, Jess—isn't that awful? I still hate him for leaving Jonathan in the lurch like that, especially."

"It isn't awful, it's human. It appears that you and Jonathan needed more than he had to give. Unconsciously, you probably measured him against Ken, and whatever else he is, your dad is a hard act to follow, Libby."

"Yes," said Libby, but she was thinking: *I didn't measure Aaron against Dad. God help me, Jess, I measured him against you.*

Jess turned over in a graceful, rolling motion, so that he was above her, his head and shoulders blocking out the light of the stars. "Enough heavy talk, woman. I came here to—"

"Buy a car?" broke in Libby, her tone teasing and full of love.

He nuzzled his face between her warm, welcoming breasts. "My God," he said, his voice muffled by her satin flesh, "what an innocent you are, Libby Kincaid!" One of his hands came down, gentle and mischievous, to squeeze her bottom. "Nice upholstery."

Libby gasped and arched her back as his mouth slid up over the rounding of her breast to claim its peak. "Not much mileage," she choked out.

Jess laughed against the nipple he was tormenting so methodically. "A definite plus." His hand moved between her thighs to assert an ancient mastery, and his breath quickened at Libby's immediate response. "Starts easily," he muttered, sipping at her nipple now, tugging it into an obedient little point.

Libby was beyond the game now, rising and falling on the velvet swells of need he was stirring within her. "I...Oh, God, Jess...what are you...ooooh!"

Somehow, Jess managed to turn on the bedside lamp without interrupting the searing pace his right hand was setting for Libby's body. "You are a goddess," he said.

The fevered dance continued, even though Libby willed herself to lie still. Damn him, he was watching her, taking pleasure from the unbridled response she could not help giving. Her heart raced with exertion, blood boiled in every vein, and Jess's lazy smile was lost in a silver haze.

She sobbed out his name, groping for his shoulders with her hands, holding on. Then, shuddering violently, she tumbled into some chasm where there was no sound but the beat of her own heart.

"You like doing that, don't you?" she snapped when she could see again, breathe again.

"Yes," replied Jess without hesitation.

Libby scrambled into a sitting position, blue eyes shooting flames. "Bastard," she said.

He met her gaze placidly. "What's the matter with you?"

Libby wasn't quite sure of the answer to that question. "It just…it just bothers me that you were…you were looking at me," she faltered, covering her still-pulsing breasts with the bedclothes.

With a deliberate motion of his hands, Jess removed the covers again, and Libby's traitorous nipples puckered in response to his brazen perusal. "Why?" he asked.

Libby's cheeks ached with color, and she lowered her eyes. Instantly Jess caught her chin in a gentle grasp, made her look at him again.

"Sweetheart, you're not ashamed, are you?"

Libby couldn't reply, she was so confused.

His hand slid, soothing, from Libby's chin to the side of her face. "You were giving yourself to me, Libby, trusting me. Is there shame in that?"

She realized that there wasn't, not the way she loved this brazen, tender, outlandish man. If only she dared to tell him verbally what her body already had.

He kissed her softly, sensing her need for greater reassurance. "Exquisite," he said. "Even ordinarily, you are exquisite. But when you let me love you, you go beyond that. You move me on a level where I've never even been touched before."

Say it now, Libby urged silently, *say you love me.*

But she had to be satisfied with what he had already said, for it was immediately clear that there would be no poetic avowals of devotion forthcoming. He'd said she was exquisite, that she moved him, but he'd made no declaration.

For this reason, there was a measure of sadness in the lovemaking that followed.

Long after Jess slept, exhausted, beside her, Libby lay awake, aching. She wanted, needed more from Jess than his readily admitted lust. So much more.

And yet, if a commitment were offered, would Libby want to accept it? Weren't there already too many conflicts complicating their lives? Though she tried to shut out the memory, Libby couldn't forget that Jess had believed her capable of carrying on with his brother and hurting her cousin and dearest friend in the process. Nor could she forget the wedge that had been driven between them the first time they'd made love, when she'd slipped and uttered words that had made him feel as though she'd used him to prove herself as a woman.

Of course, they had come together again, despite these things, but that was of no comfort to Libby. If they were to achieve any real closeness, more than just their bodies would have to be in accord.

After several hours, Libby fell into a fitful, dream-ridden sleep. When morning came, casting bright sunlight through the expanse of glass overhead, she was alone in the tousled bed.

"Lib!"

She went to the edge of the loft, peering down over the side. "What?" she retorted, petulant in the face of Jess's freshly showered, bright-and-shiny good cheer.

He waved a cooking spatula with a flourish. "One egg or two?"

"Drop dead," she replied flatly, frowning at the ladder.

Jess laughed. "Watch it. You'll get my hopes up with such tender words."

"What's this damned ladder for, anyway?"

"Are you this grouchy every morning?" he countered.

"Only when I've engaged in illicit sex the night before!" Libby snapped, scowling. "I believe I asked you about the ladder?"

"It's for climbing up and down." Jess shrugged.

Libby's head throbbed, and her eyes felt puffy and sore. "Given time, I probably could have figured out that much!"

Jess chuckled and shook his head, as if in sympathy.

Libby grasped the top of the peculiar ladder in question and gave it a vigorous shake. It was immovable. Her puzzlement made her feel even more irritable and, for no consciously conceived reason, she put out her tongue at Jess Barlowe and whirled away from the edge of the loft, out of his view.

His laughter rang out as she stumbled into the bathroom and turned on the water in the shower stall.

Once she had showered and brushed her teeth, Libby began to feel semihuman. With this came contrition for the snappish way she had greeted Jess minutes before. It wasn't his fault, after all, that he was so nauseatingly happy in the mornings.

Grinning a mischievous grin, Libby rummaged through the suitcase she had so hastily packed and found the T-shirt she had bought for Jess the day before, when she'd come to Kalispell with Cathy. She pulled the garment on over her head and, in a flash of daring, swung over the loft to climb down the ladder.

Her reward was a low, appreciative whistle.

"Now I know why that ladder was built," Jess said. "The view from down here is great.

Libby was embarrassed; she'd thought Jess was in the kitchen and thus unable to see her novel descent from the loft. Reaching the floor, she whirled, her face crimson, to glare at him.

Jess read the legend printed on the front of the T-shirt, which was so big that it reached almost to her knees, and laughed explosively. "'If it feels good, do it'?" he marveled.

Libby's glare simply would not stay in place, no matter how hard she tried to sustain it. Her mouth twitched and a chuckle escaped her and then she was laughing as hard as Jess was.

Given the situation, his words came as a shock.

"Libby, will you marry me?"

She stared at him, bewildered, afraid to hope. "What?"

The jade eyes were gentle now, still glistening with residual laughter. "Don't make me repeat it, princess."

"I think the eggs are burning," said Libby in tones made wooden by surprise.

"Wrong. I've already eaten mine, and yours are congealing on your plate. What's your answer, Kincaid?"

Libby's throat ached; something about the size of her heart was caught in it. "I...what..."

"I thought you only talked in broken sentences at the height of passion. Are you really as surprised as all that?"

"Yes!" croaked Libby after a struggle.

The broad shoulders, accentuated rather than hidden by a soft yellow sweater, moved in a shrug. "It seemed like a good solution to me."

"A solution? To what?"

"All our separate and combined problems," answered Jess airily. Persuasively. "Think about it, Lib. Stacey couldn't very well hassle you anymore, could he? And you could stay on the ranch."

Despite the companionable delivery, Jess's words made Libby's soul ache. "Those are solutions for me. What problems would marriage solve for you?"

"We're good in bed," he offered, shattering Libby with what he seemed to mean as a compliment.

"It takes more than that!"

"Does it?"

Libby was speechless, though a voice inside her kept screaming silly, sentimental things. *What about love? What about babies and leftover meatloaf and filing joint tax returns?*

"You dad would be happy," Jess added, and he couldn't have hurt Libby more if he'd raised his hand and slapped her.

"My dad? My *dad?*"

Jess turned away, seemingly unaware of the effect his convoluted proposal was having on Libby. He looked like exactly what he was: a trained, skillful attorney pleading a weak case. "You want children, don't you? And I know you like living on the ranch."

Libby broke in coldly. "I guess I meet all the qualifications. I do want children. I do like living on the Circle Bar B. So why don't you just hog-tie me and brand me a Barlowe?"

Every muscle in Jess's body seemed to tense, but he did not turn around to face her. "There is one other reason," he offered.

For all her fury and hurt, hope sang through Libby's system like the wind unleashed on a wide prairie. "What's that?"

He drew a deep breath, his hands clasped behind him, courtroom style. "There would be no chance, for now at least, of Cathy being hurt."

Cathy. Libby's knees weakened; she groped for the sofa behind her, fell into it. Good God, was his devotion to Cathy so deep that he would marry the woman he considered a threat to her happiness, just to protect her?

"I am so damned tired of hearing about Cathy," she said evenly, tugging the end of the T-shirt down over her knees for something to do.

Now Jess turned, looked at her with unreadable eyes.

Even though Libby felt the guilt she always did whenever she was even mildly annoyed with Cathy, she stood her ground. "A person doesn't have to be handicapped to hurt, you know," she said in a small and rather uncertain voice.

Jess folded his arms and the sunlight streaming in through the glass ceiling glittered in his dark hair. "I know that," he said softly. "And we're all handicapped in some way, aren't we?"

She couldn't tell whether he was reprimanding her or offering an olive branch. Huddling on the couch, feeling foolish in the T-shirt she had put on as a joke, Libby knotted her hands together in her lap. "I suppose that remark was intended as a barb."

Jess came to sit beside her on the couch, careful not to touch her. "Libby, it wasn't. I'm tired of exchanging verbal shots with you—that was fine when we had to ride the same school bus every day, but we're adults now. Let's try to act as such."

Libby looked into Jess's face and was thunderstruck by how much she cared for him, needed him. And yet, even a week before, she would have said she despised Jess and meant it. All that rancor they'd borne each other—had it really been passion instead?

"I don't understand any of this."

Jess took one of her hands into both of his. "Do you want to marry me or not?"

Both fear and joy rose within Libby. In order to look inward at her own feelings, she was forced to look away from him. She did love Jess, there was absolutely no doubt of that, and she wanted, above all things, to be his wife. She wanted children and, at thirty-one, she often had the feeling that time was getting short. Dammit, why couldn't he say he loved her?

"Would you be faithful to me, Jess?"

He touched her cheek, turning her face without apparent effort, so that she was again looking into those bewitching green eyes. "I would never betray you."

Aaron had said those words too. Aaron had been so very good with words.

But this was Jess, Libby reminded herself. Jess, not Aaron. "I couldn't give up my career," she said. "It's a crazy business, Jess, and sometimes there are long stretches of time when I don't do much of anything. Other times, I have to work ten- or twelve-hour days to meet a deadline."

Jess did not seem to be dissuaded.

Libby drew a deep breath. "Of course, I'd go on being known as Libby Kincaid. I never took Aaron's name and I don't see any sense in taking yours—should I agree to marry you, that is."

He seemed amused, but she had definitely touched a sore spot. That became immediately obvious. "Wait a minute, lady. Professionally, you can be known by any name you want. Privately, however, you'll be Libby Barlowe."

Libby was secretly pleased, but because she was angry and hurt that he didn't love her, she lifted her chin and snapped, "You have to have that Circle Bar B brand on everything you consider yours, don't you?"

"You are not a thing, Libby," he replied rationally, "but I want at least that much of a commitment. Call it male ego if you must, but I want my wife to be Mrs. Barlowe."

Libby swallowed. "Fair enough," she said.

Jess sat back on the sofa, folded his arms again. "I'm wait-ing," he said, and the mischievous glint was back in his eyes.

"For what?"

"An answer to my original question."

Fool, fool! Don't you ever learn, Libby Kincaid? Don't you ever learn? Libby quieted the voice in her mind and lifted her chin. Life was short, and unpredictable in the bargain. Maybe Jess would learn to love her the way she loved him. Wasn't that kind of happiness worth a risk?

"I'll marry you," she said.

Jess kissed her with an exuberance that soon turned to de-sire.

Jess frowned at the sleek showroom sports car, his tongue making one cheek protrude. "What do you think?" he asked.

Libby assessed the car again. "It isn't you."

He grinned, ignoring the salesman's quiet disappointment. "You're right."

Neither, of course, had the last ten cars they had looked at been "him." The sports cars seemed to cramp his long legs, while the big luxury vehicles were too showy.

"How about a truck?" Libby suggested.

"Do you know how many trucks there are on the ranch?" he countered. "Besides, some yokel would probably paint on the family logo when I wasn't looking."

Libby deliberately widened her eyes. "That would be truly terrible!"

He made a face at her, but when he spoke, his words were delivered in a touchingly serious way. "We could get an-other station wagon and fill the backseat with kids and dogs."

Libby smiled at the image. "A grungy sort of heaven," she mused.

Jess laughed. "And of course there would be lots of room to make love."

The salesman cleared his throat and discreetly walked away.

9

"I think you shocked that salesman," observed Libby, snapping the seat belt into place as Jess settled behind the wheel of their rental car.

Jess shrugged. "By wanting a station wagon?" he teased.

"By wanting *me* in the station wagon," clarified Libby.

Jess turned the key in the ignition and shifted gears. "He's lucky I didn't list all the other places I'd like to have you. The hood, for instance. And then there's the roof…"

Libby colored richly as they pulled into the slow traffic. "Jess!"

He frowned speculatively. "And, of course, on the ladder at the condo."

"The ladder?"

Jess flung her a brazen grin. "Yeah. About halfway up."

"Don't you think about anything but sex?"

"I seem to have developed a fixation, Kincaid—just since you came back, of course."

She couldn't help smiling. "Of course."

Nothing more was said until they'd driven through the quiet, well-kept streets to the courthouse. Jess parked the car and turned to Libby with a comical leer. "Are you up to a blood test and a little small-town bureaucracy, Kincaid?"

Libby felt a wild, twisting thrill in the pit of her stomach. A marriage license. He wanted to get a marriage license. In three short days, she could be bound to Jess Barlowe for life. At least, she *hoped* it would be for life.

After drawing a deep breath, Libby unsnapped her seat belt and got out of the car.

Twenty minutes later, the ordeal was over. The fact that the wedding itself wouldn't take nearly as long struck Libby as an irony.

On the sidewalk, Jess caught her elbow in one hand and helped her back into the car. While he must have noticed that she was preoccupied, he was chivalrous enough not to say so.

"Stop at that supermarket!" Libby blurted when they'd been driving for some minutes.

Jess gave her a quizzical look. "Supermarket?"

"Yes. They sell food there, among other necessary items."

Jess frowned. "Why can't we just eat in restaurants? There are several good ones—"

"Restaurants?" Libby cried with mock disdain. "How can I prove what a great catch I am if I don't cook something for you?"

Jess's right hand left the steering wheel to slide languorously up and down Libby's linen-skirted thigh. "Relax, sweetheart," he said in a rather good imitation of Humphrey Bogart. "I already know you're good in the kitchen."

The obvious reference to last night's episode in that room unsettled Libby. "You delight in saying outrageous things, don't you?" she snapped.

"I delight in *doing* outrageous things."

"You'll get no argument on that score, fella," she retorted acidly.

The car came to a stop in front of the supermarket, which

was in the center of a small shopping mall. Libby noticed that Jess's gaze strayed to a jewelry store down the way.

"I'll meet you inside," he said, and then he was gone.

Though Libby told herself that she was being silly and sentimental, she was pleased to think that Jess might be shopping for a ring.

The giddy, romantic feeling faded when she selected a shopping cart inside the supermarket, however. She was wallowing in gushy dreams, behaving like a seventeen-year-old virgin. Of *course* Jess would buy a ring, but only because it would be expected of him.

Glumly Libby went about selecting items from a mental grocery list she had been composing since she'd checked the refrigerator and cupboards at the condominium and found them all but empty.

Taking refuge in practical matters, she frowned at a display of cabbage and wondered how much food to buy. Jess hadn't said how long they would be staying in Kalispell, beyond the time it would take to find the car he wanted.

Shrugging slightly, Libby decided to buy provisions for three days. Because that was the required waiting period for a marriage license, they would probably be in town at least that long.

She looked down at her slacks and brightly colored peasant blouse. The wedding ceremony was going to be an informal one, obviously, but she would still need a new dress, and she wanted to buy a wedding band for Jess, too.

She pushed her cart along the produce aisle, woodenly selecting bean sprouts, fresh broccoli, onions. Her first wedding had been a quiet one, too, devoid of lace and flowers and music, and something within her mourned those things.

They hadn't even discussed a honeymoon, and what kind

of ceremony would this be, without Ken, without Cathy, without Senator Barlowe and Marion Bradshaw, the house-keeper?

A box seemed to float up out of the cart, but Libby soon saw that it was clasped in a strong sun-browned hand.

"I hate cereals that crunch," Jess said, and his eyes seemed to be looking inside Libby, seeing the dull ache she would rather have kept hidden. "What's wrong, love?"

Libby fought back the sudden silly tears that ached in her throat and throbbed behind her eyes. "Nothing," she lied.

Jess was not fooled. "You want Ken to come to the wedding," he guessed.

Libby lowered her head slightly. "He was hurt when Aaron and I got married without even telling him first," she said.

There was a short silence before a housewife, tagged by two preschoolers, gave Libby's cart a surreptitious bump with her own, tacitly demanding access to the cereal display. Libby wrestled her groceries out of the way and looked up at Jess, waiting for his response.

He smiled, touched her cheek. "Tell you what. We'll call the ranch and let everybody know we're getting married. That way, if they want to be there, they can. And if you want frills and flash, princess, we can have a formal wedding later."

The idea of a second wedding, complete with the trimmings, appealed to Libby's romantic soul. She smiled at the thought. "You would do that? You would go through it all over again, just for show?"

"Not for show, princess. For you."

The housewife made an appreciative sound and Libby started a little, having completely forgotten their surroundings.

Jess laughed and the subject was dropped. They walked up one aisle and down another, dropping the occasional pertinent item into the cart, arguing good-naturedly about who would do the cooking after they were married.

The telephone was ringing as Libby unlocked the front door of the condo, so she left Jess to carry in their bags of groceries and ran to answer it, expecting to hear Ken's voice, or Marion Bradshaw's, relaying some message from Cathy.

A cruel wave of *déjà vu* washed over her when she heard Aaron's smooth, confident greeting. "Hello, Libby."

"What do you want?" Libby rasped, too stunned to hang up. How on earth had he gotten that number?

"I told you before, dear heart," said Aaron smoothly. "I want a child."

Libby was conscious of Jess standing at her elbow, the shopping bags clasped in his arms. "You're insane!" she cried into the receiver.

"Maybe so, but not insane enough to let my grandmother hand over an empire to someone else. She has doubts, you know, about my dependability."

"I wonder why!"

"Don't be sarcastic, sugarplum. My request isn't really all that unreasonable, considering all I stand to lose."

"It is unreasonable, Aaron! In fact, it's sick!" At this point Libby slammed down the receiver with a vengeance. She was trembling so hard that Jess hastily shunted the grocery bags onto a side table and took her into his arms.

"What was that all about?" he asked when Libby had recovered herself a little.

"He's horrible," Libby answered, distracted and very much afraid. "Oh, Jess, he's a monster—"

"What did he say?" Jess pressed quietly.

"Aaron wants me to have his baby! Jess, he actually had the gall to ask me to come back, just so he can produce an heir and please his grandmother!"

Jess's hand was entangled in her hair now, comforting her. "It's all right, Lib. Everything will be all right."

Then why am I so damned scared? Libby asked herself, but she put on a brave face for Jess and even managed a smile. "Let's call my dad," she said.

Jess nodded, kissed her forehead. And then he took up the grocery bags again and carried them into the kitchen while Libby dialed her father's telephone number.

There was no answer, which was not surprising, considering that it was still early. Ken would be working, and because of the wide range of his responsibilities, he could be anywhere on the 150,000 acres that made up the Circle Bar B.

Sounds from the kitchen indicated that Jess was putting the food away, and Libby wandered in, needing to be near him.

"No answer?" he asked, tossing a package of frozen egg rolls into the refrigerator-freezer.

"No answer," confirmed Libby. "I should have known, I guess."

Jess turned, gave her a gentle grin. "You did know, Libby. But you needed to touch base just then, and going through the motions was better than nothing."

"When did you get so smart?"

"Last Tuesday, I think," he answered ponderously. "Know something? You look a little tired. Why don't you climb up that ladder that bugs you so much and take a nap?"

Libby arched one eyebrow. "While you do what?"

His answer was somewhat disappointing. "While I go back to town for a few hours," he said. "I have some things to do."

"Like what?"

He grinned. "Like picking up some travel brochures, so we can decide where to take our honeymoon."

Libby felt a rush of pleasure despite the weariness she was suddenly very aware of. Had it been there all along, or was she tired simply because this subtle hypnotist had suggested it to her? "Does it matter where we honeymoon?"

"Not really," Jess replied, coming disturbingly close, kissing Libby's forehead. "But I like having you all to myself. I can't help thinking that the farther we get from home right now, the better off we're going to be."

A tremor of fear brushed against Libby's heart, but it was quickly stilled when Jess caught her right earlobe between gentle teeth and then told her in bluntly erotic terms what he had wanted to do to her on the supermarket checkout counter.

When he'd finished, Libby was wildly aroused and, at the same time, resigned to the fact that when she crawled into that sun-washed bed up in the loft, she would be alone. "Rat," she said.

Jess swatted her backside playfully. "Later," he promised, and then calmly left the condo to attend to his errands.

Libby went obediently up to the bedroom, using the stairs rather than the ladder, and yawned as she stripped down to her lacy camisole and tap pants. She shouldn't be having a nap now, she told herself, when she had things of her own to do—choosing Jess's ring, for one thing, and buying a special dress, for another....

She was asleep only seconds after slipping beneath the covers.

Libby stirred, indulged in a deliciously lazy stretch. Someone was trailing soft, warm kisses across her collarbone—or was she dreaming? Just in case she was, she did not open her eyes.

Cool air washed over her breasts as the camisole was gently displaced. "Ummm," she said.

"Good dream?" asked Jess, moistening one pulsing nipple to crisp attention with his tongue.

"Oooooh," answered Libby, arching her back slightly, her eyes still closed, her head pressed into the silken pillow in eager, soft surrender. "Very good."

Jess left that nipple to subject its twin to a tender plundering that caused Libby to moan with delight. Her hips writhed slightly, calling to their powerful counterpart.

Jess heard their silent plea, slid the satiny tap pants down, down, away. "You're so warm, Libby," he said in a ragged whisper. "So soft and delicious." The camisole was unlaced, laid aside reverently, like the wrapping on some splendid gift. Kisses rained down on Libby's sleep-warmed, swollen breasts, her stomach, her thighs.

At last she opened her eyes, saw Jess's wondrous nakedness through a haze of sweet, sleepy need. As he ventured nearer and nearer to the silk-sheltered sanction of her womanhood, she instinctively reached up to clasp the brass railings on the headboard of the bed, anchoring herself to earth.

Jess parted the soft veil, admired its secret with a throaty exclamation of desire and a searing kiss.

A plea was wrenched from Libby, and she tightened her grasp on the headboard.

For a few mind-sundering minutes Jess enjoyed the swelling morsel with his tongue. "More?" he asked, teasing her, knowing that she was already half-mad with the need of him.

"More," she whimpered as his fingers strayed to the pebblelike peaks of her breasts, plying them, sending an exquisite lacelike net of passion knitting its way through her body.

Another tormenting flick of his tongue. "Sweet," he said. And then he lifted Libby's legs, placing one over each of his shoulders, making her totally, beautifully vulnerable to him.

She cried out in senseless delirium as he took his pleasure, and she was certain that she would have been flung beyond the dark sky if not for her desperate grasp on the headboard.

Even after the highest peak had been scaled, Libby's sated body convulsed again and again, caught in the throes of other, smaller releases.

Still dazed, Libby felt Jess's length stretch out upon her, seeking that sweetest and most intimate solace. In a burst of tender rebellion, she thrust him off and demanded loving revenge.

Soon enough, it was Jess who grasped the gleaming brass railings lest he soar away, Jess who chanted a desperate litany.

Wickedly, Libby took her time, savoring him, taking outrageous liberties with him. Finally she conquered him, and his cry of joyous surrender filled her with love almost beyond bearing.

His breathing still ragged, his face full of wonder, Jess drew Libby down, so that she lay beside him. With his hands he explored her, igniting tiny silver fires in every curve and hollow of her body.

This time, when he came to her, she welcomed him with a ferocious thrust of her hips, alternately setting the pace and following Jess's lead. When the pinnacle was reached, each was lost in the echoing, triumphant cry of the other, and bits of a broken rainbow showered down around them.

* * *

Sitting Indian-style on the living-room sofa, Libby twisted the telephone cord between her fingers and waited for her father's response to her announcement.

It was a soft chuckle.

"You aren't the least bit surprised!" Libby accused, marveling.

"I figured anybody that fought and jawed as much as you two did had to end up hitched," replied Ken Kincaid in his colorful way. "Did you let Cleave know yet?"

"Jess will, in a few minutes. Will you tell Cathy for me, please?"

Ken promised that he would.

Libby swallowed hard, gave Jess a warning glare as he moved to slide an exploring hand inside the top of her bathrobe. "Aren't you going to say that we're rushing into this or something like that? Some people will think it's too soon—"

"It was damned near too late," quipped Ken. "What time is the ceremony again?"

There were tears in Libby's eyes, though she had never been happier. "Two o'clock on Friday, at the courthouse."

"I'll be there, dumplin'. Be happy."

The whole room was distorted into a joyous blur. "I will, Dad. I love you."

"I love you, too," he answered with an ease that was typical of him. "Take care and I'll see you Friday."

"Right," said Libby, sniffling as she gently replaced the receiver.

Jess chuckled, touched her chin. "Tears? I'm insulted."

Libby made a face and shoved the telephone into his lap. "Call your father," she said.

Jess settled back in the sofa as he dialed the number of the senator's house in Washington, balancing the telephone on one blue-jeaned knee. While he tried to talk to his father in normal tones, Libby ran impudent fingertips over his bare chest, twining dark hair into tight curls, making hard buttons of deliciously vulnerable nipples.

With a mock-glare and a motion of his free arm, Jess tried to field her blatant advances. She simply knelt astraddle of his lap and had her way with him, her fingers tracing a path of fire around his mouth, along his neck, over his nipples.

Jess caught the errant hand in a desperate hold, only to be immediately assaulted by the other. Mischief flashed in his jade eyes, followed by an I'll-get-you-for-this look. "See you then," he said to his father, his voice a little deeper than usual and very carefully modulated. There was a pause, and then he added, "Oh, don't worry, I will. In about five seconds, I'm going to lay Libby on the coffee table and kiss her in all the best places. Yes, sir, by the time I get through with her, she'll be—"

Falling into the trap, Libby colored, snatched the receiver out of Jess's hand and pressed it to her ear. The line was, of course, dead.

Jess laughed as she assessed him murderously. "You deserved that," he said.

Libby moved to struggle off his lap, still crimson in the face, her heart pounding with embarrassment. But Jess's hands were strong on her upper arms, holding her in place.

"Oh, no you don't, princess. You're not getting out of this so easily."

"What—"

Jess smiled languidly, still holding her fast with one hand, undoing his jeans with the other. "You let this horse out of the barn, lady. Now you're going to ride it."

Libby gasped as she felt him prod her, hard and insistent, and fierce needs surged through her even as she raged at the affront. She was powerless, both physically and emotionally, to break away from him.

Just barely inside her, Jess reached out and calmly untied her bathrobe, baring her breasts, her stomach, her captured hips. His green eyes glittered as he stroked each satiny expanse in turn, allowing Libby more and more of him until she was fully his.

Seemingly unmoved himself, Jess took wicked delight in Libby's capture and began guiding her soft, trim hips up and down, endlessly up and down, upon him. All the while, he used soft words to lead her through flurries of silver snow to the tumultuous release beyond.

When her vision cleared, Libby saw that Jess had been caught in his own treachery. She watched in love and wonder as he gave himself up to raging sensation—his head fell back, his throat worked, his eyes were sightless.

Gruffly Jess pleaded with Libby, and she accelerated the up-and-down motion of her hips until he shuddered violently beneath her, stiffened and growled her name.

"Mess with me, will you?" she mocked, grinning down at him.

Jess began to laugh, between rasping breaths. When his mirth had subsided and he didn't have to drag air into his lungs, he caressed her with his eyes. In fact, it was almost as though he'd said he loved her.

Libby was still incredibly moved by the sweet spectacle she had seen played out in his face as he submitted to her,

and she understood then why he so loved to watch her respond while pleasuring her.

Jess reached up, touched away the tear that tickled on her
cheek. It would have been a perfect time for those three special words she so wanted to hear, but he did not say them.

Hurt and disappointed, Libby wrenched her bathrobe
closed and tried to rise from his lap, only to be easily
thwarted. Jess's hands opened the robe again, his eyes perused her and then came back to her face, silently daring her
to hide any part of her body or soul from him.

With an insolent finger he brushed the pink buttons at the
tips of her full breasts, smiled as they instantly obeyed him.
Apparently satisfied with their pert allegiance, Jess moved
on to trace patterns of fire on Libby's stomach, the rounding
of her hips, the sensitive hollow at the base of her throat.

Jess seemed determined to prove that he could subdue
Libby at will, and he only smiled at the startled gasp she gave
when it became apparent that all his prowess had returned in
full and glorious force.

He slid her robe off her shoulders then and removed it entirely. They were still joined, and Libby shivered as he toyed
idly with her breasts, weighing them in his hands, pressing
them together, thumbing their aching tips until they per-
formed for him.

Presently Jess left his sumptuous playthings to tamper
elsewhere, wreaking still more havoc, eliciting little anxious
cries from a bedazzled Libby.

"What do you want, princess?" he asked in a voice of liquid steel.

Libby was wild upon him, her hands clutching desperately
at his shoulders, her knees wide. "I want to be…under you.
Oh, Jess… under you…"

In a swift and graceful motion, he turned her, was upon her. The movement unleashed the passion Jess had been able to contain until then, and he began to move over her and within her, his thrusts deep and powerful, his words ragged and incoherent.

As their very souls collided and then fused together, imitating their bodies, it was impossible to tell who had prevailed over whom.

Libby awakened first, entangled with Jess, amazed that they could have slept the whole night on that narrow couch.

A smile lifted one corner of her mouth as she kissed Jess's temple tenderly and then disengaged herself, careful not to disturb him. Heaven knew, he had a right to be tired.

Twenty minutes later, when Libby returned from her shower, dressed in sandals, white slacks and a lightweight yellow sweater, Jess was still sleeping. She could empathize, for her own slumber had been fathomless.

"I love you," she said, and then she went to the kitchen and wrote a quick note on the blackboard there, explaining that she had gone shopping and would be back within a few hours.

Getting into the rented car, which was parked in the gravel driveway near the front door, Libby spotted a cluster of colorful travel brochures fanned out on the opposite seat. Each one touted a different paradise: Acapulco, the Bahamas, Maui.

As Libby slid the key into the ignition and started the car, she grinned. She had it on good authority that paradise was only a few yards away, on the couch where Jess lay sleeping.

The day was a rich mixture of blue and green, set off by the fierce green of pine trees and the riotous blooms of crocuses and daffodils in quiet front yards. Downtown, Libby found a parking place immediately, locked the car and hurried on about her business.

Her first stop was a jewelry store, and while she had anticipated a great quandary, the decision of which wedding band to buy for Jess proved an easy one. Her eyes were immediately drawn to one particular ring, forged of silver, inset with polished chips of turquoise.

Once the jeweler had assured her the band could be resized if it didn't fit Jess's finger, Libby bought it.

In an art-supply store she purchased a sketching pad and a gum eraser and some charcoal pencils. Sweet as this interlude with Jess had been, Libby missed her work and her fingers itched to draw. Too, there were all sorts of new ideas for the comic strip bubbling in her mind.

From the art store, Libby pressed on to a good-sized department store. None of the dresses there quite struck her fancy, and she moved on to one boutique and then another.

Finally, in a small and wickedly expensive shop, she found that special dress, that dress of dresses, the one she would wear when she married Jess Barlowe.

It was a clingy creation of burgundy silk, showing off her figure, bringing a glow of color to her cheeks. There were no ruffles of lace or fancy buttons—only a narrow belt made of the same fabric as the dress itself. It was the last word in elegant simplicity, that garment, and Libby adored it.

Carrying the dress box and the heavy bag of art supplies, she hurried back to the car and locked her purchases inside. It was only a little after ten, and Libby wanted to find shoes that would match her dress.

The shoes proved very elusive, and only after almost an

hour of searching did she find a pair that would do. Tired of shopping and anxious to see Jess again, Libby started home.

Some intuitive feeling made her uneasy as she drove toward the elegant condominium hidden in the tall trees. After crossing the wooden bridge and making the last turn, she knew why—Stacey's ice-blue Ferrari was parked in the driveway.

Don't be silly, Libby reprimanded herself, but she still felt alarmed. What if Stacey had come to try to talk her out of marrying Jess? What if Cathy was with him, and there was an unpleasant scene?

Determined not to let her imagination get the upper hand, Libby gathered up her loot from the shopping trip and got out of the car. As she approached the house, she caught sight of a familiar face at the window and was surprised all over again. Monica! What on earth was she doing here? Hadn't she left for Washington, D.C., with the senator?

Now Libby really hesitated. She remembered the proprietary looks the woman had given Jess as he swam that day in the pool at the main ranch house. Looks that had implied intimacy.

Libby sighed. So what if Jess and Monica had slept together? She could hardly have expected a man like him to live like a monk, and it wasn't as if Libby hadn't had a prior relationship herself, however unsatisfactory.

Despite the cool sanity of this logic, it hurt to imagine Jess making love with Monica—or with any other woman, for that matter.

Libby grappled with her purchases at the front door, reached for the knob. Before she could clasp it, the door opened.

Jess was standing there, shirtless, wearing jeans, his hair

and suntanned chest still damp from a recent shower. Instead of greeting Libby with a smile, let alone a kiss, he scowled at her and stepped back almost grudgingly, as though he had considered refusing her entrance.

Bewildered and hurt, Libby resisted a primal instinct urging her to flee and walked in.

Monica had left the window and was now seated comfortably on the couch, her shapely legs crossed at the knee, a cocktail in her hand.

Libby took in the woman's sleek designer suit and felt shabby by comparison in her casual attire. "Hello, Monica."

"Libby," replied Monica with a polite nod.

The formalities dispensed with, Libby flung a hesitant look at Jess. Why was he glaring at her like that, as though he wanted to do her bodily harm? Why was his jawline so tight, and why was it that he clenched the towel draped around his neck in white-knuckled hands?

Before Libby could voice any of her questions, Stacey came out of the kitchen, raked her with guileless caramel eyes and smiled.

"Hello," he said, as though his very presence, under the circumstances, was not an outrage.

Libby only stared at him. She was very conscious of Jess, seething somewhere on the periphery of her vision, and of Monica, taking in the whole scene with detached amusement.

Suddenly Stacey was coming toward Libby, speaking words she couldn't seem to hear. Then he had the outright gall to kiss her, and Libby's inertia was broken.

She drew back her hand and slapped him, her dress box, purse and bag of art supplies falling to the floor.

Stacey reached out for her, caught her waist in his hands.

She squirmed and flung one appealing look in Jess's direction.

Though he looked anything but chivalrous, he did intercede. "Leave Libby alone, Stacey."

Stacey paled. "I've left Cathy," he said, as though that settled everything. "Libby, we can be together now!"

Libby stumbled backward, stunned. Only when she came up against the hard barrier of Jess's soap-scented body did she stop. Wild relief went through her as he enclosed her in a steel-like protective embrace.

"Get out," he said flatly, addressing his brother.

Stacey hesitated, but then he reddened and left the condo in a huff, pulling Monica Summers behind him.

10

Furious and shaken, Libby turned to glare at Jess. It was all too clear what had happened—Stacey had been telling more of his outrageous lies and Jess had believed them.

For a few moments he stubbornly returned her angry regard, but then he spread his hands in a gesture of concession and said, "I'm sorry."

Libby was trembling now, but she stooped to pick up her dress box, and the art-store bag. She couldn't look at Jess or he would see the tears that had clouded her eyes. "After all we've done and planned, how could you, Jess? How could you believe Stacey?"

He was near, very near—Libby was conscious of him in every sense. He moved to touch her, instantly stopped himself. "I said I was sorry."

Libby forgot that she'd meant to hide her tears and looked him full in the face. Her voice shook with anger when she spoke. "Sometimes being sorry isn't enough, Jess!" She carried the things she'd bought across the room, tossed them onto the couch. "Is this what our marriage is going to be like? Are we going to do just fine as long as we aren't around Stacey?"

Jess was standing behind her; his hands came to rest on

her shoulders. "What can I say, Libby? I was jealous. That may not be right, but it's human."

Perhaps because she wanted so desperately to believe that everything would turn out all right, that a marriage to this wonderful, contradictory man would succeed, Libby set aside her doubts and turned to face Jess. The depth of her love for this erstwhile enemy still staggered her. "What did Stacey tell you?"

Jess drew in an audible breath, and for a moment there was a tightness in his jaw. Then he sighed and said, "He was sharing the glorious details of your supposed affair. And he had a remarkable grasp on what you like in bed, Libby."

The words were wounding, but Libby was strong. "Did it ever occur to you that maybe all women like essentially the same things?"

Jess didn't answer, but Libby could see that she had made her mark, and she rushed on.

"Exactly what was Monica's part in all this?" she demanded hotly. "Was she here to moderate your sexual discussion? Why the hell isn't she in Washington, where she belongs?"

Jess shrugged, obviously puzzled. "I'm not sure why she was here."

"I am! Once you were diverted from your disastrous course—marrying me—she was going to take you by the hand and lead you home!"

One side of Jess's mouth lifted in a grin. "I'm not the only one who is prone to jealousy, it appears."

"You were involved with her, weren't you?"

"Yes."

The bluntness of the answer took Libby unawares, but only for a moment. After all, had Jess said no, she would have known he was lying and that would have been devastating. "Did you love Monica?"

"No. If I had, I would have married her."

The possible portent of those words buoyed Libby's flagging spirits. "Passion wouldn't be enough?" she ventured.

"To base a marriage on? Never. Now, let's see what you bought today."

Let's see what you bought today. Libby's frustration knew no bounds, but she was damned if she was going to pry those three longed-for words out of him—she'd fished enough as it was. "I bought a wedding dress, for your information. And you're not going to see it until tomorrow, so don't pester me about it."

He laughed. "I like a woman who is loyal to her superstitions. What else did you purchase, milady?"

Libby's sense of financial independence, nurtured during the insecure days with Aaron, chafed under the question. "I didn't use your money, so what do you care?" she snapped.

Jess arched one eyebrow. "Another touchy subject rears its ugly head. I was merely curious, my love—I didn't ask for a meeting with your accountant."

Feeling foolish, Libby made a great project of opening the art-store bag and spreading its contents out on the couch.

Jess was grinning as he assessed the array of pencils, the large sketchbook. "Have I been boring you, princess?"

Libby pulled a face at him. "You could be called many things, Jess Barlowe, but you are definitely not boring."

"Thank you—I think. Shall we brave the car dealers of Kalispell again, or are you going to be busy?" The question was guileless, indicating that Jess would have understood if she wanted to stay and block out some of the ideas that had come to her.

After Aaron, who had viewed her cartooning as a childish hobby, Jess's attitude was a luxury. "I think I'd rather go with you," she said with a teasing smile. "If I don't you might come home with some motorized horror that has horns on its hood."

"Your faith in my good taste is positively underwhelming," he replied, walking toward the ladder, climbing its rungs to the loft in search of a shirt.

"You were right!" Libby called after him. "The view from down here is marvelous!"

During that foray into the jungle of car salesmen and gasoline-fed beasts, Libby spent most of her time in the passenger seat of Jess's rented car, sketching. Instead of drawing Liberated Lizzie, her cartoon character, however, she found herself reproducing Jess's image.

She imagined him looking out over the stunning view of prairies and mountains at home and drew him in profile, the wind ruffling his hair, a pensive look to his eyes and the set of his face. Another sketch showed him laughing, and still another, hidden away in the middle of the drawing pad, not meant for anyone else to see, mirrored the way Jess looked when he wanted her.

To field the responses the drawing evoked in her, Libby quickly sketched Cathy's portrait, and then Ken's. After that, strictly from memory, she drew a picture of Jonathan, full face, as he'd looked before his illness, then, on the same piece of paper, in a profile that revealed the full ravages of his disease.

She supposed it was morbid, including this aspect of the child, but to leave out his pain would have meant leaving out his courage, and Jonathan deserved better.

Touching his charcoal image with gentle, remembering fingers, Libby heard the echo of his voice in her mind. *Naturally I'm brave,* he'd told her once, at the end of a particularly difficult day. *I'm a Jedi knight, like Luke Skywalker.*

Smiling through a mist of tears, Libby added another touch to the sketch—a tiny figure of Jonathan, well and strong, wielding a light saber in valiant defense of the Rebel Alliance.

"That's terrific," observed a gentle voice.

Libby looked up quickly, surprised that she hadn't heard Jess get into the car, hadn't sensed his presence somehow. Because she couldn't speak just yet, she bit her lower lip and nodded an acknowledgment of the compliment.

"Could I take a closer look? Please?"

Libby extended the notebook and it was a gesture of trust, for these sketches were different from the panels for her comic strip. They were large pieces of her soul.

Jess was pensive as he examined the portraits of himself, Cathy, Ken. But the study of Jonathan was clearly his favorite, and he returned to it at intervals, taking in each line, each bit of shading, each unspoken cry of grief.

Finally, with a tenderness that made Libby love him even more than she had before, Jess handed the sketchbook back to her. "You are remarkably talented," he said, and then he had the good grace to look away while Libby recomposed herself.

"D-did you find a car you like?" she asked finally.

Jess smiled at her. "Actually, yes. That's why I came back—to get you."

"Me? Why?"

"Well, I don't want to buy the thing without your checking it out first. Suppose you hated it?"

It amazed Libby that such a thing mattered to him. She set the sketchbook carefully in the back seat and opened her car door to get out. "Lead on," she said, and the clean spring breeze braced her as it touched her face.

The vehicle in question was neither car nor truck, but a Land Rover. It was perfectly suited to the kind of life Jess led, and Libby approved of it with enthusiasm.

The deal was made, much to the relief of a salesman they had been plaguing, on and off, since the day before.

After some discussion, it was decided that they would keep the rental car until after the wedding, in case Libby needed it. Over a luncheon of steak and salad, which did much to settle her shaky nerves, Jess suggested that they start shopping all over again, for a second car.

Practical as it was, the thought exhausted Libby.

"You'll need transportation," Jess argued.

"I don't think I could face all those plaid sport jackets and test drives again," Libby replied with a sigh.

Jess laughed. "But you would like to have a car, wouldn't you?"

Libby shrugged. In New York, she had depended on taxis for transportation, but the ranch was different, of course. "I suppose."

"Aren't you choosy about the make, model—all that?"

"Wheels are wheels," she answered with another shrug.

"Hmmmm," Jess said speculatively, and then the subject was changed. "What about our honeymoon? Any place in particular you'd like to go?"

"Your couch," Libby said, shocked at her own audacity.

Again Jess laughed. "That is patently unimaginative."

"Hardly, considering the things we did there," Libby replied, immediately lifting a hand to her mouth. What was wrong with her? Why was she suddenly spouting these outlandish remarks?

Jess bent forward, conjured up a comical leer. "I wish we were on the ranch," he said in a low voice. "I'd take you somewhere private and make violent love to you."

Libby felt a familiar heat simmering inside her, melting through her pelvis. "Jess."

He drew some bills from his wallet, tossed them onto the table. "Let's get out of here while I can still walk," he muttered.

Libby laughed. "I think it's a good thing we're driving separate cars today," she teased, though secretly she was just as anxious for privacy as Jess was.

He groaned. "One more word, lady, and I'll spread you out on this table."

Libby's heart thudded at the bold suggestion and pumped color over her breasts and into her face. She tried to look indignant, but the fact was that she had been aroused by the remark and Jess knew it—his grin was proof of that.

As they left the restaurant, he bent close to her and described the fantasy in vivid detail, sparing nothing. And later, on the table in the condo's kitchen, he turned it into a wildly satisfying reality.

That afternoon, Libby took another nap. Due to the episode just past, her dreams were deliciously erotic.

As he had before, Jess awakened her with strategic kisses. "Hi," he said when she opened her eyes.

She touched his hair, noted that he was wearing his brown leather jacket. "You've been out." She yawned.

Jess kissed the tip of her nose. "I have indeed. Bought you a present or two, as a matter of fact."

The glee in Jess's eyes made Libby's heart twist in a spasm of tenderness; whatever he'd purchased, he was very pleased with. She slipped languid arms around his neck. "I like presents," she said.

Jess drew back, tugged her camisole down so that her

breasts were bared to him. Almost idly he kissed each dusty-rose peak and then covered them again. "Sorry," he muttered, his mouth a fraction of an inch from hers. "I couldn't resist."

That strange, magical heat was surging from Libby's just-greeted breasts to her middle, down into her thighs and even her knees. She felt as though every muscle and bone in her body had melted. "You m-mentioned presents?"

He chuckled, kissed her softly, groaned under his breath. "I was momentarily distracted. Get out of bed, princess. Said presents await."

"Can't you just…bring them here?"

"Hardly." Jess withdrew from the bed to stand at its side and wrench back the covers. His green eyes smoldered as he took in the sleep-pinkened glow of her curves, and he bent to swat her satin-covered backside. "Get up," he repeated.

Libby obeyed, curious about the gifts but disappointed that Jess hadn't joined her in the bed, too. She found a floaty cotton caftan and slipped it on over her camisole and tap pants.

Jess looked at her, made a low growling sound in his throat, and caught her hand in his. "Come on, before I give in to my baser instincts," he said, pulling her down the stairs.

Libby looked around curiously as he dragged her across the living room but saw nothing out of the ordinary.

Jess opened the front door, pulled her outside. There, beside his maroon Land Rover, sat a sleek yellow Corvette with a huge rosette of silver ribbon affixed to its windshield.

Libby gaped at the car, her eyes wide.

"Like it?" Jess asked softly, his mouth close to her ear.

"Like it?" Libby bounded toward the car, heedless of her bare feet. "I love it!"

Jess followed, opened the door on the driver's side so that

Libby could slide behind the wheel. When she did that, she got a second surprise. Taped to the gearshift knob was a ring of white gold, and the diamond setting formed the Circle Bar B brand.

"I'll hog-tie you later," Jess said.

Libby's hand trembled as she reached for the ring; it blurred and shifted before her eyes as she looked at it. "Oh, Jess."

"Listen, if you hate it…"

Libby ripped away the strip of tape, slid the ring onto her finger. "Hate it? Sacrilege! It's the most beautiful thing I've ever seen."

"Does it fit?"

The ring was a little loose, but Libby wasn't ready to part with it, not even to let a jeweler size it. "No," she said, overwhelmed, "but I don't care."

Gently Jess lifted her chin with his hand, bent to sample her mouth with his. Beneath the hastily donned caftan and her camisole, Libby's nipples hardened in pert response.

"There's only one drawback to this car," Jess breathed, his lips teasing Libby's, shaping them. "It would be impossible to make love in it."

Libby laughed and pretended to shove him. "Scoundrel!"

"You don't know the half of it," he replied hoarsely, drawing Libby out of the beautiful car and back inside the house.

There she gravitated toward the front windows, where she could alternately admire her new car and watch the late-afternoon sun catch in the very special ring on her finger. Standing behind her, Jess wrapped his arms around her waist and held her close, bending to nip at her earlobe.

"Thank you, Jess," Libby said.

He laughed, and his breath moved in Libby's hair and sent

warm tingles through her body. "No need for thanks. I'll nibble on your ears anytime."

"You know what I meant!"

His hands had risen to close over her breasts, fully possessing them. "What? What did you mean?" he teased in a throaty whisper.

Libby could barely breathe. "The car...the ring..."

Letting his hands slip from her breasts to her elbows, Jess ushered Libby over to face the mirror above the fireplace. As she watched his reflection in wonder, he undid the caftan's few buttons and slid it slowly down over her shoulders. Then he drew the camisole up over her head and tossed it away.

Libby saw a pink glow rise over her breasts to shine in her face, saw the passion sparking in her dark blue eyes, saw Jess's hands brush upward over her rib cage toward her breasts. The novelty of watching her own reactions to the sensations he was stirring inside her was erotic.

She groaned as she saw—and felt—masculine fingers rise to her waiting nipples and pluck then gently to attention.

"See?" Jess whispered at her ear. "See how beautiful you are, Libby? Especially when I'm loving you."

Libby had never thought of herself as beautiful, but now, looking at her image in the mirror, seeing how passion darkened her eyes to indigo and painted her cheeks with its own special apricot shade, she felt ravishing.

She tilted her head back against the hard breadth of Jess's shoulder, moaned as he softly plundered her nipples.

He spoke with a gruff, choked sort of sternness. "Don't close your eyes, Libby. Watch. You're beautiful—so beautiful—and I want you to know it."

It was hard for Libby not to close her eyes and give herself up to the incredible sensations that were raging through her, but she managed it even as Jess came from behind her to bend his head and take suckle at one breast.

Watching him do this, watching the heightened color in her own face, gave a new intensity to the searing needs that were like storm winds within Libby. Her eyes were fires of ink-blue, and there was a proud, even regal lift to her chin as she watched herself pleasing the man she loved.

Jess drank deeply of one breast, turned to the other. It was an earthy communion between one man and one woman, each one giving and taking.

Presently Jess's mouth slid down over Libby's slightly damp stomach, and then he was kneeling, no longer visible in the magic mirror. "Don't close your eyes," he repeated, and Libby felt her satiny tap pants sliding slowly down over her hips, her knees, her ankles.

The wide-eyed sprite in the mirror gasped, and Libby was forced to brace herself with both hands against the mantel piece, just to keep from falling. Her breathing quickened to a rasp as Jess ran skilled hands over her bare bottom, her thighs, the backs of her knees. He heightened her pleasure by telling her precisely what he meant to do.

And then he did it.

Libby's release was a maelstrom of soft sobs that finally melded together into one lusty cry of pleasure. Jess was right, she thought, in the midst of all this and during the silvery descent that followed: she *was* beautiful.

Standing again, Jess lifted Libby up into his arms. Still feeling like some wanton Gypsy princess, she let her head fall back and gloried in the liberties his mouth took with the breasts that were thrust into easy reach.

Libby was conscious of an other-worldly floating sensation as she and Jess glided downward, together, to the floor.

* * *

Rain pattered and danced on the glass ceiling above the bed, a dismal heralding of what promised to be the happiest day of Libby Kincaid's life.

Jess slept beside her, beautifully naked, his breathing deep and even. If he hadn't actually spoken of his love, he had shown it in a dozen ways. So why did the pit of Libby's stomach jiggle, as though something awful was about to happen?

The insistent ringing of the doorbell brought Jess up from his stomach, push-up style, grumbling. His dark hair hopelessly rumpled, his eyes glazed, he stumbled around the bedroom until he found his robe and managed to struggle into it.

Libby laughed at him as he started down the stairs. "So much for being happy in the mornings, Barlowe," she taunted.

His answer was a terse word that Libby couldn't quite make out.

She heard the door open downstairs, heard Senator Barlowe's deep laugh and exuberant greeting. The sounds eased the feeling of dread that had plagued Libby earlier, and she got out of bed and hurried to the bathroom for a shower.

Periodically, as Libby shampooed her hair and washed, she laughed. Having his father arrive unexpectedly from Washington, probably with Ken and Cathy soon to follow, would certainly throw cold water on any plans the groom might have had for prenuptial frolicking.

When Libby went downstairs, her hair blown dry, her makeup in place, she was delighted to see that Cathy was with the senator. They were both, in fact, seated comfortably on the couch, drinking coffee.

"Where's Dad?" Libby asked when hugs and kisses had been exchanged.

Cleave Barlowe, with his elegant, old-fashioned manners, waited for Libby to sit down before returning to his own seat near Cathy. "He'll be here in time for the ceremony," he said. "When we left the ranch, he was heading out with that bear patrol of his."

Libby frowned and fussed with her crisp pink sundress, feeling uneasy again. Jess had gone upstairs, and she could hear the water running in the shower. "Bear patrol?"

"We've lost a few calves to a rogue grizzly," Cleave said easily, as though such a thing were an everyday occurrence. "Ken and half a dozen of his best men have been tracking him, but they haven't had any luck so far."

Cathy, sitting at her father-in-law's elbow, seemed to sense her cousin's apprehension and signed that she wanted a better look at Libby's ring.

The tactic worked, but as Libby offered her hand, she at last looked into Cathy's face and saw the ravages of her marital problems. There were dark smudges under the green eyes, and a hollow ache pulsed inside them.

Libby reprimanded herself for being so caught up in her own tumultuous romance with Jess as to forget that during his visit the day before, Stacey had said he'd left Cathy. It shamed Libby that she hadn't thought more about her cousin, made it a point to find out how she was.

"Are you all right?" she signed, knowing that Cathy was always more comfortable with this form of communication than with lip reading.

Cathy's responding smile was real, if wan. She nodded and with mischievous interest assessed the ring Jess had had specially designed.

Cleave demanded a look at this piece of jewelry that was causing such an "all-fired" stir and laughed with appreciation when he saw his own brand in the setting.

Cathy lifted her hands. "I want to see your dress."

After Jess had come downstairs, dressed in jeans and the scandalous T-shirt Libby had given him, the two women went up to look at the new burgundy dress.

The haunted look was back in Cathy's eyes as she approved the garment. "I can hardly believe you're marrying Jess," she said in the halting, hesitant voice she would allow only Libby to hear.

Libby sat down on the rumpled bed beside her cousin. "That should settle any doubts you might have had about my relationship with Stacey," she said gently.

Cathy's pain was a visible spasm in her face. "He's living at the main house now," she confessed. "Libby, Stacey says he wants a divorce."

Libby's anger with Stacey was equal only to her sympathy for his wife. "I'm sure he doesn't mean any of the things he's been saying, Cathy. If only you would talk to him…"

The emerald eyes flashed. "So Stacey could laugh at me, Libby? No, thanks!"

Libby drew a deep breath. "I can't help thinking that this problem stems from a lack of communication and trust," she persisted, careful to face toward her cousin. "Stacey loves you. I know he does."

"How can you be so sure?" whispered Cathy. "How, Libby? Marriages end every day of the week."

"No one knows that better than I do. But some things are a matter of instinct, and mine tells me that Stacey is doing this to make you notice him, Cathy. And maybe because you won't risk having a baby."

"Having a baby would be pretty stupid, wouldn't it? Even if I wanted to take the risk, as you call it. After all, my husband moved out of our house!"

"I'm not saying that you should rush back to the ranch and get yourself pregnant, Cathy. But couldn't you just talk to Stacey, the way you talk to me?"

"I told you—I'd be embarrassed!"

"Embarrassed! You are married to the man, Cathy—you share his bed! How can you be embarrassed to let him hear your voice?"

Cathy knotted her fingers together in her lap and lowered her head. From downstairs Libby could hear Jess and the senator talking quietly about the vote Cleave had cast before coming back to Montana for the wedding.

Finally Cathy looked up again. "I couldn't talk to anyone but you, Libby. I don't even talk to Jess or Ken."

"That's your own fault," Libby said, still angry. "Have you kept your silence all this time—all during the years I've been away?"

Cathy shook her head. "I ride up into the foothills sometimes and talk to the wind and the trees, for practice. Do you think that's silly?"

"No, and stop being so afraid that someone is going to think you're silly, dammit! So what if they do? What do you suppose people thought about me when I stayed with a man who had girlfriends?"

Cathy's mouth fell open. "Girlfriends?"

"Yes," snapped Libby, stung by the memory. "And don't tell my dad. He'd faint."

"I doubt it," replied Cathy. "But it must have hurt terribly. I'm so sorry, Libby."

"And I'm sorry if I was harsh with you," Libby answered.

"I just want you to be happy, Cathy—that's all. Will you promise me that you'll talk to Stacey? Please?"

"I...I'll try."

Libby hugged her cousin. "That's good enough for me."

There was again a flash of delight in Cathy's eyes, indicating an imminent change of subject. "Is that car outside yours?"

Libby's answer was a nod. "Isn't it beautiful?"

"Will you take me for a ride in it? When the wedding is over and you're home on the ranch?"

"You know I will. We'll be the terror of the back roads—legends in our own time!"

Cathy laughed. "Legends? We'll be memories if we aren't careful."

Libby rose from her seat on the bed, taking up the pretty burgundy dress, slipping it carefully onto a hanger, hanging it in the back of the closet.

When that was done, the two women went downstairs together. By this time Jess and his father were embroiled in one of their famous political arguments.

Feeling uneasy again, Libby went to the telephone with as much nonchalance as she could and dialed Ken's number. There was no answer, of course—she had been almost certain that there wouldn't be—but the effort itself comforted her a little.

"Try the main house," Jess suggested softly from just behind her.

Libby glanced back at him, touched by his perception. Consoled by it. "How is it," she teased in a whisper, "that you managed to look elegant in jeans and a T-shirt that says 'If it feels good, do it'?"

Jess laughed and went back to his father and Cathy.

Libby called the main house and got a somewhat flustered Marion Bradshaw. "Hello!" barked the woman.

"Mrs. Bradshaw, this is Libby. Have you seen my father this morning?"

There was a long sigh, as though the woman was relieved to learn that the caller was not someone else. "No, dear, I haven't. He and the crew are out looking for that darned bear. Don't you worry, though—Ken told me he'd be in town for your wedding in plenty of time."

Libby knew that her father's word was good. If he said he'd be there, he would, come hell or high water. Still, something in Mrs. Bradshaw's manner was disturbing. "Is something the matter, Marion?"

Another sigh, this one full of chagrin. "Libby, one of the maids told me that a Mr. Aaron Strand called here, asking where you could be reached. Without so much as a by-your-leave, that woman came right out and told him you were in Kalispell and gave him the number. I'm so sorry."

So that was how Aaron had known where to call. Libby sighed. "It's all right, Marion—it wasn't your fault."

"I feel responsible all the same," said the woman firmly, "but I'll kick myself on my own time. I just wanted to let you know what happened. Did Miss Cathy and the senator get there all right?"

Libby smiled. "Yes, they're here. Any messages?"

"No, but I'd like a word with Jess, if it's all right."

Libby turned and gestured to the man in question. He came to the phone, took the receiver, greeted Marion Bradshaw warmly. Their conversation was a brief one, and when Jess hung up, he was laughing.

"What's so funny?" the senator wanted to know.

Jess slid an arm around Libby and gave her a quick

squeeze. "Dare I say it in front of the creator of Liberated Lizzie, cartoon cave-woman? I just got Marion's blessing— she says I branded the right heifer."

11

Libby stood at a window overlooking the courthouse parking lot, peering through the gray drizzle, anxiously scanning each vehicle that pulled in.

"He'll be here," Cathy assured her, joining Libby at the rain-sheeted window.

Libby sighed. She knew that Ken would come if he possibly could, but the rain would make the roads hazardous, and there was the matter of that rogue grizzly bear. "I hope so," she said.

Cathy stood back a little to admire the flowing silken lines of Libby's dress. "You look wonderful. Here—let's see if the flowers match."

"Flowers?" Libby hadn't thought about flowers, hadn't thought about much at all, beyond contemplating the wondrous event about to take place. Her reason said that it was insanity to marry again, especially to marry Jess Barlowe, but her heart sang a very different song.

Cathy beamed and indicated a cardboard box sitting on a nearby table.

At last Libby left her post at the window, bemused. "But I didn't…"

Cathy was already removing a cellophane-wrapped corsage, several boutonnieres, an enormous bouquet made up of burgundy rosebuds, baby's breath, and white carnations. "This is yours, of course."

Libby reached out for her bridal bouquet, pleased and very surprised. "Did you order these, Cathy?"

"No," replied Cathy, "but I did nudge Jess in the florist's direction, after seeing what color your dress was."

Moved that such a detail had been taken into consideration, Libby hugged her cousin. "Thank you."

"Thank Jess. He's the one that browbeat the florist into filling a last-minute order." Cathy found a corsage labeled with her name. "Pin this on, will you?"

Libby happily complied. There were boutonnieres for Jess and the senator and Ken, too, and she turned this last one wistfully in her hands. It was almost time for the ceremony to begin—where was her father?

A light tap at the door made Libby's heart do a jittery flip. "Yes?"

"It's me," Jess said in a low, teasing voice. "Are the flowers in there?"

Cathy gathered up the boutonnieres, white carnations wrapped in clear, crackly paper, made her way to the door. Opening it just far enough to reach through, she held out the requested flowers.

Jess chuckled but made no move to step past the barrier and see his bride before the designated moment. "Five minutes, Libby," he said, and then she heard him walking away, his heels clicking on the marble courthouse floor.

Libby went back to the window, spotted a familiar truck racing into the parking lot, lurching to a stop. Two men in rain slickers got out and hurried toward the building.

Ken had arrived, and at last Libby was prepared to join

Jess in Judge Henderson's office down the hall. She saw that august room through a haze of happiness, noticing a desk, a flag, a portrait of George Washington. In front of the rain-beaded windows, with their heavy, threadbare velvet draperies, stood Jess and his father.

Everyone seemed to move in slow motion. The judge took his place, and Jess, looking quietly magnificent in a tailored three-piece suit of dark blue, took his. His eyes caressed Libby, even from that distance, and somehow drew her toward him. At his side stood the senator, clearly tired from his unexpected cross-country trip, but proud and pleased, too.

Like a person strolling through a sweet dream, Libby let Jess draw her to him. At her side was Cathy, standing up very straight, her green eyes glistening with joyous tears.

Libby's sense of her father's presence was so strong that she did not need to look back and confirm it with her eyes. She tucked her arm through Jess's and the ceremony began.

When all the familiar words had been said, Jess bent toward Libby and kissed her tenderly. The haze lifted and the bride and groom turned, arm in arm, to face their few but much-loved guests.

Instead of congratulations, they met the pain-filled stares of two cowboys dressed in muddy jeans, sodden shirts and raincoats.

Suddenly frantic, Libby scanned the small chamber for her father's face. She'd been so sure that he was there; he had seemed near enough to touch.

"Where—" she began, but her question was broken off because Jess left her side to stride toward the emissaries from the ranch, the senator close behind him.

"The bear..." said one of them in answer to Jess's clipped

question. "We had him cornered and"—the cowboy's Adam's apple moved up and down in his throat—"and he was a mean one, Mr. Barlowe. Meaner'n the devil's kid brother."

Libby knew what was coming and the worn courthouse carpeting seemed to buckle and shift beneath her high-heeled burgundy sandals. Had it not been for Cathy, who gripped her elbow and maneuvered her into a nearby chair, she would have fallen.

"Just tell us what happened!" Jess rasped.

"The bear worked Ken over pretty good," the second cowboy confessed.

Libby gave a strangled cry and felt Cathy's arm slide around her shoulders.

"Is Ken dead?" demanded Cleave Barlowe, and as far as Libby was concerned, the whole universe hinged on the answer to that question.

"No, sir—we got Mr. Kincaid to the hospital fast as we could. But...but."

"But what?" hissed Jess.

"The bear got away, Mr. Barlowe."

Jess came slowly toward Libby, or at least it seemed so to her. As he crouched before her chair and took her chilled hands into his, his words were gentle. "Are you all right?"

Libby was too frightened and sick to speak, but she did manage a nod. Jess helped her to her feet, supported her as they left the room.

She was conscious of the cowboys, behind her, babbling an account of the incident with the bear to Senator Barlowe, of Cathy's quiet sobs, of Jess's steel arm around her waist. The trip to the hospital, made in the senator's limousine, seemed hellishly long.

At the hospital's admissions desk, they were told by a harried, soft-voiced nurse that there was no news yet and directed to the nearest waiting room.

Stacey was there, and Cathy ran to him. He embraced her without hesitation, crooning to her, smoothing her hair with one hand.

"Ken?" barked the senator, his eyes anxious on his elder son's pale face.

"He's in surgery," replied Stacey. And though he still held Cathy, his gaze shifted, full of pain and disbelief, to Libby. "It's bad," he said.

Libby shuddered, more afraid than she'd ever been in her life, her arms and legs useless. Jess was holding her up—Jess and some instinct that had lain dormant within her since Jonathan's death. "Were you there when it happened, Stacey?" she asked dully.

Stacey was rocking Cathy gently in his arms, his chin propped in her hair. "Yes," he replied.

Suddenly rage surged through Libby—a senseless, shrieking tornado of rage. "You had guns!" she screamed. "I know you had guns! Why didn't you stop the bear? Why didn't you kill it?"

Jess's arm tightened around her. "Libby—"

Stacey broke in calmly, his voice full of compassion even in the face of Libby's verbal attack. "There was too much chance that Ken would be hit," he answered. "We hollered and fired shots in the air and that finally scared the grizzly off." There was a hollow look in Stacey's eyes as they moved to his father's face and then Jess's, looking for the same understanding he had just given to Libby.

"What about the bear?" the senator wanted to know.

Stacey averted his eyes for a moment. "He got away," he breathed, confirming what one of the cowboys had said earlier at the courthouse. "Jenkins got him in the hind flank, but he got away. Ran like a racehorse, that son of a bitch. Anyway, we were more concerned with Ken at the moment."

The senator nodded, but Jess tensed beside Libby, his gaze fierce. "You sent men after the grizzly, didn't you?"

Stacey looked pained and his hold on Cathy tightened as her sobs ebbed to terrified little sniffles. "I...I didn't think—"

"You didn't think?" growled Jess. "Goddammit, Stacey, now we've got a wounded bear on the loose—"

The senator interceded. "I'll call the ranch and make sure the grizzly is tracked down," he said reasonably. "Stacey got Ken to the hospital, Jess, and that was the most important thing."

An uncomfortable silence settled over the waiting room then. The senator went to the window to stand, hands clasped behind his back, looking out. The cowboys went back to the ranch, and Stacey and Jess maneuvered their stricken wives into chairs.

The sounds and smells peculiar to a hospital were a torment to Libby, who had endured the worst minutes, hours, days, and weeks of her life in just such a place. She had lost Jonathan in an institution like this one—would she lose Ken, too?

"I can't stand it," she whispered, breaking the awful silence.

Jess took her chin in his hand, his eyes locking with hers, sharing badly needed strength. "Whatever happens, Libby, we'll deal with it together."

Libby shivered violently, looked at Jess's tailored suit, her own dress, the formal garb of Cathy and the senator. Only Stacey, in his muddy jeans, boots, shirt and sodden denim jacket, seemed dressed for the horrible occasion. The rest of the party was at ludicrous variance with the situation.

My father may be dying, she thought in quiet hysteria, *and we're wearing flowers.* The smell of her bouquet suddenly sickened Libby, bringing back memories of Jonathan's funeral, and she flung it away. It slid under a couch upholstered in green plastic and cowered there against the wall.

Jess's grip tightened on her hand, but no one made a comment.

Presently the senator wandered out, returning some minutes later with cups of vending-machine coffee balanced on a small tray. "Ken is my best friend," he announced in befuddled tones to the group in general.

The words brought a startling cry of grief from Cathy, who had been huddled in her chair until that moment, behind a curtain of tangled, rain-dampened hair. "I won't let him die!" she shrieked, to the openmouthed amazement of everyone except Libby.

Stacey, draped over the arm and back of Cathy's chair, stared down at her, his throat working. "Cathy?" he choked out.

Because Cathy was not looking at him, could not see her name on his lips, she did not answer. Her small hands flew to cover her face and she wept for the man who had loved her as his own child, raised her as his own, been her strength as well as Libby's.

"She can't hear you," Libby said woodenly.

"But she talked!" gasped Jess.

Libby lifted one shoulder in a broken shrug. "Cathy has been talking for years. To me, anyway."

"Good God," breathed the senator, his gaze sweeping over his shattered daughter-in-law. "Why didn't she speak to any of us?"

Libby was sorry for Stacey, reading the pain in his face, the shock. Of course, it was a blow to him to realize that his own wife had kept such a secret for so long.

"Cathy was afraid," Libby explained quietly. "She is very self-conscious about the way her voice sounds to hearing people."

"That's ridiculous!" barked Stacey, looking angry now, paler than before. He bolted away from Cathy's chair to stand at the windows, his back to the room. "For God's sake, I'm her husband!"

"Some of us had a few doubts about that," remarked Jess in an acid undertone.

Stacey whirled, full of fury, but the senator stepped between his two sons before the situation could get out of hand. "This is no time for arguments," he said evenly but firmly. "Libby and Cathy don't need it, and neither do I."

Both brothers receded, Stacey lowering his head a little, Jess averting a gaze that was still bright with anger. Libby watched a muscle leap in her husband's jaw and stifled a crazy urge to touch it with her finger, to still it.

"Was Dad conscious when you brought him here?" she asked of Stacey in a voice too calm and rational to be her own.

Stacey nodded, remembering. "He said that bear was almost as tough as a Mexican he fought once, down in Juarez."

The tears Libby had not been able to cry before suddenly came to the surface, and Jess held her until they passed. "Ken is strong," he reminded her. "Have faith in him."

Libby tried to believe the best, but the fact remained that Ken Kincaid was a mortal man, strong or not. And he'd been mauled viciously by a bear. Even if he survived, he might be crippled.

It seemed that Jess was reading her mind, as he so often did. His hand came up to stroke away her tears, smooth her hair back from her face. "Don't borrow trouble," he said gently. "We've got enough now."

Trying to follow this advice, Libby deliberately reviewed pleasant memories: Ken cursing a tangle of Christmas-tree lights; Ken sitting proudly in the audience while Cathy and Libby accepted their high school diplomas; Ken trying, and somehow managing, to be both mother and father.

More than two hours went by before a doctor appeared in the waiting room doorway, still wearing a surgical cap, his mask hanging from his neck. "Are you people here for Ken Kincaid?" he asked, and the simple words had the electrifying effect of a cattle prod on everyone there.

Both Libby and Cathy stiffened in their chairs, unable to speak. It was Jess who answered the doctor's question.

"Mr. Kincaid was severely injured," the surgeon said, "but we think he'll be all right, if he rests."

Libby was all but convulsed by relief. "I'm his daughter," she managed to say finally. "Do you think I could see him, just for a few minutes?"

The middle-aged physician smiled reluctantly. "He'll be in Recovery for some time," he said. "Perhaps it would be better if you visited your father tomorrow."

Libby was steadfast. It didn't matter that Ken was still under anesthetic; if she could touch his hand or speak to him, he would know that she was near. Another vigil had taught her the value of that. "I must see him," she insisted.

"She won't leave you alone until you say yes," Jess put in, his arm tight around Libby's shoulders.

Before the doctor could answer, Cathy was gripping

Libby's hands, searching her cousin's face. "Libby?" she pleaded desperately. "Libby?"

It was clear that Cathy hadn't discerned the verdict on Ken's condition, and Libby's heart ached for her cousin as she freed her hands, quickly motioned the reassurances needed.

When that was done, Libby turned back to the doctor. "My cousin will want to see my father too."

"Now, just a minute…"

Stubbornly Libby lifted her chin.

Three hours later, Ken Kincaid was moved from the recovery room to a bed in the intensive-care unit. As soon as he had been settled there, Cathy and Libby were allowed into his room.

Ken was unconscious, and there were tubes going into his nostrils, an IV needle in one of his hands. His chest and right shoulder were heavily bandaged, and there were stitches running from his right temple to his neck in a crooked, gruesome line.

"Oh, God," whimpered Cathy.

Libby caught her cousin's arm firmly in her hand and faced her. "Don't you *dare* fall apart in here, Cathy Barlowe," she ordered. "He would sense how upset you are, and that would be bad for him."

Cathy trembled, but she squared her shoulders, drew a deep breath and then nodded. "We'll be strong," she said.

Libby went to the bedside, barely able to reach her father for all the equipment that was monitoring and sustaining him. "I hear you beat up on a bear," she whispered.

There was no sign that Ken had heard her, of course, but Libby knew that humor reached this man as nothing else could, and she went on talking, berating him softly for cruelty to animals, informing him that the next time he wanted to waltz, he ought to choose a partner that didn't have fur.

Before an insistent nurse came to collect Ken's visitors, both Libby and Cathy planted tender kisses on his forehead.

Stacey, Jess and Cleave were waiting anxiously when they reached the waiting room again.

"He's going to live," Libby said, and then the room danced and her knees buckled and everything went dark.

She awakened to find herself on a table in one of the hospital examining rooms, Jess holding her hand.

"Thanks for scaring the hell out of me," he said softly, a relieved grin tilting one corner of his mouth. "I needed that."

"Sorry," Libby managed, touching the wilting boutonniere that was still pinned to the lapel of his suit jacket. "Some wedding day, huh, handsome?"

"That's the wild west for you. We like excitement out here. How do you feel, princess?"

Libby tried to sit up, but the room began to swirl, so she fell back down. "I'm okay," she insisted. "Or I will be in a few minutes. How is Cathy?"

Jess smiled, kissed her forehead. "Cathy reacted a little differently to the good news than you did."

Libby frowned, still worried. "How do you mean?"

"After she'd been assured that you had fainted and not dropped dead of a coronary, she lit into Stacey like a whirlwind. It seems that my timid little sister-in-law is through being mute—once and for all."

Libby's eyes rounded. "You mean she was yelling at him?"

"Was she ever. When they left, he was yelling back."

Despite everything, Libby smiled. "In this case, I think a good loud argument might be just what the doctor ordered."

"I agree. But the condo will probably be a war zone by the time we get there."

Libby remembered that this was her wedding night, and with a little help from Jess, managed to sit up. "The condo? They're staying there?"

"Yes. The couch makes out into a bed, and Cathy wants to be near the hospital."

Libby reached out, touched Jess's strong face. "I'm sorry," she said.

"About what?"

"About everything. Especially about tonight."

Jess's green eyes laughed at her, gentle, bright with understanding. "Don't worry about tonight, princess. There will be plenty of other nights."

"But—"

He stilled her protests with an index finger. "You are in no condition to consummate a marriage, Mrs. Barlowe. You need to sleep. So let's go home and get you tucked into bed— with a little luck, Stacey and Cathy won't keep us awake all night while they throw pots and pans at each other."

Jess's remark turned out to be remarkably apt, for when they reached the condo, Stacey and his wife were bellowing at each other and the floor was littered with sofa pillows and bric-a-brac.

"Don't mind us," Jess said with a companionable smile as he ushered his exhausted bride across the war-torn living room. "We're just mild-mannered honeymooners, passing through."

Jess and Libby might have been invisible, for all the notice they got.

"Maybe we should have stayed in a motel," Libby yawned as she snuggled into Jess's strong shoulder, minutes later, in the loft bed.

Something shattered downstairs, and Jess laughed. "And miss this? No chance."

Cathy and Stacey were yelling again, and Libby winced. "You don't think they'll hurt each other, do you?"

"They'll be all right, princess. Rest."

Too tired to discuss the matter further, Libby sighed and fell asleep, lulled by Jess's nearness and the soft sound of rain on the glass roof overhead. She awakened once, in the depths of the night, and heard the sounds of another kind of passion from the darkened living room. A smile curved her lips as she closed her eyes.

Cathy was blushing as she tried to neaten up the demolished living room and avoid Libby's gaze at the same time. Stacey, dead to the world, was sprawled out on the sofa bed, a silly smile shaping his mouth.

Libby made her way to the telephone in silence, called the hospital for a report on her father. He was still unconscious, the nurse on duty told her, but his vital signs were strong and stable.

Cathy was waiting, wide-eyed, when Libby turned away from the telephone.

Gently Libby repeated what the nurse had told her. After that, the two women went into the kitchen and began preparing a quick breakfast.

"I'm sorry about last night," Cathy said.

Standing at the stove, spatula in hand, Libby waited for her cousin to look at her and then asked, "Did you settle anything?"

Cathy's cheeks were a glorious shade of hot pink. "You heard!" she moaned.

Libby had been referring to the fight, not the lovemaking that had obviously followed, but there was no way she could clarify this without embarrassing her cousin further. She bit her lower lip and concentrated on the eggs she was scrambling.

"It was crazy," Cathy blurted, remembering. "I was *yelling* at Stacey! I wanted to hurt him, Libby—I really wanted to hurt him!"

Libby was putting slices of bread into the toaster and she offered no comment, knowing that Cathy needed to talk.

"I even threw things at him," confessed Cathy, taking orange juice from the refrigerator and putting it in the middle of the table. "I can't believe I acted like that, especially when Ken had just been hurt so badly."

Libby met her cousin's gaze and smiled. "I don't see what one thing has to do with the other, Cathy. You were angry with your husband—justifiably so, I'd say—and you couldn't hold it in any longer."

"I wasn't even worried about the way I sounded," Cathy reflected, shaking her head. "I suppose what happened to Ken triggered something inside me—I don't know."

"The important thing is that you stood up for yourself," Libby said, scraping the scrambled eggs out of the pan and onto a platter. "I was proud of you, Cathy."

"Proud? I acted like a fool!"

"You acted like an angry woman. How about calling those lazy husbands of ours to breakfast while I butter the toast?"

Cathy hesitated, wrestling with her old fear of being ridiculed, and then squared her shoulders and left the kitchen to do Libby's bidding.

Tears filled Libby's eyes at the sound of her cousin's voice. However ordinary the task was, it was a big step forward for Cathy.

The men came to the table, Stacey wearing only jeans and

looking sheepish, Jess clad in slacks and a neatly pressed shirt, his green eyes full of mischief.

"Any word about Ken?" he asked.

Libby told him what the report had been and loved him the more for the relief in his face. He nodded and then executed a theatrical yawn.

Cathy blushed and looked down at her plate, while Stacey glared at his brother. "Didn't you sleep well, Jess?" he drawled.

Jess rolled his eyes.

Stacey looked like an angry little boy; Libby had forgotten how he hated to be teased. "I'll fight with my wife if I want to!" he snapped.

Both Libby and Jess laughed.

"Fight?" gibed Jess good-naturedly. "Was that what you two were doing? Fighting?"

"*Somebody* had to celebrate your wedding night," Stacey retorted, but then he gave in and laughed too.

When the meal was over, Cathy and Libby left the dirty dishes to their husbands and went off to get ready for the day.

They were allowed only a brief visit with Ken, and even though his doctor assured them that he was steadily gaining ground, they were both disheartened as they returned to the waiting room.

Senator Barlowe was there, with Jess and Stacey, looking as wan and worried as either of his daughters-in-law. Unaware of their approach, he was saying, "We've got every available man tracking that bear, plus hands from the Three Star and the Rocking C. All we've found so far is paw-prints and dead calves."

Libby was brought up short, not by the mention of the bear but by the look on Jess's face. He muttered something she couldn't hear.

Stacey sliced an ironic look in his brother's direction. "I suppose you think you can find that son of Satan when the hands from three of the biggest ranches in the state can't turn up a trace?"

"I know I can," Jess answered coldly.

"Dammit, we scoured the foothills, the ranges…"

Jess's voice was low, thick with contempt. "And when you had the chance to bring the bastard down, you let him trot away instead—wounded."

"What was I supposed to do? Ken was bleeding to death!"

"Somebody should have gone after the bear," Jess insisted relentlessly. "There were more than enough people around to see that Ken got to the hospital."

Stacey swore.

"Were you scared?" Jess taunted. "Did the big bad bear scare away our steak-house cowboy?"

At this, Stacey lunged toward Jess and Jess bolted out of his chair, clearly spoiling for a fight.

Again, as he had before, the senator averted disaster. "Stop it!" he hissed. "If you two have to brawl, kindly do it somewhere else!"

"You can bank on that," Jess said bitterly, his green gaze moving over Stacey and then dismissing him.

"What's gotten into the two of you?" Senator Barlowe rasped in quiet frustration. "This is a hospital! And have you forgotten that you're brothers?"

Libby cleared her throat discreetly, to let the men know that she and Cathy had returned. She was disturbed by the barely controlled hostility between Jess and his brother, but with Ken in the condition that he was, she had no inclination to pursue the issue.

It was later, in the Land Rover, when she and Jess were

alone, that Libby voiced a subject that had been bothering her. "You plan to go looking for that bear, don't you?"

Jess appeared to be concentrating on the traffic, but a muscle in his cheek twitched. "Yes."

"You're going back to the ranch and track him down," Libby went on woodenly.

"That's right."

She sank back against the seat and closed her eyes. "Let the others do it."

There was a short, ominous silence. "No way."

Libby swallowed the sickness and fear that roiled in her throat. God in heaven, wasn't it enough that she'd nearly lost her father to that vicious beast? Did she have to risk losing her husband too? "Why?" she whispered miserably. "Why do you want to do this?"

"It's my job," he answered flatly, and Libby knew that there was no point in trying to dissuade him.

She squeezed her eyes even more tightly shut, but the tears escaped anyway. When they reached the condo again, Stacey's car and Cleave's pulling in behind them, Jess turned to her, brushed the evidence of her fear from her cheeks with gentle thumbs and kissed her.

"I promise not to get killed," he said softly.

Libby stiffened in his arms, furious and full of terror. "That's comforting!"

He kissed the tip of her nose. "You can handle this alone, can't you? Going to the hospital, I mean?"

Libby bit her lower lip. Here was her chance. She could say that she needed Jess now, she could keep him from hunting that bear. She did need him, especially now, but in the end, she couldn't use weakness to hold him close. "I can handle it."

An hour later, when Stacey and the senator left for the ranch, Jess went with them. Libby was now keeping two vigils instead of one.

Understanding Libby's feelings but unable to help, Cathy built a fire in the fireplace, brewed cocoa, and tried to interest her cousin in a closed-caption movie on television.

Libby watched for a while, then got out her sketchbook and began to draw with furious, angry strokes: Jess on horseback, a rifle in the scabbard of his saddle; a full-grown grizzly, towering on its hind legs, ominous muscles rolling beneath its hide, teeth bared. Try though she did, Libby could not bring herself to put Jess and that bear in the same picture, either mentally or on paper.

That evening, when Libby and Cathy went to the hospital, Ken was awake. He managed a weak smile as they came to his bedside to bestow tearful kisses.

"Sorry about missin' the wedding," he said, and for all his obvious pain, there was mirth in his blue eyes.

Libby dashed away the mist from her own eyes and smiled a shaky smile, shrugging. "You've seen one, cowboy, you've seen them all."

Ken laughed and the sound was beautiful.

12

Having assured herself that Ken was indeed recovering, Cathy slipped out to allow Libby a few minutes alone with her father.

"Thanks for scaring me half to death," she said.

Ken tried to shrug, winced instead. "You must have known I was too mean to go under," he answered. "Libby, did they get the bear?"

Libby stiffened. The bear, the bear—she was so damned sick of hearing about the bear! "No," she said after several moments, averting her eyes.

Ken sighed. He was pale and obviously tired. "Jess went after him, didn't he?"

Libby fought back tears of fear. Was Jess face to face with that creature even now? Was he suffering injuries like Ken's, or even worse? "Yes," she admitted.

"Jess will be all right, Libby."

"Like you were?" Libby retorted sharply, without thinking.

Ken studied her for a moment, managed a partial grin. "He's younger than I am. Tougher. No grizzly in his right mind would tangle with him."

"But this grizzly isn't in his right mind, is he?" Libby whispered, numb. "He's wounded, Dad."

"All the more reason to find him," Ken answered firmly. "That bear was dangerous before, Libby. He's deadly now."

Libby shuddered. "You'd think the beast would just crawl off and die somewhere."

"That would be real handy, but he won't do it, Lib. Grizzlies have nasty dispositions as it is—their eyesight is poor and their teeth hurt all the time. When they're wounded, they can rampage for days before they finally give out."

"The Barlowes can afford to lose a few cows!"

"Yes, but they can't afford to lose people, Lib, and that's what'll happen if that animal isn't found."

There was no arguing that; Ken was proof of how dangerous a bear could be. "The men from the Three Star and the Rocking C are helping with the hunt, anyway," Libby said, taking little if any consolation from the knowledge.

"That's good," Ken said, closing his eyes.

Libby bent, kissed his forehead and left the room.

Cathy was pacing the hallway, her lower lip caught in her teeth, her eyes wide. Libby chastised herself for not realizing that Stacey was probably hunting the bear too, and that her cousin was as worried as she was.

When Libby suggested a trip to the Circle Bar B, Cathy agreed immediately.

During the long drive, Libby made excuses to herself. She wasn't going just to check on Jess—she absolutely was not. She needed her drawing board, her pens and inks, jeans and blouses.

The fact that she could have bought any or all of these items in Kalispell was carefully ignored.

By the time Libby and Cathy drew the Corvette to a stop in the wide driveway of the main ranch house, the sun was starting to go down. There must have been fifty horsemen converging on the stables, all of them looking tired and discouraged.

Libby's heart wedged itself into her throat when she spotted Jess. He was dismounting, wrenching a high-powered rifle from the scabbard on his saddle.

She literally ran to him, but then she stopped short, her shoes encased in the thick, gooey mud Montanans call gumbo, her vocal cords no more mobile than her feet.

"Ken?" he asked in a hoarse whisper.

Libby was quick to reassure him. "Dad's doing very well."

"Then what are you doing here?"

Libby smiled, pried one of her feet out of the mud, only to have it succumb again when she set it down. "I had to see if you were all right," she admitted. "May I say that you look terrible?"

Jess chuckled, rubbed the stubble of beard on his chin, assessed the dirty clothes he wore in one downward glance. "You should have stayed in town."

Libby lifted her chin. "I'll go back in the morning," she said, daring him to argue.

Jess surrendered his horse to one of the ranch hands, but the rifle swung at his side as he started toward the big, well-lighted house. Libby slogged along at his side.

"Is that gun loaded?" she demanded.

"No," he replied. "Any more questions?"

"Yes. Did you see the bear?"

They had reached the spacious screened-in porch, where Mrs. Bradshaw had prudently laid out newspapers to accommodate dozens of mud-caked boots.

"No," Jess rasped, lifting his eyes to some distant thing that Libby could not see. "That sucker might as well be invisible."

Libby watched as Jess kicked off his boots, flung his sodden denim jacket aside, dispensed with his hat. "Maybe he's dead, Jess," she blurted out hopefully, resorting to the optimism her father had tacitly warned her against. "Maybe he collapsed somewhere—"

"Wrong," Jess bit out. "We found more cattle."

"Calves?"

"A bull and two heifers," Jess answered. "And the hell of it is, he didn't even kill them to eat. He just ripped them apart."

Libby shivered. "He must be enormous!"

"The men that were with Stacey and Ken said he stood over eight feet," Jess replied, and his green eyes moved wearily over Libby's face. "I don't suppose I need to say this, but I will. I don't like having you here, not now. For God's sake, don't go wandering off by yourself—not even to walk down to the mailboxes. The same goes for Cathy."

It seemed ludicrous that one beast could restrict the normal activities of human beings—in fact, the bear didn't seem real to Libby, even after what had happened to Ken. Instead, it was as though Jess was telling one of the delicious, scary stories he'd loved to terrify Libby with when they were children.

"That means, little one," he went on sternly, "that you don't go out to the barn and you don't go over to Ken's to sit and moon by that pond. Am I making myself clear?"

"Too clear," snapped Libby, following him as he carried the rifle through the kitchen, down a long hallway and into the massive billiard room where the gun cabinets were.

Jess locked the weapon away and turned to his wife. "I'm a little bit glad you're here," he confessed with a weary grin.

"Even tough cowboys need a little spoiling now and then,"

she replied, "so hie thyself to an upstairs bathroom, husband of mine, and get yourself a shower. I'll bring dinner to your room."

"And how do you know where my room is, Mrs. Barlowe?"

Libby colored a little. "I used to help Marion Bradshaw with the cleaning sometimes, remember?"

"I remember. I used to watch you bending over to tuck in sheets and smooth pillows and think what a great rear end you had."

She arched one eyebrow. "Had?"

Jess caught her bottom in strong hands, pressed her close to him. "Have," he clarified.

"Go take your shower!" Libby huffed, suddenly conscious of all the cowboys that would be gathering in the house for supper that night.

"Join me?" drawled Jess, persistent to the end.

"Absolutely not. You're exhausted." Libby broke away, headed toward the kitchen.

"Not *that* exhausted," Jess called after her.

Libby did not respond, but as she went in to prepare a dinner tray for her husband, she was smiling.

Minutes later, entering Jess's boyhood bedroom, she set the tray down on a long table under a line of windows. The door of the adjoining bathroom was open and steam billowed out like the mist in a spooky movie.

Presently Libby heard the shower shut off, the rustling sound of a towel being pulled from a rack. She sat down on the edge of Jess's bed and then bounded up again.

"Libby?"

She went cautiously to the doorway, looked in. Jess was peering into a steamy mirror, trying to shave. "Your dinner is getting cold," she said.

After flinging one devilish look at his wife, Jess grabbed the towel that had been wrapped around his hips and calmly used it to wipe the mirror. "I'll hurry," he replied.

Libby swallowed hard, as stunned by the splendor of his naked, muscle-corded frame as she had been on that first stormy night when they'd made love in the bedroom at Jess's house, the fevered motions of their bodies metered by the raging elements outside.

Jess finished shaving, rinsed his face, turned toward Libby like a proud savage. She could not look away, even though she wanted to. Her eyes were fixed on the rising, swelling shaft of his manhood.

Jess laughed. "I used to fantasize about this."

"What?" Libby croaked, her throat tight.

"Bringing the foreman's pretty daughter up here and having my way with her."

Libby's eyes were, at last, freed, and they shot upward to his face. "Oh, yeah?"

"Yeah."

"I thought you liked Cathy then."

He nodded. "I did. But even before she married Stacey, I thought of her as a sister."

"And what, pray tell, did you think of me as?"

"A hellion. But I wanted to be your lover, all the same. Since I didn't dare, I settled for making your life miserable."

"How very chivalrous of you!"

Jess was walking toward her now, holding her with the scorching assessment of those jade-green eyes even before his hands touched her. "Teenage boys are not chivalrous, Libby."

Libby closed her eyes as he reached her, drew her close. "Neither are men," she managed to say.

Her blouse was coming untucked from her jeans, rising until she felt the steamy air on her stomach and back. Finally it was bunched under her arms and Jess was tracing a brazen finger over the lines of her scanty lace bra. Beneath the fabric, her nipples sprang into full bloom, coy flowers offering their nectar.

"Y-your dinner," she reminded Jess, floating on the sensations he was stirring within her, too bedazzled even to open her eyes.

The bra slipped down, just on one side, freeing a hard-peaked, eager breast. "Yes," Jess breathed evilly, "my dinner."

"Not that. I mean—"

His mouth closed over the delicate morsel, drawing at it softly. With a pleased and somewhat triumphant chuckle, Jess drew back from the tender treat and Libby's eyes flew open as he began removing her blouse and then her bra, leaving her jeans as they were.

He led her slowly to the bed, but instead of laying her down there, as she had expected, Jess stretched out on his back and positioned her so that she was sitting up, astraddle of his hips.

Gripping her waist, he pulled her forward and lifted, so that her breasts were suspended within easy reach of his mouth.

"The age-old quandary," he breathed.

Libby was dazed. "What qu-quandary?"

"Which one," Jess mused. "How like nature to offer two when a man has only one mouth."

Libby blushed hotly as Jess nuzzled a knotted peak, a peak that ached to nourish him. "Oh, God, Jess," she whispered. "Take it…take it!"

He chuckled, flicked the nipple in question with an impertinent tongue. "I love it when you beg."

Both rage and passion moved inside Libby. "I'm…not… begging!" she gasped, but even as she spoke she was bracing herself with her hands, brushing her breast back and forth across Jess's lips, seeking admission.

"You will," he said, and then he caught the pulsing nipple between careful teeth, raking it to an almost unendurable state of wanting.

"Not on your wretched life!" moaned Libby.

"We'll see," he replied.

The opposite breast was found and thoroughly teased and Libby had to bite her lower lip to keep from giving in and pleading senselessly for the suckling Jess promised but would not give. He played with her, using his tongue and his lips, delighting in the rocking motion of her body and the soft whimpers that came from her throat.

The sweet torment became keener, and Libby both loved and hated Jess for being able to drive her to such lengths. "Make love to me… oh, Jess…make love…to me."

The concession elicited a hoarse growl from Jess, and Libby found herself spinning down to lie flat on the bed. Her remaining clothes were soon stripped away, her legs were parted.

Libby gasped and arched her back as he entered her in one ferocious, needing thrust. After gaining this warm and hidden place, Jess paused, his hard frame shuddering with restraint.

As bedazzled as she was, Libby saw her chance to set the pace, to take command, and she took it. Acting on an age-old instinct, she wrapped her legs around his hips in a fierce claiming and muttered, "Give me all of you, Jess—all of you."

He groaned in lusty surrender and plunged deep within her, seeking solace in the velvety heat of her womanhood. They were locked together for several glittering moments, each afraid to move. Soon enough, however, their bodies demanded more and began a desperate, swift rhythm.

Straining together, both moaning in fevered need, Libby and Jess reached their shattering pinnacle at the same moment, crying out as their two souls flared as one golden fire.

Twice after Jess lay still upon her, his broad back moist beneath her hands, Libby convulsed softly, whimpering.

"Some people are really greedy," he teased when, at last, her body had ceased its spasmodic clenching and unclenching.

Libby stretched, sated, cosseted in delicious appeasement. "More," she purred.

"What did I tell you?" Jess sighed. "The lady is greedy."

"Very."

He rolled, still joined with Libby, bringing her with him so that she once again sat astraddle of him. They talked, in hushed and gentle voices, of very ordinary things.

After some minutes had passed, however, Libby began to trace his nipples with feather-light fingertips. "I've always wanted to have my way with the boss's son," she crooned, teasing him as he had teased her earlier.

She bent forward, tasted those hardening nipples, each in turn, with only the merest flick of her tongue. Jess groaned and grew hard within her, by degrees, as she continued to torment him.

"How like nature," she gibed tenderly, "to offer two when a woman has only one mouth."

Jess grasped her hips in inescapable hands and thrust his own upward in a savage demand.

Libby's release came swiftly; it was soft and warm, rather than violent, and its passing left her free to bring Jess to exquisite heights. She set a slow pace for him, delighting in the look in his eyes, the back-and-forth motion of his head on the pillow, the obvious effort it took for him to lie still beneath her.

He pleaded for release, but Libby was impervious, guiding him gently, reveling in the sweet power she held over this man she so completely loved. "I'm going to love you in my own way," she told him. "And in my own time."

His head pressed back into the pillows in magnificent surrender, Jess closed his eyes and moaned. His control was awesome, but soon enough it slipped and he began to move beneath Libby, slowly at first and then quickly. Finally, his hands tangling in her hair, he cried out and his body spasmed as she purposely intensified his pleasure. His triumph seemed endless.

When Jess was still at last, his eyes closed, his body glistening with perspiration, Libby tenderly stroked a lock of hair back from his forehead and whispered, "Some people are really greedy."

Jess chuckled and was asleep before Libby withdrew from him to make her way into the bathroom for a shower of her own.

The dream was very sexy. In it, a blue-gray dawn was swelling at the bedroom windows and Libby's breast was full in Jess's hand, the nipple stroked to a pleading state.

She groaned as she felt his hard length upon her, his manhood seeking to sheathe itself in her warmth. Jess entered her, and his strokes were slow and gentle, evoking an immediate series of tremulous, velvet-smooth responses.

"Good," she sighed, giving herself up to the dream. "So good…"

The easy strokes became demanding thrusts. "Yes," said the dream Jess gruffly. "Good."

"Ooooooh," moaned Libby, as a sudden and piercing release rocked her, thrusting her into wakefulness.

And Jess was there, upon her, his face inches from her own. She watched in wonder and in love as his features grew taut and his splendid body flexed, more rapidly now. She thrust herself up to receive the fullness of his love.

Libby's hands clasped Jess's taut buttocks as he shuddered and delved deep, his manhood rippling powerfully within her, his rasping moan filling Libby's heart.

Minutes later, a languid, hazy sleep overtook Libby and she rolled over onto her stomach and settled back into her dreams. She stirred only slightly when Jess patted her derriere and left the bed.

Hours later, when she awakened fully, Libby was not entirely certain that she hadn't dreamed the whole gratifying episode. As she got out of bed, though, to take a bath and get dressed, Libby knew that Jess had loved her—the feeling of lush well-being she enjoyed was proof of that.

The pampered sensation was short-lived. When Libby went downstairs to search out a light breakfast, she found Monica Summers sitting in the kitchen, sipping coffee and reading a weekly newsmagazine.

Even though Monica smiled, her dark gray eyes betrayed her malice. "Hello…Mrs. Barlowe."

Libby nodded uneasily and opened the refrigerator to take out an apple and a carton of yogurt. "Good morning," she said.

"I was very sorry to hear about your father," Monica went

on, the tone of her voice totally belying her expression. "Is he recovering?"

Libby got a spoon for her yogurt and sat down at the table. "Yes, thank you, he is."

"Will you be staying here with us, or going back to Kalispell?"

There was something annoyingly proprietary in the way Monica said the word "us," as though Libby were somehow invading territory where she didn't belong. She lifted her chin and met the woman's stormy-sky gaze directly. "I'll be going back to Kalispell," she said.

"You must hate leaving Jess."

The pit of Libby's stomach developed an unsettling twitch. She took a forceful bite from her apple and said nothing.

"Of course, I'll be happy to…look after him," sighed Monica, striking a flame to the fuse she had been uncoiling. "It's an old habit, you know."

Libby suppressed an unladylike urge to fly over the table, teeth bared, fists flying. "Sometimes old habits have to be broken," she said, sitting very still, reminding herself that she was a grown woman now, not the foreman's little brat. Furthermore, she was Jess's wife and she didn't have to take this kind of subtle abuse in any case.

Monica arched one perfect eyebrow. "Do they?"

Libby leaned forward. "Oh, yes. You see, Ms. Summers, if you mess with my husband, I'll not only break the habit for you, I'll break a few of your bones for good measure."

Monica paled, muttered something about country girls.

"I am not a girl," Libby pointed out. "I'm a woman, and you'd better remember it."

"Oh, I will," blustered Monica, recovering quickly. "But will Jess? That's the question, isn't it?"

If there was one thing in the world Libby had absolutely no doubts about, at that moment anyway, it was her ability to please her husband in the way Monica was referring to. "I don't see how he could possibly forget," she said, and then she finished her apple and her yogurt, dropped the remnants into the trash, and left the room.

Marion Bradshaw was sweeping away residual dried mud when Libby reached the screened porch, hoping for one glimpse of Jess before she had to go back to Kalispell.

He was nowhere in sight, of course—Libby had not really expected him to be.

"How's Ken getting on?" Marion asked.

Libby smiled. "He's doing very well."

The housekeeper sighed, leaning on her broom. "Thank the good Lord for that. Me and Ken Kincaid run this place, and I sure couldn't manage it alone!"

Libby laughed and asked if Cathy was around.

Sheer delight danced in Mrs. Bradshaw's eyes. "She's where she belongs—upstairs in her husband's bed."

Libby blushed. She had forgotten how much this astute woman knew about the goings-on on the ranch. Did she know, too, why Jess had never gotten around to eating his dinner the night before?

"No shame in loving your man," Mrs. Bradshaw twinkled.

Libby swallowed. "Do you know if Stacey went with the others this morning?"

"He did. You go ahead and wake Miss Cathy right now, if you want to."

Libby was grateful for an excuse to hurry away.

Finding Stacey's room from memory, in just the way she'd found Jess's, she knocked briskly at the closed door, realized the foolishness of that, and turned the knob.

Cathy was curled up like a kitten in the middle of a bed as mussed and tangled as the one Libby had shared with Jess.

Libby bent to give Cathy's bare shoulder a gentle shake. Her cousin sat up, mumbling, her face lost behind a glistening profusion of tangled hair. "Libby? What...?"

Libby laughed and signed, "I'm going back to town as soon as I pick up some of my things at the other house. Do you want to go with me?"

Cathy's full lips curved into a mischievous smile and she shook her head.

"Things are going well between you and Stacey, then?"

Cathy's hands moved in a scandalously explicit answer.

"I'm shocked!" Libby signed, beaming. And then she gave her cousin a quick kiss on the forehead, promised to call Mrs. Bradshaw if there was any sort of change in Ken's condition, and left the room.

In Jess's room she found paper and a pen, and probably because of the tempestuous night spent in his bed, dared to write, "Jess. I love you. Sorry I couldn't stay for a proper good-bye, but I've got to get back to Dad. Take care and come to me if you can. Smiles and sunshine, Libby."

On the way downstairs, Libby almost lost her courage and ran back to rip up the note. Telling Jess outright that she loved him! What if he laughed? What if he was derisive or, even worse, pitying?

Libby denied herself the cowardice of hiding her feelings any longer. It was time she took responsibility for her own emotions, wasn't it?

The weather was crisp and bright that day, and Libby hummed as she drove the relatively short distance to her father's house, parked her car behind his truck and went in to get the things she needed.

Fitting extra clothes and her special set of pens and inks into the back of the Corvette proved easy enough, but the drawing board was another matter. She turned it this way and that way and it just wouldn't fit.

Finally Libby took it back inside the house and left it there. She would just have to make do with the kitchen table at the condo for the time being.

Libby was just passing the passenger side of Ken's truck when she heard the sound; it was a sort of shifting rustle, coming from the direction of the lilac hedge on the far side of the yard. There followed a low, ominous grunt.

Instinctively Libby froze, the hair tingling on the nape of her neck. Dear God, it couldn't be… Not here—not when there were men with rifles searching every inch of the ranch…

She turned slowly, and her heart leapt into her throat and then spun back down into the pit of her stomach. The bear stood within ten feet of her, on its hind legs.

The beast growled and lolled its massive head to one side. Its mangy, lusterless hide seemed loose over the rolling muscles beneath, and on its flank was a bloodcrusted, seeping wound.

In that moment, it was as though Libby became two people, one hysterically afraid, one calm and in control. Fortunately, it was this second Libby that took command. Slowly, ever so slowly, she eased her hand back behind her, to the door handle, opened it. Just as the bear lunged toward her, making a sound more horrifying than she could ever have imagined, she leapt inside the truck and slammed the door after her.

The raging beast shook the whole vehicle as it flung its great bulk against its side, and Libby allowed herself the luxury of one high-pitched scream before reaching for Ken's CB radio under the dashboard.

Again and again, the furious bear pummeled the side of the truck, while Libby tried frantically to make the CB radio work. She knew that the cowboys would be carrying receivers, in order to communicate with each other, and they were her only hope.

Fingers trembling, Libby finally managed to lift the microphone to her mouth and press the button. Her mind skittered over a series of movies she'd seen, books she'd read. *Mayday,* she thought with triumphant terror. *Mayday!* But the magic word would not come past her tight throat.

Suddenly a giant claw thundered across the windshield, shattering it into a glittering cobweb of cracks. One more blow, just one, and the bear would reach her easily, even though she was now crouching on the floorboard.

At last she found her voice. "Cujo!" she screamed into the radio receiver. "Cujo!" She closed her eyes, gasping, tried to get a hold on herself. *This is not a Stephen King movie,* she reminded herself. *This is reality. And that bear out there is going to tear you apart if you don't do something!*

"Libby!" the radio squawked suddenly. "Libby, come in!"

The voice was Jess's. "Th-the bear," she croaked, remembering to hold in the button on the receiver when she talked. "Jess, the bear!"

"Where are you?"

Libby closed her eyes as the beast again threw itself against the truck. "My dad's house—in his truck."

"Hold on. Please, baby, hold on. We're not far away."

"Hurry!" Libby cried, as the bear battered the windshield again and tiny bits of glass rained down on her head.

Another voice came in over the radio, this one belonging

to Stacey. "Libby," he said evenly, "honk the horn. Can you do that?"

Libby couldn't speak. There were tears pouring down her face and every muscle in her body seemed inert, but she did reach up to the center of the wheel and press the truck's horn.

The bear bellowed with rage, as though the sound had hurt him, but he stopped striking the truck and withdrew a little way. Libby knew he wasn't gone, for she could hear him lumbering nearby, growling in frustration.

Jess's men converged with Stacey's at the end of the rutted country road leading to Ken's house. When the pickup truck was in sight, they reined in their horses.

"He's mine," Jess breathed, reaching for the rifle in his scabbard, drawing it out, cocking it. He was conscious of the other men and their nervous, nickering horses, but only vaguely. Libby was inside that truck—his whole being seemed to focus on that one fact.

The bear rose up in full view suddenly, its enormous head visible even over the top of the pickup's cab. Even over the repeated honking of the truck's horn, the beast's hideous, echoing growl was audible.

"Sweet Jesus," Stacey whispered.

"Easy," said Jess, to himself more than the men around him, as he lifted the rifle, sighted in carefully, pulled back the trigger.

The thunderous shot struck the bear in the center of its nose, and the animal shrieked as it went down. The impact of its body was so solid that it seemed to shake the ground.

Instantly Jess was out of the saddle. "Make sure he's dead," he called over one shoulder as he ran toward the truck.

Stacey and several of his men reached the bear just as Jess wrenched open the door on the driver's side.

Libby scrambled out from under the steering wheel, her hair a wild, glass-spattered tangle, to fling herself, sobbing, into his arms. Jess cradled her in his arms, carried her away from the demolished truck and inside the house. His own knees suddenly weak, he fell into the first available chair and buried his face in Libby's neck.

"It's over, sweetheart," he said. "It's over."

Libby shuddered and wailed with terror.

When she was calmer, Jess caught her chin in his hand and lifted it. "What the hell did you mean, yelling 'Cujo! Cujo!'"

Libby sniffled, and the fight was back in her eyes, a glorious, snapping blue. "There was this book about a mad dog…and then there was a movie…"

Jess lifted his eyebrows and grinned.

"Oh, never mind!" hissed Libby.

13

Libby froze in the doorway of Ken's room in the intensive-care unit, her mouth open, her heart racing as fast as it had earlier, when she'd been trapped by the bear.

"Where is he?" she finally managed to whisper. "Oh, Jess, where is my father?"

Standing behind Libby, Jess lifted his hands to her shoulders and gently ushered her back into the hallway, out of sight of the empty bed. "Don't panic," he said quietly.

Libby trembled, looked frantically toward the nurses' station. "Jess, what if he...?"

There was a gentle lecture forming in Jess's features, but before he could deliver it, an attractive red-headed nurse approached, trim in her uniform. "Mrs. Barlowe?"

Libby nodded, holding her breath.

"Your father is fine. We moved Mr. Kincaid to another floor earlier today, since he no longer needs such careful monitoring. If you will just come back to the desk with me, I'll be happy to find out which room he's in."

Libby's breath escaped in one long sigh. What with spending perilous minutes cowering inside a truck, with a rogue bear doing its best to get inside and tear her to bits, and then rushing to the hospital to find her father's bed empty, she had

had more than enough stress for one day. "Thank you," she said, giving Jess a relieved look.

He got rather familiar during the elevator ride down to the second floor, but desisted when the doors opened again.

"You're incorrigible," Libby whispered, only half in anger.

"Snatching my wife from the jaws of death has that effect on me," he whispered back. "I keep thinking that I might never have gotten the chance to touch you like that again."

Libby paused, in the quest for Room 223, to search Jess's face. "Were you scared?"

"Scared? Sweet thing, I was *terrified*."

"You seemed so calm!"

He lifted one eyebrow. "Somebody had to be."

Libby considered that and then sighed. "I don't suppose we should tell Dad what actually happened. Not yet, at least."

Jess chuckled. "We'll tell a partial truth—that the bear is dead. The rest had better wait until he's stronger."

"Right," agreed Libby.

When they reached Ken's new room, another surprise was in store. A good-looking dark-haired woman was there plumping the patient's pillows, fussing with his covers. She wore well-cut jeans and a western shirt trimmed with a rippling snow-white fringe, and the way she laughed, low in her throat, said more about her relationship with Ken Kincaid than all her other attentions combined.

"Hello, Becky," said Jess, smiling.

Becky was one of those people, it seemed, who smile not just with the mouth but with the whole face. "Jess Barlowe," she crowed, "you black-hearted son-of-a-gun! Where ya been?"

Libby drew a deep breath and worked up a smile of her own. Was this the woman who had written that intriguing farewell on the condo's kitchen blackboard?

Deliberately she turned her attention on her father, who looked downright rakish as he favored his startled daughter with a slow grin and a wink.

"Who's this pretty little gal?" demanded Becky, giving Libby a friendly once-over.

For the first time, Ken spoke. "This is my daughter, Libby. Libby, Becky Stafford."

"I'll be!" cried Becky, clearly delighted. "Glad to meet ya!"

Libby found the woman's boisterous good nature appealing, and despite a few lingering twinges of surprise, she responded warmly.

"Did you get that bear?" Ken asked of Jess, once the women had made their exchange.

"Yes," Jess replied, after one glance at Libby.

Ken gave a hoot of delight and triumph. "Nail that son-of-a...nail that devil's hide to the barn door for me, will you?"

"Done," answered Jess with a grin.

A few minutes later, Jess and the energetic Becky left the room to have coffee in the hospital cafeteria. Libby lifted her hands to her hips, fixed her father with a loving glare and demanded, "Is there something you haven't told me?"

Ken laughed. "Maybe. But I'll wager that there are a few things you haven't told me, either, dumplin'."

"Who is Becky, exactly?"

Ken thought for a moment before speaking. "She's a good friend of mine, Libby. An old friend."

For some reason, Libby was determined to find something to dislike about Becky Stafford, difficult as it was. "Why does she dress like that? Is she a rodeo performer or something?"

"She's a cocktail waitress," Ken replied patiently.

"Oh," said Libby. And then she couldn't sustain her petty jealousy any longer, because Becky Stafford was a nice person and Ken had a right to like her. He was more than just her father, after all, more than just Senator Barlowe's general foreman. He was a man.

There was a brief silence, which Ken broke with a very direct question. "Do you like Becky, Lib?"

Like her? The warmth and humor of the woman still lingered in that otherwise dreary room, as did the earthy, unpretentious scent of her perfume. "Sure I do," said Libby. "Anybody with the perception to call Jess Barlowe a 'black-hearted son-of-a-gun' is okay in my book!"

Ken chuckled, but there was relief in his face, and his expression revealed that he knew how much Libby loved her husband. "How's Cathy?" he asked.

Remembering that morning's brief conversation with her cousin, Libby grinned. "She's doing fine, as far as I can tell. Bad as it was, your tussle with that bear seems to have brought Cathy and Stacey both to a point where they can open up to each other. Cathy actually talked to him."

Ken did not seem surprised by this last; perhaps he'd known all along that Cathy still had use of her voice. "I don't imagine it was peaceable," he observed dryly.

"Not in the least," confirmed Libby, "but they're communicating and…and, well, let's just say they're closer."

"That's good," answered Ken, smiling at his daughter's words. "That's real good."

Seeing that her father was getting very tired, Libby quickly kissed him and took her leave. When she reached the cafeteria, Becky was sitting alone at a table, staring sadly into her coffee cup.

Libby scanned the large room for Jess and failed to see

him, but she wasn't worried. Probably he had gone back to
Ken's room and missed seeing Libby on the way. Noticing
the pensive look on Becky's face, she was glad for a few minutes alone with the woman her father obviously liked and perhaps even loved.

"May I sit down?" she asked, standing behind the chair
that had probably been Jess's.

Becky looked up, smiled. "Sure," she said, and there was
surprise in her dark eyes.

Libby sat down with a sigh. "I hate hospitals," she said,
filled to aching with the memory of Jonathan's confinement.

"Me too," answered Becky, but her eyes were watchful.
Hopeful, in a touchingly open way.

Libby swallowed. "My…my father has been very lonely,
and I'm glad you're his friend."

Becky's smile was almost cosmic in scope. "That's good
to hear," she answered. "Lordy, that man did scare the life
out of me, going a round with that damned bear that way."

Libby thought of her own chance meeting with the creature and shivered. She hoped that she would never know that
kind of numbing fear gain.

Becky's hand came to pat hers. "It's all right now, though,
isn't it? That hairy booger is dead, thanks to Jess."

Libby laughed. Indeed, that "hairy booger" was dead, and
she did have Jess to thank for her life. When she'd tried to
voice her gratitude earlier, he had brushed away her words
and said that she was his wife and, therefore, saving her from
bears, fire-breathing dragons and the like was just part of the
bargain.

As if conjured by her thoughts of him, Jess appeared to
take Libby home.

* * *

The coming days were happy ones for Libby, if hectic. She visited her father morning and evening and worked on her cartoon strip and the panels for the book between times, her drawing board having been transported from the ranch by Jess and set up in the middle of the condo's living room.

Jess commuted between Kalispell and the ranch; many of Ken's duties had fallen to him. Instead of being exhausted by the crazy pace, however, he seemed to thrive on it and his reports on the stormy reconciliation taking place between Cathy and Stacey were encouraging. It appeared that, with the help of the marriage counselor they were seeing, their problems might be worked out.

The irrepressible Becky Stafford rapidly became Libby's friend. Vastly different, the two women nevertheless enjoyed each other—Libby found that Becky could draw her out when she became too burrowed down in her work, and just as quickly drive her back if she tried to neglect it.

"You did what?" Jess demanded archly one early-summer evening as he and Libby sat on the living-room floor consuming the take-out Chinese food they both loved.

Libby laughed with glee and a measure of pride. "I rode the mechanical bull at the bar where Becky works," she repeated.

Jess worked up an unconvincing scowl. "Hanging around bars these days, are you?" he demanded, waving a fortune cookie for emphasis.

Libby batted her eyelashes demurely. "Don't you worry one little bit," she said, feigning a musical southern drawl. "Becky guards mah virtue, y'all."

Jess's green eyes slipped to the V neck of Libby's white sweater, which left a generous portion of cleavage in full and enticing view. "Does she now? And where is she, at this very moment, when said virtue is in immediate peril?"

An anticipatory thrill gyrated in the pit of Libby's stomach and warmed her breasts, which were bare beneath her lightweight sweater. Jess had loved her often, and well, but he could still stir that sweet, needing tension with remarkable ease. "What sort of peril am I in, exactly?"

Jess grinned and hooked one finger in the V of her sweater, slid it downward into the warmth between her breasts. "Oh, the most scandalous sort, Mrs. Barlowe."

Libby's breath quickened, despite stubborn efforts to keep it even. "Your attentions are quite unseemly, Mr. Barlowe," she replied.

He moved the wanton finger up and down between the swelling softness that was Libby, and sharp responses ached in other parts of her. "Absolutely," he said. "I mean to do several unseemly things to you."

Libby tensed with delicious sensation as Jess's exploring finger slid aside, explored a still-hidden nipple.

"I want to see your breast, Libby. This breast. Show it to me."

The outrageous request made Libby color slightly, but she knew she would comply. She was a strong, independent person, but now, in this sweet, aching moment, she was Jess's woman. With one motion of her hand, she tugged the sweater's neckline down and to one side, so that it made a sort of sling for the breast that had been softly demanded.

Not touching the rounded pink-tipped treasure in any way, Jess admired it, rewarding it with an approving smile when the confectionlike peak tightened into an enticing point.

Libby was kneeling now, resting on her heels, the cartons littering the coffee table completely forgotten. She was at once too proud to plead for Jess's mouth and too needing of it to cover herself.

Knowing that, Jess chuckled hoarsely and bent to flick at

the exposed nipple with just the tip of his tongue. Libby moaned and let her head fall back, making the captured breast even more vulnerable.

"Unseemly," breathed Jess, nibbling, drawing at the straining morsel with his lips.

Libby felt the universe sway in time with his tender plundering, but she bit down hard on the garbled pleas that were rising in her throat. They escaped through her parted lips, all the same, as small gasps.

Her heartbeat grew louder and louder as Jess finally took suckle; it muffled the sounds of his greed, of the cartons being swept from the surface of the coffee table in a motion of one of his arms.

The coolness of the air battled with the heat of Libby's flesh as she was stripped of her sweater, her white slacks, her panties. Gently he placed her on the coffee table.

Entranced, Libby allowed him to position her legs wide of each other, one on one side of the low table, one on the other. Beyond the glass roof, in the dark, dark sky, a million silvery stars surged toward her and then melted back into the folds of heaven, becoming pinpoints.

Jess found the silken nest of her passion and attended it lovingly, stroking, kissing, finding, losing. Libby's hips moved wildly, struggling even as she gave herself up.

And when she had to have this singular gratification or die, Jess understood and feasted unreservedly, his hands firm under her bottom, lifting her, the breadth of his shoulders making it impossible for her to deny him what he would have from her.

At last, when the tumult broke on a lusty cry of triumph from Libby, she saw the stars above plummet toward her— or had she risen to meet them?

* * *

"Of course you're going to the powwow!" cried Becky, folding her arms and leaning over the platter of french fries in front of her. "You can't miss that and call yourself a Barlowe!"

Libby shrank down a little in the benchlike steak-house seat. As this restaurant was a part of the Barlowe chain, the name drew immediate attention from all the waiters and a number of the other diners, too. "Becky," she began patiently, "even though Dad's getting out of the hospital this afternoon, he won't be up to something like that, and I wouldn't feel right about leaving him behind."

"Leaving Ken behind?" scoffed Becky in a more discreet tone of voice. "You just try keeping him away—he hasn't missed a powwow in fifteen years."

Libby's memories of the last Indian powwow and all-day rodeo she had attended were hardly conducive to nostalgia. She remembered the dust, the hot glare of the summer sun, the seemingly endless rodeo events, the drunks—Indian and white alike—draped over the hoods of parked cars and sprawled on the sidewalks. She sighed.

"Jess'll go," Becky prodded.

Libby had no doubt of that, and having spent so much time away from Jess of late, what with him running the ranch while she stayed in Kalispell, she was inclined to attend the powwow after all.

Becky saw that she had relented and beamed. "Wait'll you see those Sioux Indians doing their war dances," she enthused. "There'll be Blackfoot, too, and Flathead."

Libby consoled herself with the thought of Indians doing their dances and wearing their powwow finery of feathers and buckskin and beads. She could take her sketchbook along and draw, at least.

Becky wasn't through with her conversation. "Did you tell Jess how you rode that electric bull over at the Golden Buckle?"

Libby tried to look dignified in the wake of several molten memories. "I told him," she said shyly.

Her friend laughed. "If that wasn't a sight! I wish I woulda took your picture. Maybe you should enter some of the events at the powwow, Libby." Her face took on a disturbingly serious expression. "Maybe barrel racing, or women's calf roping—"

"Hold it," Libby interceded with a grin. "Riding a mechanical bull is one thing and calf roping is quite another. The only sport I'm going to take part in is stepping over drunks."

"Stepping over what?" inquired a third voice, masculine and amused, from the table side.

Libby looked and saw Stacey. "What are you doing here?"

He laughed, turning his expensive silver-banded cowboy hat in both hands. "I own the place, remember?"

"Where's Cathy?" Becky wanted to know. As she had become Libby's friend, she had also become Cathy's—she was even learning to sign.

Stacey slid into the bench seat beside Libby. "She's seeing the doctor," he said, and for all his smiling good manners, he seemed nervous.

Libby elbowed her brother-in-law lightly. "Why didn't you stay there and wait for her?"

"She wouldn't let me."

Just then Becky stood up, saying that she had to get to work. A moment later, eyes twinkling over some secret, she left.

Libby felt self-conscious with Stacey, though he hadn't made any more advances or disturbing comments. She wished that Becky had been able to stay a little longer. "What's going on? Is Cathy sick?"

"She's just having a checkup. Libby…"

Libby braced herself inwardly and moved a little closer to the wall of the enclosed booth, so that Stacey's thigh wasn't touching hers. "Yes?" she prompted when he hesitated to go on.

"I owe you an apology," he said, meeting her eyes. "I acted like a damned fool and I'm sorry."

Knowing that he was referring to the rumors he'd started about their friendship in New York, Libby chafed a little. "I accept your apology, Stacey, but I truly don't understand why you said what you did in the first place."

He sighed heavily. "I love Cathy very much, Libby," he said. "But we do have our problems. At that time, things were a lot worse, and I started thinking about the way you'd leaned on me when you were going through all that trouble in New York. I liked having somebody need me like that, and I guess I worked the whole thing up into more than it was."

Tentatively Libby touched his hand. "Cathy needs you, Stacey."

"No," he answered gruffly, looking at the flickering bowl candle in the center of the table. "She won't allow herself to need me. After some of the things I've put her through, I can't say I blame her."

"She'll trust you again, if you're worthy of it," Libby ventured. "Just be there for Cathy, Stace. The way you were there for me when my whole life seemed to be falling apart. I don't think I could have gotten through those days without you."

At that moment Jess appeared out of nowhere and slid into the seat Becky had occupied before. "Now, that," he drawled acidly, "is really touching."

Libby stared at him, stunned by his presence and by the angry set of his face. Then she realized that both she and Stacey were sitting on the same side of the booth and knew that it gave an impression of intimacy. "Jess…"

He looked down at his watch, a muscle dancing furiously in his jaw. "Are you going to pick your father up at the hospital, or do you have more interesting things to do?"

Stacey, who had been as shocked by his brother's arrival as Libby had, was suddenly, angrily vocal. The candle leapt a little when he slammed one fist down on the tabletop and hissed, "Dammit, Jess, you're deliberately misunderstanding this!"

"Am I?"

"Yes!" Libby put in, on the verge of tears. "Becky and I were having lunch and then Stacey came in and—"

"Stop it, Libby," Stacey broke in. "You didn't do anything wrong. Jess is the one who's out of line here."

The long muscle in Jess's neck corded, and his lips were edged with white, but his voice was still low, still controlled. "I came here, Libby, because I wanted to be with you when you brought Ken home," he said, and his green eyes, dark with passion only the night before, were coldly indifferent now. "Are we going to collect him or would you rather stay here and carry on?"

Libby was shaking. "Carry on? *Carry on?*"

Stacey groaned, probably considering the scandal a scene in this particular restaurant would cause. "Couldn't we settle this somewhere else?"

"We'll settle it, all right," Jess replied.

Stacey's jaw was rock-hard as he stood up to let a shaken Libby out of the booth. "I'll be on the ranch," he said.

"So will I," replied Jess, rising, taking a firm grip on Libby's arm. "See you there."

"Count on it."

Jess nodded and calmly propelled Libby out of the restaurant and into the bright sunlight, where her shiny Corvette was parked. Probably he had seen the car from the highway and known that she was inside the steak house.

Now, completely ignoring her protests, he dragged her past her car and thrust her into the Land Rover beside it.

"Jess—damn you—will you *listen* to me?"

Jess started the engine, shifted it into reverse with a swift motion of his hand. "I'm afraid storytime will have to wait," he informed her. "We've got to go and get Ken, and I don't want him upset."

"Do you think I do?"

Jess sliced one menacing look in her direction but said nothing.

Libby felt a need to reach him, even though, the way he was acting, he didn't deserve reassurances. "Jess, how can you...after last night, how could you..."

"Last night," he bit out. "Yes. Tell me, Libby, do you do that trick for everybody, or just a favored few?"

It took all her determination not to physically attack him. "Take me back to my car, Jess," she said evenly. "Right now. I'll pick Dad up myself, and we'll go back to his house—"

"Correction, Mrs. Barlowe. *He* will go to his house. You, my little vixen, will go to mine."

"I will not!"

"Oh, but you will. Despite your obvious attraction to my brother, you are still my wife."

"I am not attracted to your brother!"

They had reached the hospital parking lot, and the Land Rover lurched to a stop. Jess smiled insolently and patted Libby's cheek in a way so patronizing that it made her screaming mad. "That's the spirit, Mrs. Barlowe. Walk in there and show your daddy what a pillar of morality you are."

Going into that hospital and pretending that nothing was wrong was one of the hardest things Libby had ever had to do.

Preparations for Ken's return had obviously been going on for some time. As Libby pulled her reclaimed Corvette in behind Jess's Land Rover, she saw that the front lawn had been mowed and the truck had been repaired.

Ken, still not knowing the story of his daughter, his truck, and the bear, paused after stepping out of Jess's Land Rover, his arm still in a sling. He looked his own vehicle over quizzically. "Looks different," he reflected.

Jess rose to the occasion promptly, smoothly. "The boys washed and waxed it," he said.

To say the very least, thought Libby, who would never forget, try though she might, how that truck had looked before the repair people in Kalispell had fixed and painted it. She opened her mouth to tell her father what had happened, but Jess stopped her with a look and a shake of his head.

The inside of the house had been cleaned by Mrs. Bradshaw and her band of elves; every floor and stick of furniture had been either dusted or polished or both. The refrigerator had been stocked and a supply of the paperback westerns Ken loved to read had been laid in.

As if all this wasn't enough to make Libby's services completely superfluous, it turned out that Becky was there too. She had strung streamers and dozens of brightly colored balloons from the ceiling of Ken's bedroom.

Her father was obviously pleased, and Libby's last hopes of drumming up an excuse to stay the night, at least, were dashed. Becky, however, was delighted with her surprise.

"I thought you were working!" Libby accused.

"I lied," replied Becky, undaunted. "After I left you and Stacey at the steak house, I got a friend to bring me out here."

Libby shot a glance in Jess's direction, knew sweet triumph as she saw that Becky's words had registered with him. After only a moment's chagrin, however, he tightened his jaw and looked away.

While Becky was getting Ken settled in his room and generally spoiling him rotten, Libby edged over to her husband. "You heard her," she whispered tersely, "so where's my apology?"

"Apology?" Jess whispered back, and there was nothing in his face to indicate that he felt any remorse at all. "Why should I apologize?"

"Because I was obviously telling the truth! Becky said—"

"Becky said that she left you and Stacey at the steak house. It must have been a big relief when she did."

Heedless of everything but the brutal effect of Jess's unfair words, Libby raised one hand and slapped him, hard.

Stubbornly, he refused her the satisfaction of any response at all, beyond an imperious glare, which she returned.

"Hey, do you guys…?" Becky's voice fell away when she became aware of the charged atmosphere of the living room. She swallowed and began again. "I was going to ask if you wanted to stay for supper, but maybe that wouldn't be such a good idea."

"You can say that again," rasped Jess, catching Libby's arm in a grasp she couldn't have broken without making an even more embarrassing scene. "Make our excuses to Ken, will you, please?"

After a moment's hesitation and a concerned look at Libby, Becky nodded.

"You overbearing bastard!" Libby hissed as her husband squired her out of the house and toward his Land Rover.

Jess opened the door, helped her inside, met her fiery blue gaze with one of molten green. Neither spoke to the other, but the messages flashing between them were all too clear anyway.

Jess still believed that Libby had been either planning or carrying on a romantic tryst with Stacey, and Libby was too proud and too angry to try to convince him otherwise. She was also too smart to get out of his vehicle and make a run for hers.

Jess would never hurt her, she knew that. But he would not allow her a dramatic exit, either. And she couldn't risk a screaming fight in the driveway of her father's house.

Because she was helpless and she hated that, she began to cry.

Jess ignored her tears, but he too was considerate of Ken— he did not gun the Land Rover's engine or back out at a speed that would fling gravel in every direction, as he might have at another time.

When they passed his house, with its window walls, and started up a steep road leading into the foothills beyond, Libby was still not afraid. For all his fury, this man was too tender a lover to touch her in anger.

"Where are we going?" she demanded.

He ground the Land Rover into a low gear and left the road, now little more than a cow path, for the rugged hillside. "On our honeymoon, Mrs. Barlowe."

Libby swallowed, unnerved by his quiet rage and the jostling, jolting ascent of the Land Rover itself. "If you take me in anger, Jess Barlowe, I'll never forgive you. Never. That would be rape."

The word "rape" got through Jess's hard armor and stung him visibly. He paled as he stopped the Land Rover with a lurch and wrenched on the emergency brake. "Goddammit, you *know* I wouldn't do anything like that!"

"Do I?" They were parked at an almost vertical angle, it seemed to Libby. Didn't he realize that they were almost straight up and down? "You've been acting like a maniac all afternoon!"

Jess's face contorted and he raised his fists and brought them down hard on the steering wheel. "Dammit it all to hell," he raged, "you drive me crazy! Why the devil do I love you so much when *you drive me crazy?*"

Libby stared at him, almost unable to believe what she had heard. Not even in their wildest moments of passion had he said he loved her, and if he had found that note she'd left for him, betraying her own feelings, the day the bear was killed, he'd never mentioned it.

"What did you say?"

Jess sighed, tilted his head back, closed his eyes. "That you drive me crazy."

"Before that."

"I said I loved you," he breathed, as though there was nothing out of the ordinary in that.

"Do you?"

"Hell, yes." The muscles in his sun-browned neck corded as he swallowed, his head still back, his eyes still closed. "Isn't that a joke?"

The words tore at Libby's heart. "A joke?"

"Yes." The word came, raw, from deep within him, like a sob.

"You idiot!" yelled Libby, struggling with the door, climbing out of the Land Rover to stalk up the steep hillside. She trembled, and tears poured down her face, and for once she didn't care who saw them.

At the top of the rise, she sat down on a huge log, her vision too blurred to take in the breathtaking view of mountains and prairies and an endless, sweeping sky.

She sensed Jess's approach, tried to ignore him.

"Why am I an idiot, Libby?"

Though the day was warm, Libby shivered. "You're too stupid to know when a woman loves you, that's why!" she blurted out, sobbing now. "Damn! You've had me every way but hanging from a chandelier, and you still don't know!"

Jess straddled the log, drew Libby into his arms and held her. Suddenly he laughed, and the sound was a shout of joy.

14

Drunken cowboys and Indians notwithstanding, the pow-wow of the Sioux, Flathead and Blackfoot was a spectacle to remember. Held annually in the same small and otherwise unremarkable town, the meeting of these three tribes was a tradition that reached back to days of mist and shadow, days recorded on no calendar but that of the red man's legends.

Now, on a hot July morning, the erstwhile cow pasture and ramshackle grandstands were churning with activity, and Libby Barlowe's fingers ached to make use of the sketchbook and pencils she carried.

Craning her neck to see the authentic tepees and their colorfully clad inhabitants, she could hardly stand still long enough for the plump woman at the admission gate to stamp her hand.

There was so much noise—laughter, the tinkle of change in the coin box, the neighing and nickering of horses that would be part of the rodeo. Underlying all this was the steady beat of tom-toms and guttural chants of Indian braves.

"Enjoy yourself now, honey," enjoined the woman tending the cashbox, and Libby jumped, realizing that she was holding up the line behind her. After one questioning look at the hat the woman wore, which consisted of panels cut from various beer cans and crocheted together, she hurried through the gate.

Jess chuckled at the absorbed expression on Libby's face. There was so much to see that a person didn't know where to look first.

"I think I see a fit of creativity coming on," he said.

Libby was already gravitating toward the tepees, plotting light angles and shading techniques as she went. In her heart was a dream, growing bigger with every beat of the tom-toms. "I want to see, Jess," she answered distractedly. "I've got to *see*."

There was love in the sound of Jess's laughter, but no disdain. "All right, all right—but at least let me get you a hat. This sun is too hot for you to go around bareheaded."

"Get me a hat, get me a hat," babbled Libby, zeroing in on a group of small Indian children, who wore little more than loincloths and feathers as they sat watching fathers, uncles and elder brothers perform the ancient rites for rain or success in warfare or hunting.

Libby was taken with the flash of their coppery skin, the midnight black of their hair, the solemn, stalwart expressions in their dark eyes. Flipping open her sketchbook, she squatted in the lush summer grass and began to rough in the image of one particular little boy.

Her pencil flew, as did her mind. She was thinking in terms of oil paints—vivid, primitive shades that would do justice to the child's coloring and the peacock splendor of his headdress.

"Hello," she said when the dark eyes turned to her in dour question. "My name is Libby, what's yours?"

"Jimmy," the little boy responded, but then he must have remembered the majesty of his ancestry, for he squared his small shoulders and amended, "Jim Little Eagle."

Libby made a hasty note in the corner of his sketch. "I wish I had a name like that," she said.

"You'll have to settle for 'Barlowe,'" put in a familiar

voice from behind her, and a lightweight hat landed on the top of her head.

Libby looked up into Jess's face and smiled. "I guess I can make do with that," she answered.

Jess dropped to his haunches, assessed the sketch she'd just finished with admiring eyes. "Wow," he said.

Libby laughed. "I love it when you're profound," she teased. And then she took off the hat he'd given her and inspected it thoroughly. It was a standard western hat, made of straw, and it boasted a trailing tangle of turquoise feathers and crystal beads.

Jess took the hat and put it firmly back on, then arranged the feathers so that they rested on her right shoulder, tickling the bare, sun-gilded flesh there in a pleasant way. "Did you wear that blouse to drive me insane, or are you trying to set a world record for blistering sunburns?" he asked unromantically.

Libby looked down at the brief white eyelet suntop and wondered if she shouldn't have worn a western shirt, the way Becky and Cathy had. The garment she had on had no shoulders or sleeves; it was just a series of broad ruffles falling from an elasticized band that fitted around her chest, just beneath her collarbone. Not even wanting to think about the tortures of a sunburn, she crinkled her nose and said, "I wore it to drive you insane, of course."

Jess was going to insist on being practical; she saw it in his face. "They're selling T-shirts on the fairway—buy one."

"Now?" complained Libby, not wanting to leave the splendors of the recreated Indian village even for a few minutes.

Jess looked down at his watch. "Within half an hour," he said flatly. "I'm going to find Ken and the others in the grandstands, Rembrandt. I'll see you later."

Libby squinted as he rose against the sun, towering and magnificent even in his ordinary jeans and worn cowboy shirt. "No kiss?"

Jess crouched again, kissed her. "Remember. Half an hour."

"Half an hour," promised Libby, turning to a fresh page in her sketchbook and pondering a little girl with coal-black braids and a fringed buckskin shift. She took a new pencil from the case inside her purse and began to draw again, her hand racing to keep up with the pace set by her heart.

When the sketch was finished, Libby thought about what she meant to do and how the syndicate that carried her cartoon strip would react. No doubt they would be furious.

"Portraits!" her agent would cry. "Libby, Libby, there is no *money* in portraits."

Libby sighed, biting her lower lip. Money wasn't a factor really, since she had plenty of that as it was, not only because she had married a wealthy man but also because of prior successes in her career.

She was tired of doing cartoons, yearning to delve into other mediums—especially oils. She wanted color, depth, nuance—she wanted and needed to grow.

"Where the hell is that T-shirt I asked you to buy?"

Libby started, but the dream was still glowing in her face when she looked up to meet Jess's gaze. "Still on the fairway, I would imagine," she said.

His mouth looked very stern, but Jess's eyes were dancing beneath the brim of his battered western hat. "I don't know why I let you out of my sight," he teased. And then he extended a hand. "Come on, woman. Let's get you properly dressed."

Libby allowed herself to be pulled through the crowd to

one of the concession stands. Here there were such thrilling offerings as ashtrays shaped like the state of Montana and gaudy scarves commemorating the powwow itself.

"Your secret is out," she told Jess out of the corner of her mouth, gesturing toward a display of hats exactly like her own. The colors of their feather-and-bead plumage ranged from a pastel yellow to deep, rich purple. "This hat is not a designer original!"

Jess worked up an expression of horrified chagrin and then laughed and began rifling through a stack of colorful T-shirts. "What size do you wear?"

Libby stood on tiptoe, letting her breath fan against his ear, delighting as that appendage reddened visibly. "About the size of the palm of your hand, cowboy."

"Damn," Jess chuckled, and the red moved out from his ear to churn under his suntan. "Unless you want me to drag you off somewhere and make love to you right now, you'd better not make any more remarks like that."

Suddenly Libby was as pink as the T-shirt he was measuring against her chest. Coming from Jess, this was no idle threat—since their new understanding, reached several weeks before on the top of the hill behind his house, they had made love in some very unconventional places. It would be like him to take her to one of the small trailers brought by some of the cowboys from the Circle Bar B and follow through.

Having apparently deemed the pink T-shirt appropriate, Jess bought it and gripped Libby's hand, fairly dragging her across the sawdust-covered fairgrounds. From the grandstands came the deafening shouts and boot-stompings of more than a thousand excited rodeo fans.

Reaching the rest rooms, which were housed in a building of their own, Jess gave an exasperated sigh. There must have been a hundred women waiting to use the facilities, and he clearly didn't want to stand around in the sun just so Libby could exchange her suntop for a T-shirt.

Before she could offer to wait alone so that Jess could go back and watch the rodeo, he was hauling her toward the nest of Circle Bar B trailers at such a fast pace that she had to scramble to keep up with him.

Thrusting her inside the smallest, which was littered with boots, beer cans and dirty clothes, he ordered, "Put on the shirt."

Libby's color was so high that she was sure he could see it, even in the cool darkness of that camper-trailer. "This is Jake Peterson's camper, isn't it? What if he comes back?"

"He won't come back—he's entered in the bull-riding competition. Just change, will you?"

Libby knew only too well what would happen if she removed that suntop. "Jess…"

He closed the camper door, flipped the inadequate-looking lock. Then he reached out, collected her befeathered hat, her sketchbook, her purse. He laid all these items on a small, messy table and waited.

In the distance, over the loudspeaker system, the rodeo announcer exalted, "This cowboy, folks, has been riding bulls longer'n he's been tying his shoes."

There was a thunderous communal cry as the cowboy and his bull apparently came out of their chute, but it was strangely quiet in that tiny trailer where Jess and Libby stood staring at each other.

Finally, in one defiant motion of her hands, Libby wrenched the suntop off over the top of her head and stood still before her husband, her breasts high and proud and completely bare. "Are you satisfied?" she snapped.

"Not yet," Jess retorted.

He came to stand very close, his hands gentle on her breasts. "You were right," he said into her hair. "You just fit the palms of my hands."

"Oh," said Libby in sweet despair.

Jess's hands continued their tender work, lulling her. It was so cool inside that trailer, so intimate and shadowy.

Presently Libby felt the snap on her jeans, and then the zipper, give way. She was conscious of a shivering heat as the fabric glided downward. Protesting was quite beyond her powers now; she was bewitched.

Jess laid her on the narrow camper bed, joining her within moments. Stretched out upon her, he entered her with one deft thrust.

Their triumph was a simultaneous one, reached after they'd both traveled through a glittering mine field of physical and spiritual sensation, and it was of such dizzying scope that it seemed natural for the unknowing crowd in the grandstands to cheer.

Furiously Libby fastened her jeans and pulled on the T-shirt that had caused this situation in the first place. She gathered up her things, plopped her hat onto her head, and glared into Jess's amused face.

He dressed at a leisurely pace, as though they weren't trespassing.

"If Jake Peterson ever finds out about his, I'll die," Libby said, casting anxious, impatient looks at the locked door.

Jess pulled on one boot, then the other, ran a hand through his rumpled hair. His eyes smoldering with mischief and lingering pleasure, he stood up, pulled Libby into his arms and kissed her. "I love you," he said. "And your shameful secret is safe with me, Mrs. Barlowe."

Libby's natural good nature was overcoming her anger. "Sure," she retorted tartly. "All the same, I think you should know that every man who had ever compromised me in a ranch hand's trailer has said that selfsame thing."

Jess laughed, kissed her again, and then released her. "Go back to your Indians, you little hellion. I'll find you later."

"That's what I'm afraid of," Libby tossed back over one shoulder as she stepped out of the camper into the bright July sunshine. Almost before her eyes had adjusted to the change, she was sketching again.

Libby hardly noticed the passing of the hours, so intent was she on recording the scenes that so fascinated her: braves festooned with colorful feathers, doing their war and rain dances; squaws, plump in their worn buckskin dresses, demonstrating the grinding of corn or making their beaded belts and moccasins; children playing games that were almost as old as the distant mountains and the big sky.

Between the residual effects of that scandalous bout of lovemaking in the trailer and the feast of color and sound assaulting her now, Libby's senses were reeling. She was almost relieved when Cathy came and signed that it was time to leave.

As they walked back to find the others in the still-dense crowd, Libby studied her cousin out of the corner of her eye. Cathy and Stacey were living together again, but there was a wistfulness about Cathy that was disturbing.

There would be no chance to talk with her now—there were too many distractions for that—but Libby made a mental vow to get Cathy alone later, perhaps during the birthday party that was being held on the ranch for Senator Barlowe that evening, and find out what was bothering her.

As the group made plans to stop at a favorite café for an

early supper, Libby grew more and more uneasy about Cathy. What was it about her that was different, besides her obviously downhearted mood?

Before Libby could even begin to work out that complex question, Ken and Becky were off to their truck, Stacey and Cathy to their car. Libby was still staring into space when Jess gently tugged at her hand.

She got into the Land Rover, feeling pensive, and laid her sketchbook and purse on the seat.

"Another fit of creativity?" Jess asked quietly, driving carefully through a maze of other cars, staggering cowboys and beleaguered sheriff's deputies.

"I was thinking about Cathy," Libby replied. "Have you noticed a change in her?"

He thought, shook his head. "Not really."

"She doesn't talk to me anymore, Jess."

"Did you have an argument?"

Libby sighed. "No. I've been so busy lately, what with finishing the book and everything, I haven't spent much time with her. I'm ashamed to say that I didn't even notice the change in her until just a little while ago."

Jess gave her a gentle look. "Don't start beating yourself up Libby. You're not responsible for Cathy's happiness or unhappiness."

Surprised, Libby stared at him. "That sounds strange, coming from you."

They were pulling out onto the main highway, which was narrow and almost as choked with cars as the parking area had been. "I'm beginning to think it was a mistake, our being so protective of Cathy. We all meant well, but I wonder sometimes if we didn't hurt her instead."

"Hurt her?"

One of Jess's shoulders lifted in a shrug. "In a lot of ways, Cathy's still a little girl. She's never had to be a grown-up, Libby, because one of us was always there to fight her battles for her. I think she uses her deafness as an excuse not to take risks."

Libby was silent, reflecting on Cathy's fear of being a mother.

As though he'd looked into her mind, Jess went on to say, "Both Cathy and Stacey want children—did you know that? But Cathy won't take the chance."

"I knew she was scared—she told me that. She's scared of so many things, Jess—especially of losing Stacey."

"She loves him."

"I know. I just wish she had something more—something of her own so that her security as a person wouldn't hinge entirely on what Stacey does."

"You mean the way your security doesn't hinge on what I do?" Jess ventured, his tone devoid of any challenge or rancor.

Libby turned, took off her hat and set it down between them with the other things. "I love you very, very much, Jess, but I could live without you. It would hurt unbearably, but I could do it."

He looked away from the traffic only long enough to flash her one devilish grin. "Who would take shameful liberties with your body, if it weren't for me?"

"I guess I would have to do without shameful liberties," she said primly.

"Thank you for sidestepping my delicate male ego," he replied, "but the fact of the matter is, there's no way a woman as beautiful and talented as you are would be alone for very long."

"Don't say that!"

Jess glanced at her in surprise. "Don't say what?"

It was his meaning that had concerned Libby, not his exact words. "I don't even want to think about another man touching me the way you do."

Jess's attention was firmly fixed on the road ahead. "If you're trying to make me feel secure, princess, it's working."

"I'm not trying to make you feel anything. Jess, before we made love that first time, when you said I was really a virgin, you were right. Even the books I've read couldn't have prepared me for the things I feel when you love me."

"It might interest you to know, Mrs. Barlowe, that my feelings toward you are quite similar. Before we made love, sex was just something my body demanded, like food or exercise. Now it's magic."

She stretched to plant a noisy kiss on her husband's cheek. "Magic, is it? Well, you're something of a sorcerer yourself, Jess Barlowe. You cast spells over me and make me behave like a wanton."

He gave an exaggerated evil chuckle. "I hope I can remember the hex that made you give in to me back there at the fairgrounds."

Libby moved the things that were between them into the backseat and slid closer, taking a mischievous nip at his earlobe. "I'm sure you can," she whispered.

Jess shuddered involuntarily and snapped, "Dammit, Libby, I'm driving."

She was exploring the sensitive place just beneath his ear with the tip of her tongue. "Umm. You like getting me into situations where I'm really vulnerable, don't you, Jess?" she breathed, sliding one hand inside his shirt. "Like today, for instance."

"Libby…"

"Revenge is sweet."

And it was.

Shyly Libby extended the carefully wrapped package that contained her personal birthday gift to Senator Barlowe. She had not shown it to anyone else, not even Jess, and now she was uncertain. After all, Monica had given Cleave gold cufflinks and Stacey and Cathy planned to present him with a bottle of rare wine. By comparison, would her offering seem tacky and homemade?

With the gentle smile that had won him so many hearts and so many votes over the years, he took the parcel, which was revealingly large and flat, and turned it in his hands. "May I?" he asked softly, his kind eyes twinkling with affection.

"Please do," replied Libby.

It seemed to take Cleave forever to remove the ribbons and wrapping paper and lift the lid from the box inside, but there was genuine emotion in his face when he saw the framed pen-and-ink drawing Libby had been working on, in secret, for days. "My sons," he said.

"That's us, all right," commented Jess, who had appeared at the senator's side. "Personally, I think I'm considerably handsomer than that."

Cleave was examining the drawing closely. It showed Jess looking forward, Stacey in profile. When the senator looked up, Libby saw the love he bore his two sons in his eyes. "Thank you," he said. "This is one of the finest gifts I've ever received." He assessed the drawing again, and when his gaze came back to meet hers, it was full of mischief. "But where are my daughters? Where are you and Cathy?"

Libby smiled and kissed his cheek. "I guess you'll have to wait until your *next* birthday for that."

"In that case," rejoined the senator, "why not throw in a couple of grandchildren for good measure?"

Libby grinned. "I might be able to come up with one, but a couple?"

"Cathy will just have to do her part," came the immediate reply. "Now, if you'll excuse me, I want to take this picture around and show all my guests what a talented daughter-in-law I have."

Once his father had gone, Jess lifted his champagne glass and one eyebrow. "'Talented' is definitely the word," he said.

Libby knew that he was not referring to her artwork and hastily changed the subject. "You look so splendid in that tuxedo that I think I'd like to dance with you."

Jess worked one index finger under the tight collar of his formal shirt, obviously uncomfortable. "Dance?" he echoed dryly. "Lead me to the organ grinder and we're in business."

Laughing, Libby caught at his free hand and dragged him into the spacious living room, which had been prepared for dancing. There was a small string band to provide the music.

Libby took Jess's champagne glass and set it aside, then rested both hands on his elegant satin lapels. The other guests—and there were dozens—might not have existed at all.

"Dance with me," she said.

Jess took her into his arms, his eyes never leaving hers. "You know," he said softly, "you look so wonderful in that silvery dress that I'm tempted to take you home and make damned sure my father gets that grandchild he wants."

"When we start a baby," she replied seriously, "I want it to be for us."

Jess's mouth quirked into a grin and his eyes were alight with love. "I wasn't going to tape a bow to the little stinker's head and hand it over to him, Libby."

Libby giggled at the picture this prompted in her mind. "Babies are so funny," she dreamed aloud.

"I know," Jess replied. "I love that look of drunken wonder they get when you lift them up high and talk to them. About that time, they usually barf in your hair."

Before she could answer, Ken and Becky came into the magical mist that had heretofore surrounded Libby and Jess.

"All right if I cut in?" Ken asked.

"How soon do you want a grandchild?" Jess countered.

"Sooner the better," retorted Ken. "And, Jess?"

"What?" demanded his son-in-law, eyes still locked with Libby's.

"The music stopped."

Jess and Libby both came to a startled halt, and Becky was so delighted by their expressions that her laughter pealed through the large room.

When the band started playing again, Libby found herself dancing with her father, while Jess and Becky waltzed nearby.

"You look real pretty," Ken said, beaming down at her.

"You're pretty fancy yourself," Libby answered. "In fact, you look downright handsome in that tuxedo."

"She says that to everybody," put in Jess, who happened to be whirling past with Becky.

Ken's laugh was low and throaty. "He never gets too far away from you, does he?"

"About as far as white gets from rice. And I like it that way."

"That's what I figured. Libby..."

The serious, tentative way he'd said her name gave Libby pause. "Yes?"

"Becky and I are going to get married," he blurted out, without taking a single breath.

Libby felt her eyes fill. "You were afraid to tell me that? Afraid to tell me something wonderful?"

Ken stopped, his arms still around his daughter, his blue eyes bright with relief and delight. Then, with a raucous shout that was far more typical of him than tuxedos and fancy parties, her father lifted her so high that she was afraid she would fall out of the top of her dress.

"That was certainly rustic," remarked Monica, five minutes later, at the refreshment table.

Libby saw Jess approaching through the crowd of guests and smiled down at the buttery crab puff in her fingers. "Are you making fun of my father, Ms. Summers?"

Monica sighed in exasperation. "This *is* a formal party, after all—not a kegger at the Golden Buckle. I don't know why the senator insists on inviting the help to important affairs."

Slowly, and with great deliberation, Libby tucked her crab puff into Monica's artfully displayed cleavage. "Will you hold this, please?" she trilled, and then walked toward her husband.

"The foreman's brat strikes again," Jess chuckled, pulling her into another waltz.

Cathy was sitting alone in the dimly lit kitchen, her eyes fixed on something far in the distance. Libby was careful to let her cousin see her, rather than startle her with a touch.

"Hi," she said.

Cathy replied listlessly.

Libby took a chair opposite Cathy's and signed, "I'd like to help if I can."

Cathy's face crumbled suddenly and she gave a soft cry that tore at Libby's heart. Her hands flew as she replied, "Nobody can help me!"

"Don't I even get to try?"

A tendril of Cathy's hair fell from the soft knot at the back of her head and danced against a shoulder left bare by her Grecian evening gown. "I'm pregnant," she whispered. "Oh, Libby, I'm pregnant!"

Libby felt confusion and just a touch of envy. "Is that so terrible? I know you were scared before, but—"

"I'm still scared!" Cathy broke in, her voice unusually loud.

Libby drew a deep breath. "Why, Cathy? You're strong and healthy. And your deafness won't be the problem you think it will—you and Stacey can afford to hire help, if you feel it's necessary."

"All of that is so easy for you to say, Libby!" Cathy flared with sudden and startling anger. "You can hear! You're a whole person!"

Libby felt her own temper, always suppressed when dealing with her handicapped cousin, surge into life. "You know something?" she said furiously. "I'm sick of your 'Poor Cathy' number! A child is just about the best thing that can happen to a person and instead of rejoicing, you're standing here complaining!"

"I have a reason to complain!"

Libby's arms flew out from her side in a gesture of wild annoyance. "All right! You're deaf, you can't hear! Poor, poor Cathy! Now, can we get past singing your sad song? Dammit, Cathy, I know how hard it must be to live in silence, but can't you look on the positive side for once? You're married to a successful, gentle-hearted man who loves you very much. You have everything!"

"Said the woman who could hear!" shouted Cathy.

Libby sighed and sat back in her chair. "We're all handicapped in some way—Jess told me that once, and I think it's true."

Cathy was not going to be placated. "What's your handicap, Libby?" she snapped. "Your short fingernails? The fact that you freckle in the summer instead of getting tan?"

The derisive sarcasm of her cousin's words stung Libby. "I'm as uncertain of myself at times as you are, Cathy," she said softly. "Aaron—"

"Aaron!" spouted Cathy with contempt. "Don't hand me that, Libby! So he ran around a little—I had to stand by and watch my husband adore my own cousin for months! And I'll bet Jess has made any traumas you had about going to bed with a man all better!"

"Cathy, please…"

Cathy gave a guttural, furious cry of frustration. "I'm so damned tired of you, Libby, with your career and your loving father and your…"

Libby was mad again, and she bounded to her feet. "And my what?" she cried. "I can't help that you don't have a father—Dad tried to make up for that and I think he did a damned good job! As for a career—don't you dare hassle me about that! I worked like a slave to get where I am! If you want a career, Cathy, get off your backside and start one!"

Cathy stared at her, stunned, and then burst into tears. And, of course, Jess chose exactly that moment to walk in.

Giving Libby one scalding, reproachful look, he gathered Cathy into his arms and held her.

15

After one moment of feeling absolutely shattered, Libby lifted her chin and turned from Jess's annoyance and Cathy's veiled triumph to walk out of the kitchen with dignity.

She encountered a worried-looking Marion Bradshaw just on the other side of the door. "Libby...Mrs. Barlowe...that man is here!"

Libby drew a deep breath. "What man?" she managed to ask halfheartedly.

"Mr. Aaron Strand, that's who!" whispered Marion. "He had the nerve to walk right up and ring the bell..."

Libby was instantly alert, alive in every part of her being, like a creature being stalked in the wilds. "Where is he now?"

"He's in the senator's study," answered the flushed, quietly outraged housekeeper. "He says he won't leave till he talks with you, Libby. I didn't want a scene, what with all these people here, so I didn't argue."

Wearily Libby patted Marion's shoulder. Facing Aaron Strand, especially now, was the last thing in the world she wanted to do. But she knew that he would create an awful fuss if his request was denied, and besides, what real harm could he do with so many people in the house? "I'll talk to him," she said.

"I'll get Jess," mused Mrs. Bradshaw, "and your daddy, too."

Libby shook her head quickly, and warm color surged up over her face. Jess was busy lending a strong shoulder to Cathy, and she was damned if she was going to ask for his help now, even indirectly. And though Ken was almost fully recovered from his confrontation with the bear, Libby had no intention of subjecting him to the stress that could result from a verbal round with his former son-in-law. "I'll handle this myself," she said firmly, and then, without waiting for a reply, she started for the senator's study.

Aaron was there, tall and handsome in his formal clothes.

"At least when you crash a party, you dress for it," observed Libby dryly from the doorway.

Aaron set down the paperweight he had been examining and smiled. His eyes moved over her in a way that made her want to stride across the room and slap him with all her might. "That dress is classy, sugarplum," he said in acid tones. "You're definitely bunkhouse-calendar material."

Libby bit her lower lip, counted mentally until the urge to scream passed. "What do you want, Aaron?" she asked finally.

"Want?" he echoed, pretending pleasant confusion.

"Yes!" hissed Libby. "You flew two thousand miles—you must want something."

He sighed, leaned back against the senator's desk, folded his arms. "Are you happy?"

"Yes," answered Libby with a lift of her chin.

Again he assessed her shiny silver dress, the hint of cleavage it revealed. "I imagine the cowboy is pretty happy with you, too," he said. "Which Barlowe is it, Libby? The steak-house king or the lawyer?"

Libby's head began to ache; she sighed and closed her eyes for just a moment. "What do you want?" she asked again insistently.

His shoulders moved in a shrug. "A baby," he answered, as though he was asking for a cup of coffee or the time of day. "I know you're not going to give me that, so relax."

"Why did you come here, then?"

"I just wanted a look at this ranch. Pretty fancy spread, Lib. You do know how to land on your feet, don't you?"

"Get out, Aaron."

"Without meeting your husband? Your paragon of a father? I wouldn't think of it, Mrs. Barlowe."

Libby was off balance, trying to figure out what reason Aaron could have for coming all the way to Montana besides causing her added grief. Incredible as it seemed, he had apparently done just that. "You can't hurt me anymore, Aaron," she said. "I won't let you. Now, get out of here, please."

"Oh, no. I lost everything because of you—everything. And I'll have my pound of flesh, Libby—you can be sure of that."

"If your grandmother relieved you of your company responsibilities, Aaron, that's your fault, not mine. I should think you would be glad—now you won't have anything to keep you from your wine, women and song."

Aaron's face was tense. Gone was his easy, gentlemanly manner. "With the company went most of my money, Libby. And let's not pretend, sweetness—I can make your bright, shiny new life miserable, and we both know it."

"How?" asked Libby, poised to turn and walk out of the study.

"By generating shame and scandal, of course. Your father-in-law is a prominent United States senator, isn't he? I should think negative publicity could hurt him very badly—and you know how good I am at stirring that up."

Rage made Libby tremble. "You can't hurt Cleave Barlowe, Aaron. You can't hurt me. Now, get out before I have you thrown out!"

He crossed the room at an alarming speed, had a hold on Libby's upper arms before she could grasp what was happening. He thrust her back against the heavy door of the study and covered her mouth with his own.

Libby squirmed, shocked and repulsed. She tried to push Aaron away, but he had trapped her hands between his chest and her own. And the kiss went on, ugly and wet, obscene because it was forced upon her, because it was Aaron's.

Finally he drew back, smirking down at her, grasping her wrists in both hands when she tried to wriggle away from him. And suddenly Libby was oddly detached, calm even. Mrs. Bradshaw had been right when she'd wanted to let Jess know that Aaron was here, so very right.

Libby had demurred because of her pride, because she was mad at Jess; she'd thought she could handle Aaron Strand. Pride be damned, she thought, and then she threw back her head and gave a piercing, defiant scream.

Aaron chuckled. "Do you think I'm afraid of your husband, Libby?" he drawled. Incredibly, he was about to kiss her again, it appeared, when he was suddenly wrenched away.

Libby dared one look at Jess's green eyes and saw murder flashing there. She reached for his arm, but he shook her hand away.

"Strand," he said, his gaze fixed on a startled but affably recovering Aaron.

Aaron gave a mocking half-bow. It didn't seem to bother him that Jess was coldly furious, that half the guests at the senator's party, Ken Kincaid included, were jammed into the study doorway.

"Is this the part," Aaron drawled, "where we fight over the fair lady?"

"This is the part," Jess confirmed icily.

Aaron shrugged. "I feel honor-bound to warn you," he said smugly, "that I am a fifth-degree black belt."

Jess spared him an evil smile, but said nothing.

Libby was afraid; again she grasped at Jess's arm. "Jess, he really is a black belt."

Jess did not so much as look at Libby; he was out of her reach, and not just physically. She felt terror thick in her throat, and flung an appealing look at Ken, who was standing beside her, one arm around her waist.

Reading the plea in his daughter's eyes, he denied it with an almost imperceptible shake of his head.

Libby was frantic. As Jess and Aaron drew closer to each other, circling like powerful beasts, she struggled to free herself from her father's restraining arm. For all his weaknesses of character, Aaron Strand was agile and strong, and if he could hurt Jess, he would, without qualms of any kind.

"Jess, no!" she cried.

Jess turned toward her, his jaw tight with cold annoyance, and Aaron struck in that moment. His foot came up in a graceful arc and caught Jess in the side of the neck. Too sick to stand by herself or run away, Libby buried her face in Ken's tuxedo jacket in horror.

There were sounds—terrible sounds. Why didn't someone stop the fight? Why were they all standing around like Romans thrilling to the exploits of gladiators? Why?

When the sounds ceased and Libby dared to look, Jess was still standing. Aaron was sitting on the floor, groaning theatrically, one corner of his lip bleeding. It was obvious that he wasn't badly hurt, for all his carrying on.

Rage and relief mingled within Libby in one dizzying sweep. "Animals!" she screamed, and when she whirled to flee the ugliness, no one moved to stop her.

Libby sat on the couch in the condo's living room, her arms wrapped around her knees, stubbornly ignoring the ringing of the telephone. She couldn't help counting, though—that had become something of a game in the two days since she'd left the ranch to take refuge here. Twenty-six rings. It was a record.

She stood up shakily, made her way into the kitchen, where she had been trying to sketch out the panels for her cartoon strip. "Back to the old drawing board," she said to the empty room, and the stale joke fell flat because there was no one there to laugh.

The telephone rang again and, worn down, Libby reached out for the receiver affixed to the kitchen wall and snapped, "Hello!"

"Lib?" The voice belonged to her father, and it was full of concern. "Libby, are you all right?"

"No," she answered honestly, letting a sigh carry the word. "As a matter of fact, I'm not all right. How are you?"

"Never mind me—why did you run off like that?"

"You know why."

"Are you coming back to the ranch?"

"Why?" countered Libby, annoyed. "Am I missing some bloody spectacle?"

Ken gave a gruff sigh. "Dammit, Libby, do you love Jess Barlowe or not?"

Tears stung her eyes. Love him? These two days away from him had been hell, but she wasn't about to admit that. "What does it matter?" she shot back. "He's probably so busy holding Cathy's hand that he hasn't even noticed I'm gone."

"That's it. Cathy. Standing up for her is a habit with Jess, Lib—you know that."

Libby did know; in two days she'd had plenty of time to come to the conclusion that she had overreacted in the kitchen the night of the party when Jess had seemed to take Cathy's part against her. She shouldn't have walked out that way. "There is still the fight—"

"You screamed, Libby. What would you have done, if you'd been in Jess's place?" Without waiting for an answer, her father went on, "You're just being stubborn, and so is Jess. Do you love him enough to make the first move, Lib? Do you have the gumption?"

Libby reached out for a kitchen chair, sank into it. "Where is he?"

There was a smile in her father's voice. "Up on that ridge behind your place," he answered. "He's got a camp up there."

Libby knew mild disappointment; if Jess was camping, he hadn't been calling. She had been ignoring the telephone for two days for nothing. "It's nice to know he misses me so much," she muttered petulantly.

Having said his piece, Ken was silent.

"He does miss me, doesn't he?" demanded Libby.

"He misses you," chuckled Ken. "He wouldn't be doing his hermit routine if he didn't."

Libby sighed. "The ridge, huh?"

"The ridge," confirmed Ken with amusement. And then he hung up.

I shouldn't be doing this in my condition, Libby complained to herself as she made her way up the steep hillside. *But since the mountain won't come to me...*

She stopped, looked up. The smoke from Jess's campfire

was curling toward the sky; the sun was hot and bright. What the devil did he need with a fire, anyway? It was broad daylight, for heaven's sake.

Muttering, holding on to her waning courage tenaciously, Libby made her way up over the rise to the top of the ridge. Jess was standing with his back to her, looking in the opposite direction, but the stiffness of his shoulders revealed that he knew she was there.

And suddenly she was furious. Hadn't she climbed up this cursed mountain, her heart in her throat, her pride God-only-knew-where? Wasn't the current situation as much his fault as her own? Hadn't she found out, the very day after she'd left him, that she was going to have his baby?

"Damn you, Jess Barlowe," she hissed, "don't you dare ignore me!"

He turned very slowly to face her. "I'm sorry," he said stiffly and with annoying effort.

"For what?" pressed Libby. Damned if she was going to make it easy!

Jess sighed, idly kicked dirt over his campfire with one booted foot. There was a small tent pitched a few feet away, and a coffeepot sat on a fallen log, along with a paperback book and a half-eaten sandwich. "For assuming that the scene with Cathy was your fault," he said.

Libby huffed over to the log, which was a fair distance from Jess, and sat down, folding her arms. "Well, praise be!" she murmured. "What about that stupid fistfight in your father's study?"

His green eyes shot to her face. "You'll grow horns, lady, before you hear me apologize for that!"

Libby bit her lower lip. Fighting wasn't the ideal way to settle things, it was true, but she couldn't help recalling the pleasure she herself had taken in stuffing that crab puff down the front of Monica Summers' dress at the party. If Monica had made one move to retaliate, she would have gladly tangled with her. "Fair enough," she said.

There was an uncomfortable silence, which Libby finally felt compelled to break. "Why did you have a fire going in the middle of the day?"

Jess laughed. "I wanted to make damned sure you found my camp," he replied.

"Dad told you I was coming!"

He came to sit beside her on the log and even though he didn't touch her, she was conscious of his nearness in every fiber of her flesh and spirit. "Yeah," he admitted, and he looked so sad that Libby wanted to cry.

She eased closer to him. "Jess?"

"What?" he asked, looking her squarely in the eyes now.

"I'm sorry."

He said nothing.

Libby drew a deep breath. "I'm not only sorry," she went on bravely, "I'm pregnant, too."

He was quiet for so long that Libby feared she'd been wrong to tell him about their child—at least for now. It was possible that he wanted to ask for a separation or even a divorce, but he might stay with her out of duty now that he knew. To hold him in that manner would break Libby's heart.

"When did you find out?" he asked finally, and the lack of emotion in his face and in his voice made Libby feel bereft.

"Day before yesterday. After Cathy said she was pregnant, I got to thinking and realized that I had a few symptoms myself."

Jess was silent, looking out over the trees, the ranges, the far mountains. After what seemed like an eternity, he turned to her again, his green eyes full of pain. "You weren't going to tell me?"

"Of course I was going to tell you, Jess. But, well, the time didn't seem to be right."

"You're not going to leave, are you?"

"Would I have climbed a stupid mountain, for pity's sake, if I wanted to leave you?"

A slow grin spread across Jess's face, and then he gave a startling hoot of delight and shot to his feet, his hands gripping Libby's and pulling her with him. If he hadn't caught her in his arms and held her, she would probably have fallen into the lush summer grass.

"Is it safe to assume you're happy about this announcement?" Libby teased, looking up at him and loving him all the more because there were tears on his face.

He lifted her into his arms, kissed her deeply in reply.

"Excuse me, sir," she said when he drew back, "but I was wondering if you would mind making love to me. You see, I'd like to find out if I'm welcome here."

In answer, Jess carried her to the tent, set her on her feet. "My tent is your tent," he said.

Libby blushed a little and bent to go inside the small canvas shelter. Since there wasn't room enough to stand, she sat on the rumpled sleeping bag and waited as Jess joined her.

She was never sure exactly how it came about, but within moments they were both lying down, facing each other. The weight of his hand was bliss on her breast, and so were the hoarse words he said.

"I love you, Libby. I need you. No matter how mad I make you, please don't leave me again."

Libby traced the strong lines of his jaw with a fingertip.

"I won't, Jess. I might scream and yell, but I won't leave. I love you too much to be away from you—if I learned anything in the last two days, it was that."

He was propped up on one elbow now, very close, and he was idly unbuttoning her blouse. "I want you."

Libby feigned shock. "In a tent, sir?"

"And other novel places." He paused, undid the front catch of her bra.

Libby sighed, then gasped as the warmth of his mouth closed over the straining peak of her breast. The sensation was exquisite, sweeping through her, pushing away the weariness and confusion and pain. She tangled her fingers in his rumpled hair, holding him close.

Jess finally left the breast he had so gently plundered to remove his clothes, and then, more slowly, Libby's. When she lay naked before him in the cool shadows of the tiny tent, he took in her waiting body with a look of rapt wonder. "Little enchantress," he breathed, "let me worship you.

Libby could not bear to be separate from him any longer. "Be close to me, Jess," she pleaded softly, "be part of me."

With a groan, he fell to her, his mouth moist and commanding upon hers. His tongue mated with Libby's and his manhood touched her with fire, prodding, taking only partial shelter inside her.

At last Jess broke the kiss and lifted his head, and Libby saw, through a shifting haze, that he was savoring her passion as well as his own. She was aware of every muscle in his body as he struggled to defy forces that do not brook the rebellion of mere mortals.

Finally these forces prevailed, and Jess was thrust, with a raspy cry, into Libby's depths. They moved together wildly, seeking and reaching and finally breaking through the barriers that divide this world from the glories of the next.

Cathy assessed the large oil painting of Jim Little Eagle, the Indian child Libby had seen at the powwow months before, her hands resting on her protruding stomach.

Libby, whose stomach was as large as Cathy's, was wiping her hands on a rag reserved for the purpose. The painting was a personal triumph, and she was proud of it. "What do you think?" she signed, after setting aside the cloth.

Cathy grinned. "What do I think?" she asked aloud, sitting down on the tall stool behind Libby's drawing board. "I'll tell you what I think. I think you should sell it to me instead of letting that gallery in Great Falls handle it. After all, they've got your pen-and-ink drawings and the other paintings you did."

Libby tried to look stern. "Are you asking for special favors, Cathy Barlowe?"

Cathy laughed. "Yes!" Her sparkling green eyes fell to the sketch affixed to Libby's drawing board and she exclaimed in delighted surprise. "This is great!"

Libby came to stand behind her, but her gaze touched only briefly on the drawing. Instead, she was looking out at the snow through the windows of her studio in Ken and Becky's house.

"What are you going to do with this?" Cathy demanded, tugging at Libby's arm.

Libby smiled, looking at the drawing. It showed her cartoon character, given over to the care of another artist now. Liberated Lizzie was in an advanced state of pregnancy, and the blurb read, "If it feels good, do it."

"I'm going to give it to Jess," she said with a slight blush. "It's a private joke."

Cathy laughed again, then assessed the spacious, well-equipped studio with happy eyes. "I'm surprised you work down here at your dad's place. Especially with Jess home almost every day, doing paperwork and things."

Libby's mouth quirked in a grin. "That's *why* I work down here. If I tried to paint there, I wouldn't get anything done."

"You're really happy, aren't you?"

"Completely."

Cathy enfolded her in a hug. "Me, too," she said. And when her eyes came to Libby's face, they were dancing with mischief. "Of course, you and Jess have to understand that you will never win the Race. Stacey and I are ahead by at least a nose."

Libby stood straight and tried to look imperious. "We will not concede defeat," she said.

Before Cathy could reply to this, Stacey came into the room, pretending to see only Libby. "Pardon me, pudgy person," he began, "but has my wife waddled by lately?"

"Is she kind of short, with long, pretty hair and big green eyes and a stomach shaped rather like a watermelon?"

Stacey snapped his fingers and a light seemed to go on in his face. "That's a pretty good description."

"Haven't seen her," said Libby.

Cathy gave her a delighted shove and flung herself at her husband, laughing. A moment later they were on their way out, loudly vowing to win what Jess and Stacey had dubbed the Great Barlowe Baby Race.

Through with her work for the day and eager to get home to Jess, Libby cleaned her brushes and put them away, washed her hands again, and went out to find her coat. The first pain struck just as she was getting into the car.

At home, Jess was standing pensively in the kitchen, star-

ing out at the heavy layer of snow blanketing the hillside behind the house. Libby came up as close behind him as her stomach would allow and wrapped her arms around his lean waist.

"I've just had a pretty good tip on the Baby Race," she
said.

The muscles beneath his bulky woolen sweater tightened,
and he turned to look down at her, his jade eyes dark with
wonder. "What did you say?"

"We're on the homestretch, Jess. I need to go to the hospital. Soon."

He paled, this man who had hunted wounded bears and
fire-breathing dragons. "My God!" he yelled, and suddenly
they were both caught up in a whirlwind of activity. Phone
calls were made, suitcases were snatched from the coat-closet
floor, and then Jess was dragging Libby toward his Land
Rover.

"Wait, I'm sure we have time—"

"I'm not taking any chances!" barked Jess, hoisting her
pear-shaped and unwieldy form into the car seat.

"Jess," Libby scolded, grasping at his arm. "You're panicking!"

"You're damned right I'm panicking!" he cried, and then
they were driving over the snowy, rutted roads of the ranch
at the fastest pace he dared.

When they reached the airstrip, the Cessna had been
brought out of the small hangar where it was kept and fuel
was being pumped into it. After wrestling Libby into the
front passenger seat, Jess quickly checked the engine and the
landing gear. These were tasks, she had learned, that he never
trusted to anyone else.

"Jess, this is ridiculous!" she protested when he scrambled

into the pilot's seat and began a preflight test there. "We have plenty of time to drive to the hospital."

Jess ignored her, and less than a minute later the plane was taxiing down the runway. Out of the corner of one eye Libby saw a flash of ice blue.

"Jess, wait!" she cried. "The Ferrari!"

The plane braked and Jess craned his neck to see around Libby. Sure enough, Stacey and Cathy were running toward them, if Cathy's peculiar gait could be called a run.

Stacey leapt up onto the wing and opened the door. "Going our way?" he quipped, but his eyes were wide and his face was white.

"Get in," replied Jess impatiently, but his eyes were gentle as they touched Cathy and then Libby. "The race is on," he added.

Cathy was the first to deliver, streaking over the finish line with a healthy baby girl, but Libby produced twin sons soon after. Following much discussion, the Great Barlowe Baby Race was declared a draw.

* * * * *

Turn the page for
an exciting preview
of
New York Times Bestselling author
Linda Lael Miller's
newest historical romance

McKettrick's Choice

Available now at your
favorite book outlet
from HQN Books

CHAPTER

Arizona Territory, August 12, 1888

HOLT MCKETTRICK hooked a finger under his fancy collar in a vain effort to loosen it a little. Wedding guests milled on the wide, grassy stretch of ground alongside the Triple M ranch house, their finery dappled by shivering patches of shade from the young oaks thriving there. Two fiddlers played a mournful rendition of "Lorena," and there was a whole hog roasting in the pit Holt's three half brothers had dug in the ground and lined with flat rocks from the creek. The wedding cake, baked by Holt's sisters-in-law, was the size of a buckboard, and a long table—an improvised arrangement of planks supported by half a dozen fifty-gallon barrels—wobbled under the weight of a week's worth of fancy grub.

The old man and the rest of the McKettrick outfit had spared no effort or expense to make the gathering memorable. Holt reckoned he might have enjoyed it as much as the next fellow—if he hadn't been the bridegroom.

A hand struck his back in jovial greeting, and Holt nearly spilled his cup of fruit punch, generously laced with whiskey from his brother Rafe's flask, down the front of his dandy suit.

"I reckon that's the preacher, yonder," said Holt's father, Angus Mc-Kettrick, nodding toward an approaching rider splashing across the sun-dazzled creek, driving his horse hard. "'Bout time he showed up. I was beginning to think we'd have to send somebody out to the mission to fetch that crippled-up padre."

Holt swallowed, squinted. Heat prickled the back of his neck. Something stirred in him, a sweet, aching feeling like he got on hot summer nights, when a high-country breeze curled around his brain like a voice calling him back to Texas.

"I reckon," he muttered. Holt wondered where Rafe had gotten to with that flask, though he didn't look away from the rider to search the crowd.

The newcomer, his features hidden in the glare of midafternoon light, spurred his horse up the creek bank on the near side, man and mount flinging off diamonds of water as they came.

"Margaret is a fine woman," Angus said. He had a way of cutting a statement loose without laying any groundwork first.

"Who?" Holt asked, distracted. The skin between his shoulder blades itched, and his chest felt wet beneath the starched cotton of his shirtfront.

"Your bride," Angus answered, with a note of exasperation. Out of the corner of his eye, Holt saw his father tug at the knot in his string tie. Like as not, his wife, Concepcion, had cinched it tight as a corset ribbon.

The rider gained the edge of the yard and dismounted with the hasty grace of a seasoned cowpuncher, leaving the reins to dangle. He came straight for Holt.

"That ain't the preacher," Angus remarked unnecessarily, and with concern. Though he had almost no formal education, the old man read till his eyes gave out, and when he let his grammar slip, it meant he was agitated.

Holt glanced toward the house, where Miss Margaret Tarquin, his bride-to-be, was shut away in an upstairs bedroom getting herself gus-sied up for the wedding, then went to meet the messenger. The fiddle-playing ground to a shrill halt, and a silence settled over the crowd. Even the kids and the dogs were quiet.

"I'm lookin' for Holt Cavanagh," the newly arrived young man announced. His denim trousers were wet with creek water, and he shivered, despite the shimmering heat of that August afternoon. "You'd be him, I reckon?"

Holt nodded in brusque acknowledgment. It didn't occur to him to explain that he'd set aside the name Cavanagh, once he and the old man had made their blustery peace, and went by McKettrick these days.

Angus stuck close, bristly brows lowered, and Rafe, Kade and Jeb, elusive until then, seemed to materialize out of the rippling mirages haunting the grounds like ghosts. Holt and his brothers had had their differences in the three years they'd been acquainted—still did—but blood was blood. If the rider brought good news, they'd celebrate. If it was bad, they'd do what they could to help. And if there was trouble in the offing, they'd wade right into the fray and ask for the particulars later.

Holt's affection for them, though sometimes grudging, was in his marrow.

The visitor handed over a slip of paper. "Frank Corrales told me to give you this. He sent you a telegram, and when you didn't answer, he figured it didn't go through and told me to hit the trail. I carried that there letter all the way from Texas."

A shock of alarm surged through Holt, like venom from an invisible snake. He hesitated slightly, then snatched the soggy sheet of brown paper and unfolded it with a snap of his wrist. He felt his father and brothers move a stride closer.

He took in the words in a glance, absorbed the implications, and read them again to make sure he had the right of the situation.

JOHN CAVANAGH ABOUT TO BE DRIVEN OFF HIS LAND.
GABE TO HANG FOR A HORSE THIEF AND A MURDERER ON THE FIRST OF OCTOBER. COME QUICK.
FRANK CORRALES

Holt was still digesting the news when a feminine voice jarred him out of his stupor, and a slender hand came to rest on his coat sleeve. "Holt? Is something wrong?"

Holt started slightly, turned his head to look down into the upturned face of his bride-to-be, resplendent in her lacy finery and gossamer veil. She was a pretty woman, with fair hair and expressive blue eyes, a sent-for wife, imported all the way from Boston. Holt never looked at her without a stab of guilt; Margaret deserved a man who loved her, not one who wanted a mother for his young daughter, a bed companion for himself and not much else.

"I've got to go back to Texas," he said. The words had been shambling along the far borders of his mind for a long while, but this was the first time he'd let them come to the fore, let alone find their way out of his mouth.

Angus cleared his throat, and the whole party started up again, like it was some sort of signal. Reluctantly, Rafe, Kade and Jeb moved off, and Angus handed the rider a five-dollar gold piece, then steered him toward the food table.

One of the ranch hands took care of the exhausted horse.

Margaret's smile faltered a little as she gazed up at Holt, waiting.

"Maybe when I get back..." he began awkwardly, but then his voice just fell away.

She sighed, shook her head. "I don't believe I want to wait, Holt," she said. "If that's what you're asking me to do, I mean."

He touched her face, let his hand fall back to his side. "I'm sorry," he rasped, and he was, truly, though he doubted it would count for much in the grand scheme of things. At his brothers' urging, he'd brought this woman out from the east, and now here she was, all got up in a bridal gown, with half the territory in attendance, and there wasn't going to be a wedding.

"I'll go ahead and marry you anyhow," he said, against his every instinct, because he was Angus McKettrick's son and a deal was a deal. But he couldn't make himself sound like that was what he wanted, and Margaret was no fool. "I've still got to leave, though, either way."

A tear shimmered on her cheek, but Margaret held her chin high, shook her head again. "No," she said, with sad pride. "If you really wanted me for a wife, you'd have gone ahead with the ceremony, put a ring on my finger so everybody would know I was taken, maybe even asked me to come along."

"It'll be a hard trip," Holt said. From a verbal standpoint, he felt like a lame cow, turning in fruitless circles, trying to find its way out of a narrow place in the trail. Nonetheless, he kept right on struggling. "Hard things to attend to, too, once I get there."

She worked up another smile. "Godspeed, Holt McKettrick," she said. Then, to his profound chagrin, she turned to face the gathering.

All attempts at merriment ceased, and a hush fell.

"There will be no wedding today," Margaret announced, in a clear voice, while everyone stared back at her in bleak sympathy. Her spine, Holt noted, with admiration, was straight as a new fence post. "But there *will* be a party. I'm going upstairs right now and change out of this silly dress, and when I come back down again, I expect to find every last one of you making merry."

With that, Margaret started for the house. Holt's sisters-in-law, Emmeline, Mandy and Chloe, all flung poisonous glances in his direction and hurried after his retreating almost-bride.

Only Lizzie, Holt's twelve-year-old daughter, had the temerity to approach him, and her cheeks glowed pink with indignation.

"Papa," she demanded, coming to a stop directly in front of him, "how *could* you?"

Holt loved his child, though he hadn't known she'd existed until last year, and except for Margaret herself, Lizzie was the hardest person in the crowd to face just then. "I've got business in Texas," he said, because that was the stark truth and he had nothing else to offer. "It can't wait."

Lizzie stiffened, blinked her large hazel eyes, and bit her lower lip. "You're leaving?"

He reached out to lay a hand on her shoulder, but she shrank from him.

"Lizzie," he whispered.

She turned on her heel, fled to her grandfather. Angus put an arm around the child and glowered at Holt. The old man looked like Zeus himself, shooting thunderbolts from his eyes.

"Hell," Holt muttered, and started for the barn.

His brothers fell in beside him, their faces hard. Holt lengthened his stride, but they stuck to his heels like barn muck. Stubborn cusses, cut from the same itchy cloth as their pa, every one of them.

"What the hell is going on here?" Rafe snarled. The firstborn of Angus's three younger sons, Rafe was a bull of a man, and always the first to demand an accounting. He and Kade and Jeb formed a semicircle in front of Holt, barring his way into the barn, where his horse was stabled, blissfully unaware of the long, arduous ride ahead.

Holt might have shoved his way through, if he hadn't figured that would lead to a fight. He wasn't afraid of tangling, but a brawl would mean a delay, and the need to get where he was going made an urgent clench in the pit of his belly.

He pulled out the crumpled letter, thrust into his vest pocket earlier, and shoved it at Kade, who happened to be the one standing directly in front of him. "See for yourself," he said.

Kade scanned the page, while Jeb and Rafe peered at it from either side.

"I'll saddle your horse," Kade said, handing it back. He was the middle brother, the thoughtful, practical one. "Best pack yourself some of that wedding grub, too, for the trail."

"Have a word with Lizzie before you go, Holt," Rafe interjected. "She doesn't look like she's taking this real well."

"I could ride along," Jeb put in, with typical eagerness. The youngest of the brood, he was also the fastest gun, and hands-down the best rider. Jeb was handy to have around in a tight place, for those reasons and a few others, but the plain and simple truth was that Holt didn't want to have to look out for him. He wasn't fool enough to say so, though.

He might have grinned, if he hadn't just humiliated a fine woman and learned that two of the best friends he'd ever had were in trouble. Jeb had a wife to look after, and a baby daughter, barely walking. Rafe and Kade were in the same situation, since all three of their brides had managed to come a-crop with babies a year ago last Independence Day.

"This is my fight," Holt said. "I'll handle it."

Rafe looked thoughtful. "John Cavanagh. That's the man who raised you, isn't it?"

Holt nodded, though Rafe's assessment didn't begin to cover what Cavanagh meant to him. "He's got a spread outside San Antonio."

"And this Gabe yahoo...?" Jeb fished. "Who's he?"

"We were Rangers together," Holt explained. Gabe Navarro was a wild man—part Comanche, part Mexican, part devil—but he was neither a murderer nor a horse thief. Holt had known him too long and too well ever to believe either accusation.

Apparently satisfied, Kade headed into the barn to get Holt's horse, Traveler, ready.

Rafe and Jeb went to the feast table and commenced gathering food for the journey. Holt looked for Lizzie and found her still in Angus's arms, her head resting against the old man's broad shoulder.

"Here, now," Angus murmured, giving his eldest son an unfriendly but resigned glance as Holt approached. "You talk to your papa, Lizzie-beth. It's no good parting without saying what needs to be said."

Lizzie sniffled, raised her head, and met Holt's gaze.

Angus squeezed her upper arm, then favoring Holt with a withering glare, he walked away.

"Are you coming back?" Lizzie wanted to know.

"Yes," Holt said, with certainty. He wasn't through with Texas—he'd left too many things undone there—but in the deepest part of his heart, he knew the Arizona Territory and the Triple M were home. He belonged on this stretch of red, rocky dirt, with his impossible father, his rowdy brothers and his spirited daughter.

She dashed at her face with the back of one hand. "You promise?"

"You have my word."

"What if you *can't* come home? What if somebody shoots you?"

"I *will* come back, Lizzie."

"I guess I have to believe you."

He chuckled, extended an arm. Lizzie hesitated, then curled against his chest, clinging a little. "You be a good girl," he said, resting his chin on top of her dark head, wishing he didn't have to leave her behind. "Mind Concepcion and your grandfather."

She trembled, tugged a cherished blue ribbon from her hair and tucked it into Holt's vest pocket. "A remembrance," she said softly, and Holt's heart ached. Before he could find words to assure his daughter that forgetting her would be impossible, she went on, "Are you going to visit Mama's grave? She's buried in San Antonio, in the cemetery behind Saint Ambrose's."

He nodded, still choked up. Lizzie's mother, Olivia, was part of the unfinished business waiting for him in Texas. He needed to say a proper goodbye to her, put her to rest in his mind and his heart, even though it was too late for her to hear the words.

"Will you take her flowers—the best you can find—for me?"

Holt's throat still wouldn't open. He nodded again.

Lizzie stared into his face, looking, perhaps, for the half-truths people tell to children, or even a bold-faced lie. Finding only truth, she straightened her shoulders and hoisted her chin.

"All right, then," she said. "I guess you'd better ride while there's still enough daylight to see the trail."

He smiled, cupped her chin in one hand. "Don't eat too much cake," he said.

Her eyes glistened with tears. "Don't get yourself shot," she countered.

And that was their farewell.

Lizzie was a woman-child, with the run of one of the biggest ranches in the Arizona Territory. She could already ride like a pony soldier, and Kade's wife, Mandy, a sharpshooter, had taught her niece to handle a shotgun as well as a side arm. Lizzie had lost her mother to a fever and seen her aunt murdered in cold blood alongside a stagecoach. She knew only too well that life was fragile, the world was a dangerous place and that some partings were permanent.

This one wouldn't be, Holt promised himself as he rode out, Lizzie's ribbon in his pocket.

HQN™

We *are* romance™

From the *New York Times* bestselling author of
Secondhand Bride comes the latest title in the
McKettrick family saga!

LINDA LAEL MILLER

Independent and strong-willed Lorelai Fellows has had it with
men, but setting fire to her wedding dress probably wasn't
the best way to make her point. Yet when Holt McKettrick
comes to town looking to save his best friend from the
gallows, the sparks between him and Lorelai are flying...
and two people determined never to believe in love can't
believe they've gone this long without it.

The wayward McKettrick brother is back in town,
and things will never be the same....

McKettrick's Choice

Available in hardcover in bookstores this June.

www.HQNBooks.com

PHLLM029

HQN™

We *are* romance™

New York Times bestselling author

DIANA PALMER

brings readers eight beloved titles in four books
featuring the infamous Long, Tall Texans,
including the charming Hart Brothers!

Specially priced at only **$4.99**,
each classic 2-in-1 collection contains a special sneak peek of Diana Palmer's newest title from **HQN Books**!

Available in bookstores in June.

www.HQNBooks.com

PHDP0505

HQN™

We *are* romance™

Return to Jacobsville, Texas, with
the *New York Times* bestseller

Renegade,

the eagerly anticipated sequel to *Desperado* and *Lawless*.
Now available for the first time in paperback!

DIANA PALMER

Cash Grier takes nothing at face value—especially not
Tippy Moore. As quickly as their relationship began, it
abruptly ends. But circumstances soon demand that Cash set
aside his bitterness to save the woman who broke his heart.

Don't miss the newest Long, Tall Texans story. Coming this June.

www.HQNBooks.com

PHDP050

HQN™

We *are* romance™

The Bad Luck Brides are back
by *USA TODAY* bestselling author

GERALYN DAWSON

Mari McBride would never be so foolish as to travel solo
through the badlands of Texas in search of her missing
sister. But as she looks at her choice of bodyguard—
Luke Garrett, the most notorious and insufferable man
in town—she has to wonder if she wasn't better off
going it alone…until the notorious McBride "curse"
strikes yet again…

Her Bodyguard

Don't miss this original story in the popular
Bad Luck Brides series, in stores this June!

www.HQNBooks.com

PHGD043

HQN™

We *are* romance™

First there was *Endgame*.
Now award-winning author

DEE DAVIS

introduces the second title in the Last Chance series

CIA operative Payton Reynolds is none too pleased when
assigned to protect bomb specialist Samantha Waters,
recently called in to investigate a series of bombs
detonating around the city. She's not exactly a dream
assignment—stubborn, willful and far too attractive for
his peace of mind—yet as the situation escalates, Payton will
do anything to protect her…no matter the cost.

Enigma

**Visit your nearest bookstore in June for this nail-biting
romantic-suspense title from Dee Davis!**

And keep an eye out for *Exposure*, coming in September.

www.HQNBooks.com

PHDD048

If you enjoyed what you just read,
then we've got an offer you can't resist!

Take 2 bestselling novels FREE!
Plus get a FREE surprise gift!

Clip this page and mail it to MIRA®

IN U.S.A.
3010 Walden Ave.
P.O. Box 1867
Buffalo, N.Y. 14240-1867

IN CANADA
P.O. Box 609
Fort Erie, Ontario
L2A 5X3

YES! Please send me 2 free MIRA® novels and my free surprise gift. After receiving them, if I don't wish to receive anymore, I can return the shipping statement marked cancel. If I don't cancel, I will receive 4 brand-new novels every month, before they're available in stores! In the U.S.A., bill me at the bargain price of $4.99 plus 25¢ shipping and handling per book and applicable sales tax, if any*. In Canada, bill me at the bargain price of $5.49 plus 25¢ shipping and handling per book and applicable taxes**. That's the complete price and a savings of over 20% off the cover prices—what a great deal! I understand that accepting the 2 free books and gift places me under no obligation ever to buy any books. I can always return a shipment and cancel at any time. Even if I never buy another The Best of the Best™ book, the 2 free books and gift are mine to keep forever.

185 MDN DZ7J
385 MDN DZ7K

Name _____ (PLEASE PRINT)

Address _____ Apt.#

City _____ State/Prov. _____ Zip/Postal Code

*Not valid to current The Best of the Best™, Mira®,
suspense and romance subscribers.*

Want to try two free books from another series?
Call 1-800-873-8635 or visit www.morefreebooks.com.

* Terms and prices subject to change without notice. Sales tax applicable in N.Y.
** Canadian residents will be charged applicable provincial taxes and GST. Offer limited to one per household.
   All orders subject to approval. Offer limited to one per household.
® and ™are registered trademarks owned and used by the trademark owner and or its licensee.

BOB04R
©2004 Harlequin Enterprises Limited

HQN™

We *are* romance™

New York Times bestselling author

LINDA LAEL MILLER

presents four titles that have become reader favorites along with a special sneak preview of her newest release in June.

Specially priced at only $4.99

Collect all four!

Available in bookstores in June.

www.HQNBooks.com

PHLLM0505